Blues of Autumn

RICHARD ADAMSON

Black Rose Writing | Texas

First printing

ISBN: 978-1-68433-448-3
PUBLISHED BY BLACK ROSE WRITING
www.blackrosewriting.com

Printed in the United States of America
Suggested Retail Price (SRP) $18.95

Blues of Autumn is printed in Garamond

*As a planet-friendly publisher, Black Rose Writing does its best to eliminate unnecessary waste to reduce paper usage and energy costs, while never compromising the reading experience. As a result, the final word count vs. page count may not meet common expectations.

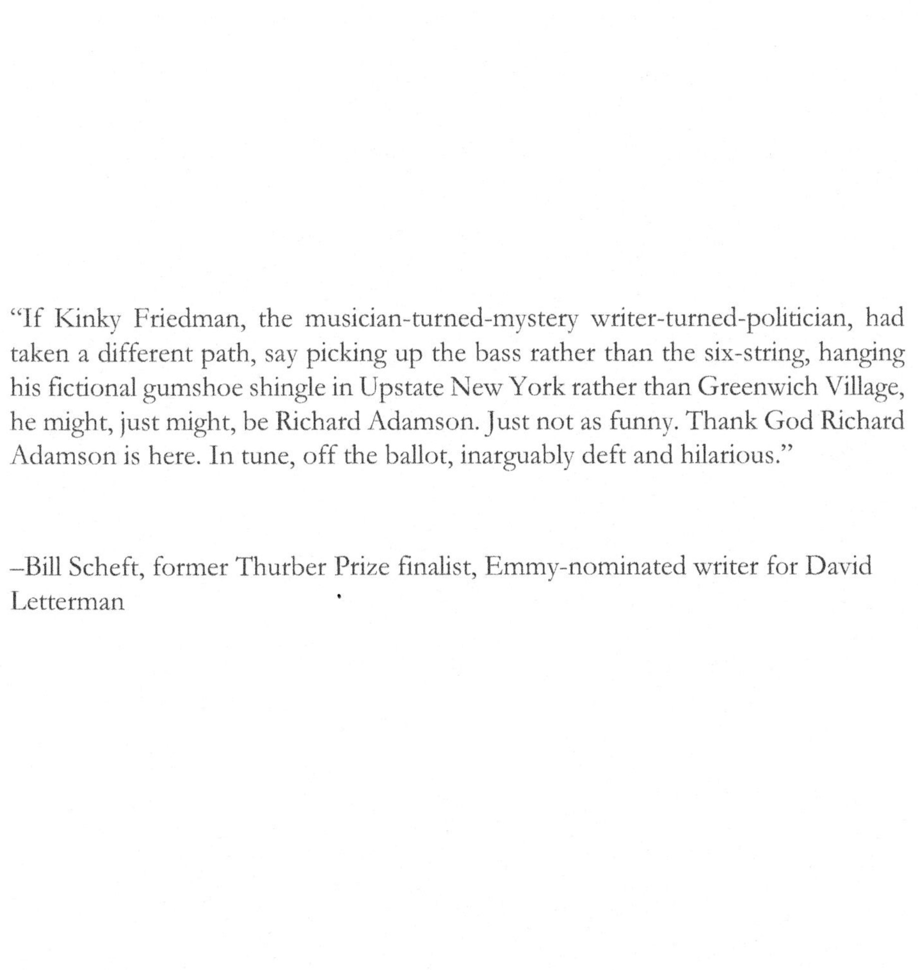

"If Kinky Friedman, the musician-turned-mystery writer-turned-politician, had taken a different path, say picking up the bass rather than the six-string, hanging his fictional gumshoe shingle in Upstate New York rather than Greenwich Village, he might, just might, be Richard Adamson. Just not as funny. Thank God Richard Adamson is here. In tune, off the ballot, inarguably deft and hilarious."

–Bill Scheft, former Thurber Prize finalist, Emmy-nominated writer for David Letterman

For Helene

Blues of Autumn

CHAPTER ONE

Fists flew. Punches landed. The dust did not. It just hung in the air and enjoyed the brief but welcome change of address. The whole thing lasted only a few seconds. Bar fights are like that. Finished in the blink of a swollen eye. There was nothing I could do. Not a damned thing. Honest. Don't believe me? Neither did he.

I owed the man an explanation. Granted, it wasn't my fight. Not directly, that is. But indirectly, all fights in this town are my fights. So as soon as my band tossed away the last remaining beats of *Standing On Shaky Ground* I unstrapped my bass guitar, jumped off the portable riser the boss calls a stage, and weaved my way to the man's table to make sure there were no hard feelings. You see, the way most people figure it, cops are like hookers – just because we're no longer wearing the big, silly shoes doesn't necessarily mean we're off duty.

He was sitting alone at the back of the room. Next to the rack of pool cues. He was the straight one. As soon as I had a clear shot I started firing off excuses. "I hope you understand. I couldn't just drop everything."

"Quite all right." Paul Briar didn't bother to look up – he was too busy fussing over the fresh cigarette burn in his snazzy silk sports jacket. I figured that's what the fight had been about. The fancy duds. In the Blues and Cues Roadhouse, a designer label is a *Kick Me* sign.

I thumbed toward the bar area where the club's two owners were uncapping domestic beer and listening to hunters lie. "I figured Jack and Vanessa could handle it." And I wasn't kidding. Jack was built like a twelve-screen multiplex, and his wife, Vanessa, like the candy counter.

"Don't give it a second thought." Briar poked a well-manicured finger through the fresh burn hole in his jacket.

Now that I'd stepped closer I could see that, although Paul Briar's spiffy threads hadn't fared well, the guy's spiffy face seemed to have escaped injury. I guess either Briar was better with his fists than he looked or Jack and Vanessa had managed to cool things down pretty quickly. I hadn't actually seen the tussle, you understand. I tend to close my eyes when I'm playing. That way I can pretend people are listening.

I still felt that my own lack of action needed further explanation: "It's not like I'm just a guitarist or something. I'm the bass player."

"Uh, huh…"

"Take piano players..." I glanced toward the stage where Simon Reesor, our keyboard player, was fiddling with some knobs on his synth. "Simon can drop out anytime. Hell, he can leave the stand, stroll out to his car, light up a joint, and hump a passing moose if they're both in the mood. The world isn't going to end. I mean, who's going to miss a keyboard player, right?"

"Only the moose."

"Right," I chuckled. I was glad to see Briar hadn't lost his sense of humor over the summer. Considering the horror he'd been through last spring I wouldn't have been surprised if he never smiled again. Anyway, I continued pleading my own immediate case, "When the bass player drops out, that means trouble. No bass, no foundation. No foundation, the whole structure collapses. You do understand, right?"

Briar nodded his agreement. He'd obviously grown tired of lying out loud.

I surveyed the room. "The boys still here?"

"I believe your bartender escorted the two gentlemen out. They'd had quite a lot to drink."

"Yeah, sometimes Clive and Robbie can get pretty blitzed." I gazed at the room's front wall as if I could see straight through it out into the graveled black swamp of motorcycles, muscle cars, and pickup trucks. "Hate to see the boys drive home like that, but…" I gave this sad and somber conjecture the moment's silence I thought it deserved before clapping my hands to summon back reality. "But hey, whatcha gonna do? I mean, it *is* a bar, right?"

Briar replied, somewhat sarcastically I thought, "And you *are* a police officer, right?"

I chuckled. "Yeah, I know what you mean, but—"

"*Chief* of Police, if I'm not mistaken." Now the guy was getting downright snarky. He knew darn well who I was. Over the past couple of months I'd been chatting with him by text, email, Facebook, you name it. We'd met in person, however, just a couple days ago.

"Technically, you are right," I said. "I am indeed the big hard cheese around here." I pulled up a chair. The thing wiggled. Everything in here does. Except the women. I sat down so I could plead my case face to face. "You see, when I took this gig Jack and Vanessa had certain reservations…"

"You being in law enforcement and all."

"Exactly. They felt that having a police officer on stage two nights a week might put a crimp in the evening's festivities — some of their more-discriminating clientele might think twice about patronizing such an establishment. So I promised to keep a low profile, look the other way whenever I could. I try not to forget that Blues and Cues is a working man's bar. Or more correctly, a *saloon*."

"I'm told in your case it's more correctly an *office*."

I laughed. "Yeah. People like to say that. But no, we have a proper police station. Quaint. Unobtrusive. It's downtown. Somewhere near city hall, I'm told."

Paul Briar would have laughed out loud at my little quip, but he probably didn't want to expose his gleaming white laminates to the smoky air. I had the same concern when I repainted my Volvo. Briar's white teeth sparkled all the brighter framed by his dark, even tan – the kind of perfect, even tan you get indoors from a UV lamp, certainly not outdoors in Upstate New York in November. He sported freshly-trimmed eyebrows and just enough sideburns to say, *I could have real sideburns if I wanted to, but I just don't want to.* Curiously, the only part of Paul Briar that was not meticulously groomed was his shaggy blonde hair which sprouted haphazardly and tumbled over his forehead like a root-bound spider plant.

I picked up his silk sports jacket and checked out the cigarette burn. As I examined the offended garment I lowered my voice and mumbled… no, more like whispered, "You, uh… you don't want to file charges, do you?"

"Best leave well enough alone," he answered. "I didn't come to Glen Echo to make trouble."

"Good man." My voice returned to its normal volume. "I think that's best for all concerned." And by *all*, of course, I meant *me*. If there's one thing I hate worse than being interrupted while I'm playing it's having to spend my break between sets filling out complaint reports. After all, cops need down time, too. At least, that's what I told the department shrink back in Buffalo when I handed her my badge, gas card, and yo-yo. She didn't agree, though. Oh, she thought I was nuts, all right. But not nuts enough to warrant psychiatric leave. Neither, for that matter, did my department supervisor. So I had no choice but to resign from the force and look for a more perceptive employer, one who recognized bat-shit crazy when he saw it.

Ironically, I am now my own boss.

I handed Briar's sports jacket back to him, saying, "For future reference, this establishment may not be the best venue in which to display such fine haberdashery."

He countered with, "I don't dress down to accommodate others."

Yeah, I'd asked for that, I suppose. After all, who wants fashion tips from a guy who's wearing a free promotional beer t-shirt? Domestic beer, at that. "Let me buy you a drink," I said. Hell, snippy attitude or not, I was truly grateful to the guy for not pressing charges.

I turned to Casey, our waitress, who was doing her best to encourage a substantial tip by leaning over a nearby customer's substantial table and wiping it off with her substantial breasts. "Hey, Case, how's 'bout a beer. And whatever my friend Paul, here, is hooked up to."

Casey bounced off without further comment, which is all that is smart or necessary in a place like this, and I turned back to Briar. "So how'd it start? Clive Holand make some crack about your fancy threads?"

"I believe the incident was sparked by my request that they extinguish their cigarettes. The shorter one decided to make his feelings clear by using my jacket pocket as an ash tray."

My jaw fell to my belt buckle. "You asked Clive and Robbie Holand to butt out?"

"This *is* a non-smoking establishment, is it not?"

Technically, he was right – smoking has long been prohibited in all bars and restaurants in New York State. But to point out this legal detail to a couple of hard-drinking, hard-hitting pool players like the Holand brothers takes a special kind of balls. Or a special kind of death wish. So I asked him, "Why didn't you just mention the problem to one of the staff? Let them handle it."

"I'm more of a hands-on type." Briar took a sip from his martini glass. "I don't delegate well."

Wow. I was truly impressed. For one thing, I didn't know this place had martini glasses. And for another… well, it never fails. Just when I think I'm the nuttiest squirrel in the tree some critter like Briar scampers along. Maybe the guy really did have a death wish. Hell, considering what he'd been through over the summer, I wouldn't have been surprised.

The tragedy happened months before I got here, early last spring. Briar and his wife had come up here from the city for a weekend break. One morning the guy's sweetie decides to go off for an early morning paddle. In a canoe. Or maybe it was a kayak. I'm not an outdoors guy. Whatever it was, she took it out for a ride down a river. A fast river. Alone. She never came back. Searchers found the craft busted up at the bottom of a set of white water rapids. Her body was never found. Now, six months later, this guy, the grieving husband, shows up at the very same B&B where he and his late wife last stayed. I have no idea why he's back. Closure, he says. Bullshit, I say. Not to his face, of course. Like I say, the man's had a hell of rough time. But he's hanging out here in the mountains for some reason, and I don't think it's for the autumn colors or for the imported beer and domestic blues music.

Casey flounced by with our drinks and placed them on our table without flashing her usual dessert tray of cleavage. She probably figured I was paying and she knows musicians don't tip. Come to think of it, neither do cops.

Paul Briar took one quick gander at my cold bottle of Moretti and remarked, "Off duty, I presume?"

I clinked my beer bottle against his martini glass and started to say, "Here's to off-duty." But the words never made it past my dry lips.

An explosion rocked the building. My rickety chair trembled like an old man's cane. Beer bottles rolled across table tops. Glasses leapt to their deaths. Plaster fell like snow. Men screamed. Women cursed. A brass cymbal tumbled off the stage and hit the linoleum dance floor with a sizzling crash that clearly announced the end of civilization as we knew it.

And I was back on duty.

CHAPTER TWO

Like many buildings in the Adirondack mountains, the Blues and Cues Roadhouse sits directly upon solid rock. Two-billion-year-old gneiss and granite. No sand or clay to buffer shock waves. As a result, whenever there's a loud noise outside – say, when a clap of thunder rolls down the valley or a Harley Davidson grumbles to life – we don't just hear the roar, we feel the roar. Through our feet if we're standing. Through our butts if we're sitting. Tonight's explosion knocked our asses off our chairs.

The women reached the door first – not running away from the blast, running toward it. Unlike the boys at the bar, the girls were not ashamed of their curiosity. They were the first to look. The first to react. The first to speak.

"A fuckin' car," announced the first young woman as she held the door open with one hand and shielded her face from the heat with the other.

A second woman, her pale white face washed crimson from the fire's glow, opened her mouth wide in amazement. The firelight danced off her tongue stud as she added, "Fuckin' awthome." She proceeded to pull out her camera phone. I pushed past her. Out the door and into the parking lot. But I didn't get far. What I saw stopped me dead.

In all my years on the job, including my early years on traffic, I'd never seen a vehicle fire quite like this one. A car usually catches fire under the hood or, more frighteningly, under the grease-covered chassis near the fuel line. But this blaze was contained solely inside the cabin, its long hungry tongues of flame poking through blown-out windows trying to lick black liquorice off the night sky.

I strained my eyes to see if anyone was inside the vehicle, but the thick smoke smudged my view. What I could make out with no trouble was the color, make, and model of the car. And that's what melted my heart. That's what stopped me dead.

A late model Audi. Pale gold. *Desert Pearl.* That's the name he'd quoted to me with a chuckle when he showed it to me two months ago. The car, even back then, was parked at the far end of the lot, same place as it was sitting now. Sheltered by the stand of birches. Far from the front door of the club. Safe, he'd said, from the careless drunks and jealous assholes with keys in their hands.

I blinked hard to moisten my parched eyes as I pressed closer to the flames. Behind me the growing crowd of onlookers, which was now intermixed with both sexes, followed slowly in my trail, most of them shuffling ahead like zombies while they watched the whole scene unfold on the screen of their phones. I yelled at the pack to keep back – the gas tank might blow. The men, at least, were quick to comply.

I edged closer to the flames, pushing against the heat with my shoulder as though I were pushing into a hurricane, until I could finally get a decent look. But of course there was nothing decent about it.

The figure sat motionless in the front seat – leaning slightly forward as if it were trying to tune in a better radio station. I couldn't tell yet who exactly was in there, but I could make a damn good guess. Seeing as how the vehicle was Simon's Audi, and seeing as how I'd just left Simon himself inside the club seated at his keyboard, this had to be Evelyn, his wife.

I ripped off my cotton t-shirt. Wrapped it around my right hand as an oven mitt. Grabbed the door handle. I pulled.

But the door didn't budge. I tried again, this time ramming my foot up against the doorpost for leverage. The thing still refused to give up. I stepped back to rewind my hand and to silently curse Simon. He'd always cautioned Evelyn to lock the car doors the moment she got in, before she even turned on the ignition.

I reached in through the already-broken driver's window, grabbed the latch, and yanked. This time the door popped open. And the flames said *thank you.* They appreciated the brand new supply of oxygen.

This fresh blast of heat ripped my breath away. With empty lungs unable to expand for another gulp, I quickly reached in and started to lift her out. But she wouldn't budge – her shoulder harness and seat belt were still cinched up tight. That was Simon's fault too. He always took good care of his girl.

I reached across to unbuckle her seatbelt, and in so doing I noticed that the porcelain skin around Evelyn's neck and shoulders was still unmarred by the blast and flames. Sure, she had a few splatters of blood on her face, but they were pretty small, and for a moment I found this encouraging. Then I noticed that the clothes on the lower half of her body were in tatters. Especially her blood-soaked slacks. Most of the explosion must have come from under the dash. In a nanosecond of useless thought I remembered how proud Evelyn had been of those legs. She would often wear skirts that, according to some, were far too short for a middle-aged woman to wear. Only middle-aged women said this, of course.

Shit. Where was that damn seatbelt buckle? Was it caught under her coat? I stuck my head farther inside. But the searing heat and greasy smoke soon clouded my vision with a mudpack of tears and soot. I pulled my head back out to wipe the crud from my eyes and catch my breath.

Then I dove back inside again.

The flames, happy to see me return, licked the back of my head like a lonely puppy welcoming its master. I worked away and this time managed to get the seatbelt buckle popped. I wrapped my arms around Evelyn's waist and was just in the process of lifting her up off the seat when the second explosion hit.

This time the blast came from just inches away. It wasn't a bomb, of course. It was the driver's front airbag, the one that was housed in the middle of the steering wheel. My own fault. In my haste I had gotten careless. I should have remembered that the heat sets them off.

The bag's hard plastic cover booted me in the back of the head like a place kicker converting a touchdown, sending my skull crashing straight into Evelyn's abdomen, forcing the air out of her lungs and the contents of her stomach streaming down my neck. On the plus side, the vomit extinguished the flames in my hair.

The bag deflated almost as quickly as it had inflated, and I was soon free to lift Evelyn up once again. Only difference was, now everything had gone quiet. Stone dead silent. I could no longer hear the crackle of the flames. Nor could I hear the voices of my fellow rescuers. I just saw their outstretched arms as they reached in to help me pull Evelyn out.

I noticed two sets of hands slip under her torso besides mine. Together, we carried Evelyn to a soft spot on the grass where we could lay her down. As I pulled my arms out from under her torn and insulted body I noticed my fingers were stinging. At the time, I figured this was just because they were badly burned.

Anyway, now that we finally had Evelyn taken care of, I could straighten up and finally take a nice deep breath of fresh cool air.

I immediately collapsed. Too much of a good thing. I wasn't completely out. Just a little dizzy. My legs had turned to rubber and had slowly lowered me to the ground. But this was okay. Now.

I closed my eyes and struggled to catch more breath. It wasn't easy. My lungs didn't want to work. The super-heated air must have scorched my bronchials. I took short gulps. The grass, cool, crisp, and white with frost, felt good on the back of my scorched head.

After managing a couple of good deeper breaths I opened my eyes and scanned the faces hovering above me. I was anxious to see who the men were who had risked their lives to give me a hand.

I saw that they were both bending over Evelyn's body. One of them was Simon. No surprise there, of course. He must have followed me out. He was now on his knees tending to his wife with help from the other brave good Samaritan to have lent me a hand, Paul Briar. I admit this was indeed a surprise. It shouldn't have been. After all, Briar did say he was a hands-on type of guy. And here I'd thought he was just another bar room bullshitter.

As my chest gradually accepted deeper lungfuls of air I turned my head and watched Simon go to work. He checked his dear wife's airways for obstructions. Then he started giving her mouth-to-mouth. He performed the procedure expertly, pausing every few breaths to feel for a pulse or to put his ear to her chest. In with the good air, out with the bad. I watched as Evelyn's chest rose and fell in perfect rhythm, thinking of how Simon always did have good meter, which was unusual for a keyboard player. I also noted that every time his lips touched hers, Simon closed his eyes as if he were kissing her goodnight. Or goodbye.

I'm sure Simon knew that his efforts were pointless. But he kept trying just the same. Even when his eyes had filled with tears he kept trying. And even when those tears dripped from his cheeks and washed dog-leg pathways down his sweetie's soot-smeared face, the guy kept trying.

But not so hard anymore. Not with the same desperation. Not with the same hope. Simon was no fool. He's a realist. In his line of work he has to be. Simon knew better than any of us. He dealt with this sort of thing every day. A man like Simon knows when there's hope and when there isn't. Same as he knows a guy can't pay the bills solely by playing blues two nights a week in a cruddy roadhouse. That's why, some thirty-odd years ago, Simon transferred his major at Syracuse

University from music performance to pre-med. The way he tells it, he figured if he couldn't pay the rent by helping people forget their troubles he could at least do something that might lessen their pains. And who knows? Maybe one day, especially after he had jumped through all the hoops necessary to become a highly-respected surgeon, as he certainly has, he might even be able to save a life or two.

But not tonight, he couldn't.

I guess there are flaws to every plan.

CHAPTER THREE

The sour wail of the siren was sweet music to my hungry ears. Hearing that fire truck come screaming down the highway meant my auditory loss had been only temporary. I would indeed bop to Aretha and Ray and Jaco once again. That was the good news. The bad news was that I would never again hear the lilt of Evelyn Reesor's laughter. Moments ago I had watched Simon pull the EMS team's blanket up over her face. He did it gently, as if he were tucking her in for the night. A long, lonely night.

Glen Echo Fire Department's Pumper Number Three had arrived as first responder. To tell the truth, there is no Pumper Number One. No Number Two either, but our local real estate agents don't generally tell you this until after the deal is signed.

Our lone fire truck was closely followed by an ambulance crew from the closest trauma unit – the Adirondack Center in Saranac Lake. The hospital could offer no help to the deceased victim, of course, but still, I instructed the medics to whisk Evelyn's body off as quickly as possible with her husband riding along. I didn't want poor Simon stuck here when the press and other morons with camera phones showed up. Our band's guitarist, Rodger, followed the ambulance in his own car so he could keep a close eye on Simon.

The New York State Troopers were the last to arrive on scene, but that's understandable. Their closest station, Tupper Lake, was a good twenty minutes' drive from Glen Echo which was why the town of Glen Echo insists on maintaining its own police department. Trouble is, at this particular moment, the entire Glen Echo Police Department was sitting on the running board of the town's only fire truck getting his only head bandaged.

When the ambulance attendant was through wrapping up my blistered scalp, he turned his rubber-gloved skills to dressing a spray of scratches and pinpricks on my fingers and palms – injuries I'd suffered when I'd yanked Evelyn out of the wreckage. Turns out the bastard who'd made the pipe bomb had loaded it with carpet tacks thereby assuring the victim's torso would be additionally lethal to first responders.

While the medic took my blood pressure for the fourth time, an unmarked car crunched into the gravel parking lot. I recognized the vehicle, but my blood pressure probably stayed where it was anyway. I basically liked this next guy. In small doses, at least.

Detective Manny Manwaring of the New York State Police Major Crimes Division, Troop K, stepped out of the car. The driver's side, of course. Manny rarely lets anyone else sit behind the wheel. Manny didn't pause to get his bearings and assess the big picture. He rarely does that, either. He lumbered over to the nearest uniform and asked a question. The uniform pointed a finger at me.

I waved a big howdy and waited for my old friend to stroll my way. I was sure he would approve of how I'd handled things so far and why I'd let the deceased victim and her distraught, newly-widowed husband depart the scene.

I was wrong.

"For shit's sake, Tanager. Is this how you mountain folk deal with Persons Of Interest out here in Upper Lower Moose Groin? You just let them go off for a wagon ride holding the vic's cold, dead hand?" The frigid night air condensed Manwaring's words into clouds of steam that rose toward heaven. Luckily for all concerned, the words dissolved long before they got there.

"Manny, the guy just lost his wife. I thought we could cut him a break." I added, "And don't worry, Simon's not going anywhere." I adjusted my turban bandage but purely for recreational reasons. It had slipped down over my eyes, greatly inhibiting my ability to watch the veins on Detective Manwaring's neck pop out.

"A friggin' buddy of yours, I take it."

"I've known Simon for a while," I admitted. "Not nearly as long as I've known you, of course. But on the plus side, I like him a whole lot better." I smiled to let him know I was serious.

Manwaring suggested we continue our interview inside the warm restaurant. This seemed like a peachy fine idea to me, but as soon as the paramedic helped me get to my feet, my world started spinning. The medic insisted I lie down in his EMS vehicle. Apparently my blood pressure was pretty low.

The ambulance attendant kindly left the engine running to keep me cozy warm, and before I knew it I was fast asleep. When I woke up, I took one look out the back window of the vehicle and assumed I'd slept through the entire night. But no. What I had mistaken for daylight was just the tungsten-halogen light fixtures the investigations crew had set up. I could hear their auxiliary generator chugging away like it was operating a carnival ride. Still a bit wobbly, I wrapped a blanket around myself and wriggled out of the ambulance to go join the circus.

The cold night air quickly slapped me awake. At the far end of the parking lot I could see Detective Manwaring standing beside the burned-out shell of Simon's Audi. I hitched up my blanket to keep it clear of the fresh-mixed mud and slowly waltzed over to him.

Manny took one look at the turban of bandage that encased my cranium and said with undisguised glee, "You're gonna have to get your noggin shaved, you know." His smile stretched ear-to-ear, almost bursting with delight. Manny Mankowski's own head was bald as an Olympic swimmer's ass.

"What we got?" I asked.

Manny answered by holding up a short length of copper pipe. It was about six inches long and three-quarters of an inch in diameter. One end had been blasted apart like a trick cigar.

"Not very big," I said with some surprise. "What about all those flames?"

"Found a jug of barbecue starter on the floor, under the dash."

I looked around the wreck to see what else I'd missed while I was napping. Judging by the current state of the investigation it looked like I'd been out for a good hour or two.

I noticed something missing. I turned to Manwaring, "No broadcast crews here yet?" At a spectacular incident like this I'd expected to see a least one or two television cameras looking for blood, guts, and tears to feed news-hungry America.

Manwaring pointed towards a young woman taking photos with her phone. Barely out of her teens, she looked as if she was snapping vacation shots for her Instagram. "Go say howdy to Kiley from The Lake Placid Shopper."

I stayed where I was.

Overall, the scene was static. Rather like a movie shoot. Bright lights, lots of people milling about, all focused on their own individual jobs. A few members of the New York State Violent Crimes Investigation Team who were unfortunate enough to answer their phones at this ridiculous hour, were poking about, tagging evidence, and unrolling yellow tape. The volunteer fire fighters were rolling up their hoses, walking stiff-legged so as not to slip on the muddy skating rink their water had slicked up. A tow truck beeped as it backed into position to crank the burned-out Audi onto its flatbed for the trip downstate to the labs in Albany.

Mankowski bent down and picked up a carpet tack from the half-frozen sludge of wet leaves, pine needles, and motor oil that had pooled around the car. He twirled the half-inch long, blue-black steel shaft between his fingers. "Christ, her legs musta been hamburger."

I had nothing to add to his expert assessment.

Mankowski dropped the nail back onto the ground. "Next time I wouldn't mind examining the body on site, if you don't mind."

"All the important forensics will be on that vehicle, not the victim." Then I added, "We can drive down have a look at the car tomorrow."

"We?" Manwaring raised an eyebrow. Or lowered his face. With Manwaring it's hard to tell which.

He had a point, of course. The crime had not occurred in my actual jurisdiction. And even if it had, no sane D.A. was going to hand over a homicide like this to a village cop on a one-man force even if that particular cop was once a major crimes detective himself.

I circled the car's mortal remains for a final tour before it was carried off. In the mud by the door I noticed something shiny, a tiny glint of brass. It was a spent rifle cartridge. I picked it up. "Looks like a Remington .233."

Manwaring lifted the shell from my hand for his own perusal. Then he said with some resentment, "You didn't say anything about shots fired."

"Home-made blasting cap?" I suggested.

Like a morning glory growing in the weeds beside a junk yard fence, a smile slowly blossomed on Manwaring's craggy face. He then tapped my bandaged head like he was checking it for ripeness. "Good to see it still works."

I grabbed a latex glove from Manwaring's pocket and snapped it on as if I was now going to ask the car to turn its grill and cough. I opened the car's driver-side door.

The interior of the car had been completely gutted by the fire. I leaned inside and fished around under steering column.

Manwaring was ahead of me. "Ignition looks fine," he said. "Must have wired it to something under the hood."

I straightened up. "You may be right. Ignition harness is pretty tough to access on these models." I went around to the passenger side. "But working under the hood would attract a lot of attention. Too much traffic coming and going from the club." I leaned into the car again and, using my good right hand, the one that wasn't bandaged, reached deep inside the cavern of Swiss cheese that used to be the car's glove compartment. After a moment's fishing I found what I was looking for. Gently, I pulled out a single wire. It was charred, of course, but I could still see where it had been neatly trimmed and stripped.

I showed it to Manwaring. "Wired it to the light fixture inside the glove compartment. Left the compartment door ajar so the switch would already be in the 'on' position. The moment she turned on her headlights…" I didn't have to finish the sentence.

Manwaring asked me, "You up to telling me more about your musician pal?"

We turned and walked toward the entrance of the club. "I've known Simon and Evelyn for about five months."

"He's a doctor. "

"OBGYN."

Manwaring looked like he was trying to sound that out. So I added, "Obstetrician/gynecologist. On staff at Glen Echo Samaritan. Has his own clinic as well."

"And her?"

"Real estate. Residential. Mostly vacation properties."

"Kids?"

"One. A daughter. Going to Paul Smith's." Paul Smith's is a college of hotel management located an hour north of here.

"OBGYN…" The gears in Manwaring's head were whirring so loudly I could actually hear them grind. Then I realized it was just the tow truck's winch. Manwaring said, "Those guys do abortions, right?"

"Among other duties."

"Have any trouble with the pro-lifers?"

"Don't they all?"

"Anything recently?"

I shrugged. "You'll have to check with his office."

Yeah, I knew I was being evasive on my friend Simon's behalf. This was another reason I shouldn't be chief investigating officer on this case.

By now we had reached the bar's entrance. Manwaring held the door open for me, a gesture which I appreciated considering my left hand was wrapped in a bandage the size of a canned ham. As we stepped inside the club, Mankowski paused to survey the room. His hard gaze scraped across the thin, worn carpet, over the broken, mismatched chairs, and across the chipped wooden tables that were carved up like benches in a bad neighborhood. When he finished his visual tour he turned to me and said, "So, you're telling me a big, wealthy twat surgeon spends his weekends in a toilet like this playing rock and roll for free beer?"

I was offended by his choice of words. "Not rock and roll," I said. "Rhythm and blues. And he'd play even if the beer weren't free. We all would. But don't let that get around."

We continued walking across the dance floor. Things seemed busier in here than outside, although busy might not be the right word. Several investigative officers milled about, both in and out of uniform, some taking a welcome break over hot coffee, others still interviewing witnesses. A couple dozen civilians, including bar patrons and staff, hung patiently in the dark shadows, waiting to make statements about whether or not they'd noticed any suspicious strangers walking around with dynamite in their back pockets.

Manwaring pulled out a chair for me. Casey the waitress dropped by our table to see how I was doing, make sure I was all right. We exchanged a few words about the evening's tragedy, both agreeing that Evelyn Reesor was a sweetheart and that Simon was going to be devastated by her death. I assured Casey that Rodger, our guitarist, was staying with Simon tonight and that I'd make sure to keep a close eye on our good friend over the next few days.

After Casey left I turned to Manwaring and stated the obvious. "You know that bomb wasn't meant for Evelyn Reesor, right?"

Manwaring jammed his big hand into a small bowl of pretzels. "I'm listening."

"Simon was supposed to be the one starting that vehicle, not Evelyn. It was his car. Nobody knew Evelyn was going to be here tonight."

"Nobody? Not even the husband?"

"Well, sure, Simon knew. He brought her. But he would be the only one who knew. Evelyn didn't come out to see us play that often."

"Sounds like a lady with taste." Manwaring bit into his pretzel. It didn't break – it just bent. Realizing his mistake, he put the uneaten half back in the bowl. "So, what brought the lady out here tonight?"

"They'd been out to dinner. Evelyn had wanted to talk about…" I hesitated for only a nanosecond, "…about something or other. I don't know. But they'd been out to dinner."

That was a close one. Until this very moment I hadn't given this particular detail any thought. But now I suddenly realized that if I said any more I would be digging a hole for Simon. A deep hole he might have trouble climbing his way out of.

"So, what was it?" Manwaring picked up another pretzel and licked off the salt. "What'd she want to talk about?"

My mind did some quick dancing. It thought about how, since I'd arrived here, Simon had become just about my closest new friend in town. Musically, and personally, we had clicked from the start. We both liked the same good music, laughed at the same bad jokes, and we both agreed that chiropractors, naturopaths, pop psychologists, and pop radio programmers were universally full of shit. So, I really didn't want to say anything that might incriminate my new pal. On the other hand, if Manwaring didn't hear it from me he was surely going to hear it from someone else. Hell, from *every*one else. There are no secrets in small towns like Glen Echo. So, for Simon's sake, I decided it would be best coming from me. I only hoped Simon would one day agree.

"Simon and Evelyn were having problems," I said.

"Problems?"

"Marital problems."

"Marital problems?"

"Right. Marital problems." I wasn't going to make this dance too easy. I was uncomfortable talking this way about my friend. Besides, I was sure it led nowhere.

"He was fucking around?"

"Something like that."

Manwaring shook his head slowly, probably because it was too big to shake fast. "Geez, the guy was a gynecologist. You'd think he'd see enough pussy on the job." Then Manny stopped shaking his head and shook his shoulders, "But hey, I guess even if a guy works all day at Ben and Jerry's, he's still going to want to step out for a lick of *Haagen Dazs* every now and—"

"Her," I said. "*He* caught *her*."

Manwaring said nothing. He couldn't. His brain was now otherwise occupied. Our dance had finished. We were now in the bedroom. Conception was now occurring. A fresh new motive was forming. Complete with villain. The cuckolded husband. It was obvious. The doctor killed his wife because she was screwing around on him.

After waiting through the proper gestation period for this brand new idea to reach full fetal magnificence I then terminated it with, "It's not what you're thinking."

"No?"

"He loved her. Crazy for her. So crazy he was willing to overlook her occasional transgressions." I corrected myself, "Well, maybe not willing, but certainly able."

"Transgressions? You mean there was more than one?"

"Simon wasn't home much. He worked hard at his day gig. And when he wasn't at the hospital or at his clinic he was here, playing with the band."

"When he should have been home playing with his wife."

"All I know is, Simon would never do anything to hurt Evelyn. Like I say, he was devoted to her. Nuts about the woman. Wanted to save the marriage. In fact, I believe that's what they went to dinner tonight to discuss. He was afraid she wanted a divorce. I think he figured she was just going through a stage. Mid-life crisis. You know. Reaffirming her youth. Some people get plastic surgery. Some start riding Harleys. Some take up skydiving..."

"Some play rock and roll."

I let that one go. "Take it from me," I said as I adjusted the bandage on my hand. "This was not a domestic. Simon Reesor did not murder his wife. Somebody else blew up that car."

Manwaring had had enough of me and my input, so he let me know I was dismissed by saying, "You look like shit, Tanager."

"Yeah? Well, your mother dresses you funny."

"Want one of my guys to drive you home?"

"I'm cool." And I was. I stood up, walked up onto the stage, and got my leather jacket from where I'd stashed it behind my speaker cabinet. With some difficulty, I put it on and zipped it up. Then I waved goodnight to Casey and saw myself to the door.

The night's chill bit hard. The first thing I did after I started my car was turn on the heater. Then I waited for the engine to warm up. Then I did some thinking.

Now, in my own defence I must say that when I left the bar that early morning, I had every intention of dropping by the hospital to see how Simon was doing. Honest. But by the time I'd climbed into my car, wincing with every move, I'd had second thoughts. I was dead beat. My hand hurt. My head hurt. My neck hurt. My hair hurt. Besides, I knew Rodger would be watching over our pal Simon for the rest of the night, so I decided to head for home. Besides, I had someone waiting up for me. Someone warm.

Technically, I am single. But that does not mean I am unattached. I do have what is referred to as a *significant other*, significant in that he shares my home and my bed. His name is Stanley, and he has become known around town as my unofficial deputy. Luckily, considering the tight budget I operate on, Stanley is happy to be paid in pats to the head and dog biscuits.

Usually when I get home late at night like this, Stanley is on me like white on country music. But tonight when I opened the front door of my little rented house I saw no sign of the pooch. This usually means only one thing – that he has gotten ahold of something he shouldn't have and has taken it to his favorite hiding place, his cardboard box den under the sink in my living room. Yes, there's a sink in my living room. The house used to belong to a lady who ran a hairdressing salon from her home. I still get women of a certain age knocking on my door with hopes of a rinse and a tint. Anyway, I looked in the makeshift cardboard dog house and there was Stanley. Caught red-handed. Or red-pawed.

I gave him my best, most authoritative show-me-your-license-and-registration voice. "Bad dog."

But he wasn't buying the bust. His big brown eyes looked up at me with glee, and his tail propped into high gear. The perp pup was proud of himself, but he couldn't brag about it - his mouth was full. The furry idiot had my shiny, brand new police chief's hat clamped between his jaws – the very same hat that had sparked a three-hour debate at the special Glen Echo town council meeting called last month to decide whether the item's capital cost should come out of my salary or out of the town's operating budget. The verdict was close, with the mayor finally casting the deciding vote in my favor. He's been holding the hat over my head ever since. So to speak.

"Give that to me," I barked in my best alpha male voice.

Stanley dutifully dropped the hat at my feet.

I picked it up and wiped off the doggy spittle. The imitation patent leather peak had Stanley's tooth marks pressed into it like Braille for a blind cop. Meanwhile, Stanley was already spinning with joy. He knew what was coming.

Yup, I always reward the dog when he follows my orders like this. So, I gave him his biscuit and wondered whether I was teaching him to give up items on command or to steal my hats and chew them up on command. Either way, it's probably a good thing I've never had children.

I took the pooch for a quick walk around the block. Then we both went to bed. But only one of us got any sleep. For what was left of that short night I lay watching my window shade grow lighter and my thoughts grow darker. Stanley, as usual, had dropped off to sleep as soon as his head hit my ankles. But then, his furry cranium wasn't filled with high-def images of an ex-dancer's lower torso ripped to bloody shreds by some maniac's demented home workshop project. Evelyn had once told Simon that, if she was ever mortally injured in a car accident or something, she wanted her organs donated for transplant. That's the kind of person she was. Generous to the grave and beyond. And that is the final insult in this crime. Seems like the bomber has robbed his victim of her last selfless gesture: I'm sure Evelyn's lacerated, crushed, and charred lungs, heart, liver, and kidneys would be of no use to anyone now.

I obviously wasn't going to fall asleep this way. So I tried more positive thoughts.

Hey, that Paul Briar turned out to be quite a guy, huh? Diving into those flames the way he did took guts, especially considering he didn't know Evelyn Reesor. Nor did he know her husband. But Paul Briar and Simon Reesor have a lot in common now – both having lost their wives so tragically. It looks like both men will miss their wives quite a bit. I know that sounds like an odd thing to say, but if there's one thing I've learned in my twenty-odd years of scrounging through other people's psyches and sock drawers, it is this: love is not an absolute. Hate is, but not love. Love comes in as many colors, hues, and intensities as an Adirondack hillside in autumn. And it follows that grief suffered from the loss of a loved one would also vary in intensity. To be frank, I've known some men who, when their wife passed on, lost nothing more than a live-in cook, a housekeeper, and a social secretary. But others lost a vital part of themselves, a vital organ they couldn't live without and no transplant can replace. I hate it when some amateur psych 101 student starts spouting nonsense about the five stages of grief as if such a dense emotion can be reduced to some sort of simple formula. The way I look at it, when a man falls to pieces after his wife dies it isn't a sign of weakness – it's a sign of strength, the strength of a relationship very few of us will ever experience.

Funny, the horseshit that runs through a guy's head when he's listening to the birdies tune up their morning vocals outside his bedroom window, huh?

I lay with my hat-chewing mutt at my feet and wondered if I would ever love someone as deeply as Simon Reesor and Paul Briar seemed to have loved their wives.

Or if I really wanted to.

CHAPTER FOUR

"Sorry to wake you, Chief."

"That's okay," I lied. "You didn't wake me." I yanked the cord of my old landline phone to gain some slack and in the process knocked the electric alarm clock off my night stand. *Play time*, barked Stanley, as he used my groin as a handy springboard from which to leap to the floor. He immediately grabbed the clock and run off with it.

"I know it's early, Chief, but thought you'd want to know…"

"Know what – that's it's early?" I rearranged my bruised balls to a feng shui that might bring more luck and less pain. "No problem," I assured. "I've been up for hours."

I waited for Marlene to make a wisecrack about my being awake at this ungodly hour. As my executive assistant, she knows that we executives never get to the police station before ten in the morning. She knows this because she's always there by eight. Or so she claims.

"I just got off the phone with Karen at EMS."

"Uh, huh?" I swung my legs around and sat on the edge of the bed. "EMS, you say?" I was stalling for time so I could conduct a medical inventory. I tapped my knuckles gently on the outside of my bandaged head to see if it still hurt. At first, it didn't.

"I'm afraid I have some bad news," Marlene said.

"Right, I know. Evelyn Reesor." Marlene didn't always remember which nights I played at Blues and Cues, so I filled her in, "I was there."

"It's not about *Evelyn* Reesor."

It was the way she accented the word *Evelyn* that chilled my blood to ice water. If she wasn't calling with bad news about *Evelyn* Reesor then she must be calling with bad news about…

"What is it?" I asked.

"It's Doctor Reesor…"

I waited. Afraid to take a breath.

"He's, uh… He's dead."

Stanley let out a little whimper. Or maybe it was me.

"How?" I asked. "Where? When?"

"This morning. His home. Gun shot."

"Shot? I don't… But I thought… Is Rodger okay?"

"Rodger?"

"Rodger McGibney. He was with Simon."

"The man who found the body said Doctor Reesor was alone."

"Alone? But how… I mean… Aw, shit."

Marlene waited for me to say more. It was a long wait. My brain had gone numb. Or maybe it was full of too many questions to pick just one. Finally, I thought of something to say.

"I'm on my way."

*****

Simon and Evelyn Reesor's modest three-bedroom ranch home did not scream *successful surgeon.* But I guess, having only the one child, Simon and Evelyn never felt the need to upgrade. Besides, they also keep a winter hideaway in Barbados plus a condo in Baton Rouge which is where Evelyn originally came from. Evelyn is, or was, Simon's second wife. They met seven years ago when she was vacationing up here. Golfing, not skiing. As far as I know, she never fully surrendered herself to the North Country. Simon said she was always after him to pack up his latex gloves and woolen mittens and move his practice down to Louisiana. Sure, she used to say, the tornadoes and hurricanes down there can mess things up a bit, but she'd take them over an Adirondack blizzard anytime. Simon, on the other hand, once told me he'd rather shovel through the snow up here than shovel through the shit he'd have to take down there from the Southern anti-abortion people. In light of last night's events his words might ring ironic.

I pulled my old Ford Crown Vic into Simon's circular drive behind the ambulance that had beat me here. No evidence of the State troopers yet, but they were on their way. Simon's house is outside the town limits of Glen Echo, so this was officially the state's affair not mine. Marlene had called me only because she knew I was a friend of the victim.

The front door was open. I knew my way around inside the house, of course. Our band used to rehearse here. Evelyn, always the gracious southern hostess, would keep us well fueled with cold beer and hot Cajun cooking. She always hated having to substitute walleye for catfish.

As I walked down the hallway I could hear a woman's voice ricocheting from the kitchen.

"Seventy-five yards. Heavy overcast. Not enough light to use my scope, just the peep on my 30-06. But shit, that was enough. That big ol' buck's legs folded like cheap furniture. Straight through the heart. That was three years ago. Have not taken one damn thing since."

"Yeah. Last couple of culls sucked," a man's voice said.

Another man's voice added, "Looks like it's going to be a better harvest this season."

"Hope so," said the woman. "Sure like to pop me another buck."

I've been having to listen to this kind of shit a lot up here. Hunters have as many euphemisms for the word *kill* as the Bible has for the word *fuck*.

I stepped inside the kitchen. Three startled heads turned my way. Two belonged to paramedics: one male, one female. I recognized the male as having dressed my wounds last night at Evelyn's car bombing. Poor guy must be working the tail end of a double shift. I guessed the third person at the table, a big fellow with strong, rough hands, must be the finder. According to Marlene, a stonemason had arrived early this morning to continue some scheduled repair work on the fireplace wall in Simon's billiard room when he stumbled upon Simon's body.

Something about this static tableau facing me struck me as wrong. Off kilter. Three people were seated around the kitchen table, each with a cup of coffee. Trouble was, nobody had served a cup to the fourth person at the table. In fact, nobody was paying much attention to him at all. And that was just not right. Sure, I knew the guy was dead and all, but Simon was always the leader in any group. The guy you look to for his reaction to whatever idiocy was happening around you. A quiet-spoken guy, yes, but Simon could never be ignored. We always wanted his take on things. And now here he was – slumped forward, his head resting on one forearm, his other arm wedged awkwardly underneath his chest, nobody paying the least bit of attention to him. It was just wrong.

"Where'd you get the coffee?" was my first question.

The male medic indicated a large thermos bottle that obviously belonged to him or to one of his friends. "Sorry. None left. Found the mugs in the cupboard." He looked at my bandaged head. "How you feeling?"

"You guys should know better. Please, don't touch anything else." I pulled on a latex glove.

"We didn't touch the vic," the female medic announced in her own defense.

"Except his neck," the male medic added. "Check for cardio."

"Colder'n a Lake Placid hooker's knees," the female medic said. "Saw no reason to poke around any further."

"Ain't none in Lake Placid," the stonemason said.

"None what?" asked the female medic.

"Hookers. There's ski pros. Golf pros. But no sex pros. Gotta drive to Watertown."

"That's on account o' Fort Drum," the female medic explained. "Anywhere's there's soldiers there's hookers."

The other medic asked, "It cost a lot to get laid in Watertown?"

"Depends," the stonemason said. "What grade gas your truck take?"

"Premium."

"Shit. Why'd you buy a truck like that?"

"Didn't know I'd have to drive all the way to Watertown."

I snapped on my latex gloves and tried to tune out the inanity. I was anxious to know whether I was right about cause of death.

"Cops coming?" the stonemason asked someone.

The female medic slapped him on the shoulder and pointed to me. "What the fuck you think *he* is?"

"I mean, like, state cops."

I answered, "They're on their way." I didn't take offense. My uniform is rather subtle, just a light blue shirt with a shoulder crest, no striped pants, and thanks to my hungry dog I wasn't wearing my cap this morning. Most days I tend to look more like a security guard than like a chief of police.

I leaned in for a closer look at my pal Doctor Simon Reesor, henceforth to be referred to as *the victim.* He had collapsed face-forward onto the table. A newspaper, soaked with blood, lay under his head.

I looked to the stonemason, "What time you get here?"

"Little after eight."

The date on the newspaper under Simon's head was today's. Our morning papers, even out here in the boonies, are delivered surprisingly early, often at five or six, which meant Simon had died sometime between six and eight.

The female medic noticed that I was examining the newspaper. "Looks like he was reading it when they shot him," she said.

The male medic, the one who'd attended Evelyn and me eight hours ago, asked me, "Think the shooter was the same guy killed his wife?"

I shook my head, no. "Simon was a doctor. A man of science. They do things neatly. He didn't want to leave a mess."

At this news the woman medic punched her male partner in his arm. "Told ya. Fucker offed himself. You owe me a beer."

The male medic wasn't going down without a fight. He got up from his chair and examined the tile floor under the table. "So, where's the gun? Somebody show me the weapon."

So I did. Simon was a large man with large hands. Too large for a surgeon. Or even a piano player, for that matter. Better for a linebacker. I gently lifted his thorax up from the table while supporting his head. Lying under his chest, clutched tightly in his big left hand, was his wife's tiny twenty-two caliber Smith and Wesson pistol, the one he insisted she carry in her purse when she sat on an open house or went out into the mountains to show a property.

While holding his heavy chest up, I tried not to look at Simon's mouth. I'd rather read the M.E.'s report later. For now, I just left the gunpowder-scorched porcelain tooth crown and the piece of upper lip right where they were, lying on the newspaper next to today's *Morning Smile* – the little joke the paper always prints to get the reader's day off to a light start.

I gently lowered Simon's head back onto the table and noted that there was no exit wound on the back of his skull.

"Fuckin' hell," said the stonemason, speaking for the whole room.

The lady medic/moose murderer was also impressed. "Imagine. A big fucker like him cappin' himself dead with a pea shooter like that."

"He's a physician," I said. "He knew exactly where to point the gun." I'd known it would be suicide, of course. I'd known it long before I had arrived here. Last night I'd watched the last glowing embers of life start fading from his eyes. Smothered out not just by grief but by a heavy blanket of unbearable guilt.

Simon knew the car bomb had been meant for him. He knew it was his fault and his fault alone that his darling wife had been blown to pieces and was now lying in the morgue. How could any man live with a burden like that? Simon had no choice but to finish the job the bomber had started. Any idiot could have seen this coming.

Any idiot.

I turned to the kitchen sink.

"You don't look so good," commented the male medic.

I rinsed my face under the tap. Somebody handed me a towel. I turned back to address my audience. "The police will be here any minute. The *real* police. They'll want to talk with you." And I left the room.

I stepped outside onto the front porch and saw a state patrol car cruising this way, its rooftop lights flashing but no siren. Two more cars popped over the rise behind it.

I got into my car and dialed Rodger on my cell. Rodger was understandably shaken when I gave him the news about Simon. "I don't get it," he sputtered. "I mean, like… I saw how much Sy had to drink. It was a lot. Four, maybe five doubles. Scotch. Straight up. And you know Sy. He's not much of a drinker. When I left the house he was fried, man. Not falling-down drunk but pissed enough that I was sure he couldn't do anything but pass out the minute his head hit that pillow. I… I'm sorry, man. I'm really, really sorry. Fuck, I… I never guessed he might… I mean… Shit, man." Rodger's voice trailed off.

In my rear-view mirror I watched the first State Police unit pull into the drive behind me. I closed my door.

"Don't beat yourself up over it," I said. "It wasn't your fault." And I meant it. Rodger wasn't an experienced cop. This wasn't his error at all. It was purely mine. I knew better. I've seen it all before. I should have stayed with the guy. But I didn't. I was too tired. And my head was sore. And my hand hurt. And my dog needed walking. And…

A bang on the rear fender of my car was followed by a male voice calling out, "Mornin', sunshine."

I bid Roger a quick and gentle goodbye then rolled down my window. An icy breeze blew a dry yellow birch leaf onto my lap. "You still on the job?" I asked with genuine surprise. I didn't expect to see Manwaring here this morning. As head of last night's team he must have been at Blues and Cues until at least dawn. He couldn't have gotten more than a couple of hours sleep.

He leaned into my car and announced, "Looks like you were right." Even at nine in the morning Manny's breath smelled of garlic. Probably breakfast sausages.

I said, "I'm right, huh? That's always nice to hear. About anything in particular?" I picked the dead birch leaf off my lap.

"The bomb. You said it was meant for the Doc." Manny indicated Simon's house. "Looks like they came back to finish the job."

I crushed the leaf in my hands and dropped the crumbs out the window. "Suicide. Swallowed his gun."

"Ha." Manwaring slapped my car's roof. "Told ya. Couldn't live with what he'd done."

I had to admit, Manwaring was flexible. The way he now saw it, or *wanted* to see it, Doctor Simon Reesor, ravaged by guilt, had killed himself, thereby completing the murder/suicide combo and doing the State a huge favor by saving us all the cost of an extensive homicide investigation and murder trial.

"You get any sleep last night?" I asked.

"Sleep? What's that?" Manwaring chuckled. "Maybe I should become a small-town Chief of Police. Sleep late, hand out a few jay-walking citations, chase some skateboarders off the town hall steps, and call it a day by six."

I said nothing to his good-natured jibe. I wasn't in the mood to trade quips. Manwaring misinterpreted my silence. He thought he'd insulted me. So he tried to make nice.

"Look," his voice softened. "I know officially the ball has once again bounced outside your fence. But why don't you throw in with us. You knew the principals involved. I'm sure you've got plenty to add to the mix. I would welcome your help."

"You would? Seriously?"

"Well…" Manwaring always was a lousy liar. "Truth is, I just don't think there's any great mystery here. Husband catches wife spreadin' it around. Husband murders wife. Guy feels guilty about what he's done. Blows his brains out. No brainer…" He laughed. "Literally." Manwaring immediately realized he'd gone too far with his joke. He got serious again. "But hey, maybe I'm wrong. Maybe there's something to this abortion provider angle. Right-to-lifers got a right to be nuts, too. Every group has its extremists. Which reminds me, Chuckles Yasuda wants to see you."

"You called the Bureau?" Chuck Yasuda was an FBI agent stationed in Utica, New York. If Manwaring has already called the feds, he must truly suspect a tie-in to abortion terrorism is possible.

"No, he called me."

Now, that made much more sense. Word must have gotten out. If last night's car-bombing did, indeed, prove to be an act of terrorism, the case would be a matter for the FBI. In particular, for their National Task Force on Violence Against Health Care Providers.

"Johansen called too," Manwaring added.

"Johansen? This isn't a matter for the Sheriff's department."

"It is when an election is coming up. And get ready for lots more. The show has just started. If this thing gets national coverage every elected dickhead in the county is going to want to stick his fat face into the spotlight. Exposure is what it's all about for these guys." Manwaring opened my car door to invite me out. "Come on, Tanager. Join the party. Get your name in the papers. You're already all over the Internet."

"Me? What the–"

"Video. Last night. Somebody caught some nice HD footage of you pulling the vic out of the burning vehicle. Gone viral. You're a big hero."

"Aw, shit." This was not good news. And I wasn't thinking of myself.

"Hey, a little publicity never hurts. Who knows – you may want to run for mayor of Hooterville one day, replace your boss, the priest."

"Minister."

"Whatever. Come on. I'll tell His Holiness the mayor that you're vital to the investigation. He'll have to find another boy to help cats cross the street and pull old ladies out of trees. Let's go." Manwaring started up the front walk.

But I stayed seated right where I was. I called out to him, "You notified next of kin yet?"

Manwaring pointed toward a young woman in uniform who was standing waiting for him by the front door of Simon's house. "Moira. She's very good. College girl. Knows all the right shit to say. She could tell you your grandmother's been eaten by poodles and you'd be ready to donate your inheritance to the ASPCA."

"Make sure she gets hold of their daughter. Fast. Name's Rebecca. Paul Smith's. Number's on Simon's phone. Photo's on top of the piano."

Manwaring nodded as if to say, *You can shut the fuck up now, Chief – I know what I'm doing.*

"And hurry." I pointed to an orange SUV that was pulling off the highway. It boasted the call letters of a TV station down in Watertown. "'Cause here come more cameras."

Manwaring pulled an imaginary comb out of his pocket and pretended to run it through his imaginary hair as he called to me, "You not coming along?"

I turned the keys in the ignition. The old Crown Vic's eight-cylinders barked to life. I yelled out the window, "I'm afraid you'll have to handle this one without me. I'm far too busy."

"What, you got some unlicensed dogs to chase down?"

"Exactly. Gotta round up a couple of pit bulls that have been running around town unleashed."

Manwaring laughed.

But I wasn't joking.

CHAPTER FIVE

If I'd taken the quick route to my next call I would have been there in fifteen minutes, but I didn't. I took the scenic route. I needed scenic. Plenty of scenic. Enough scenic to burn some ugly images off the backs of my eyelids. But today even the beautiful Adirondack mountains weren't scenic enough for this job, so I threw a CD into the player of my old Ford and cranked up the volume. Of course, this didn't work either. Billy Preston's classic grooves just made me think of what a great keyboard player Simon had been. I'll bet the man had been a damn good surgeon, too.

Simon never talked much about his day gig. None of us do. We get together every weekend to forget about our daily grinds not to rehash them. Occasionally, though, during rehearsals or while we were setting up our gear, one of us might mention some particularly interesting event from his work week. That's how I first heard about the letters.

Nowadays, most of these sorts of messages come by text and email, but they used to come by post. I'm not sure exactly how long ago it was we talked about them, but I remember we were outdoors and there were still lots of mosquitoes around. I had swatted one of the little buggers while I was helping Simon lug his keyboard monitor into the club and I almost dropped the thing. I made some crack to Simon about hoping he could fix me up if I suffered a hernia. This steered our conversation to the type of medical procedures Simon performed.

He mentioned that part of his time was spent doing terminations. This, of course, was the white-smocked word for abortions. When I asked him if he ever caught any flack for performing the controversial procedure Simon said that, like many specialists in his chosen field, he occasionally received letters from anti-abortion groups. Most of these communications, he said, were of a non-violent nature – the writer was usually threatening to organize a picket line or some such demonstration out front of Simon's clinic to encourage the Good Doctor to go into some other line of medical practice. Simon said he was always sympathetic toward these anti-abortion groups. He understood their viewpoint. In fact, when he first started his practice, and for purely practical reasons, he didn't perform the operation at all. The way he looked at it, why complicate his professional life with a procedure that, depending purely on the prevailing political wind direction, might blow legal this week but suddenly spin around and gust illegal next week? No other medical specialist has to live with that sort of uncertainty. Besides, at the time, Simon had no strong feelings on the subject, for or against. So he took the easy route and sailed clear of the storm. Eventually, however, he had to change course. It was brought to Simon's attention that teenage pregnancy in America was bursting out of control and preventing a lot of young women, especially disadvantaged young women, from staying in school and finishing their education. Simon thought about his own daughter and what would happen if she became pregnant while still in school. Simon decided it was his duty as a responsible physician to help women out no matter what their decision. But still, whenever he received a letter from some Pro-Life group, he would thank them for their concern. He would go on to explain to the letter writer that less than fifteen percent of his procedures involved terminations and that any protestors wishing to demonstrate at his clinic would only succeed in inconveniencing the eighty-five percent of his patients who were coming to him for assistance in growing nice, fat healthy babies. Simon said this usually cooled down the protestors and enabled him to carry on with his work peacefully.

But then there were the other letters. The ones with no return address. The envelopes addressed to *Baby Killer* and written with pens pressed so hard they almost tore through the envelope paper. Simon's staff was instructed to leave such envelopes untouched so that Simon could open them himself. Outdoors. Under water. He said this mail usually came from individuals, not groups. And curiously, most of these individuals were men, not women.

Simon understood that 99.99 percent of the violent threats were as empty as the heads that made them and that if someone were truly serious about doing a physician harm he or she would not first send a note bragging about it. These people were not legit pro-lifers but illegit nutbars. I told Simon, that if he ever wanted to track down one of these misguided zealots I had friends at the FBI who would look into the matter for him. But Simon didn't seem to think he needed the help, so our conversation turned to matters more immediate – matters such as whether the boobs on Casey, the waitress, were natural or man-made. In this regard, Simon was surprisingly easy to fool. But then his area of medical specialty did lie farther south.

And now here I was, driving through the gloriously all-natural cleavage of the Adirondack mountains, wishing Simon and I had spoken a little more about those letters and a little less about the waitress's impressive topography. I didn't know if Simon kept those threatening letters, but I did know I should have told Detective Manwaring about them. Of course, I would have told him last night when Evelyn was murdered, but I assumed my grieving pal Dr. Simon Reesor would bring the subject up himself today when Manwaring interviewed him. Now, of course, that wasn't going to happen. I also could have told Manwaring about the letters this morning, but I didn't do that, either. Why not, I wondered. Was I playing games? Was I pissed off with Manwaring's patronizing attitude towards me as a small-town cop? Was I holding back the info as a means of holding onto some power for myself? Was I that big an asshole?

Wouldn't surprise me.

I picked up my phone and dialed Manwaring's number so I could un-asshole myself. But my cell couldn't find a tower to connect with – this happens a lot in these mountains – so I vowed to call him as soon as I returned to civilization. Or when I crowned a high hill. But first, I had a little peacekeeping chore to take care of. A task I had been avoiding. A task where I was about to be out-assholed.

* * * * *

The Torrence flats is one of those small sections of the Adirondacks where the Canadian Shield, that great granite invader from the north, tucks itself under a thin quilt of topsoil thereby giving local farmers a few cozy acres of soft arable land, a garden plot where the odd person can scratch a living out of the dirt. And one of the oddest of these odd persons was a man named Len Holand.

I'd never met the man in person, mind you, but I'd heard about him, and what I'd heard was not good. But it wasn't just Len Holand I was coming out here to see today. I was actually coming to talk with his two sons, Clive and Robbie, the two toughs who had remodeled Paul Briar's sports jacket for him last night at the bar.

I dragged my tired eyes off the passing scenery long enough to check my GPS. The little screen told me I had just passed Al Levesque's Chiropractic Clinic and Taxidermy shop. Up here, a lot of people have to hold down two or three gigs to pay the bills. Anyway, according to Marlene I was now supposed to keep my sleepy eyes open for the Holand farm. I slowed down so I could check out the passing addresses. Most people out here post their names on their mailbox, their gate post, barn roof, or dead horse, but after driving a good quarter mile without seeing the Holand family name, I deduced that this particular family wasn't seeking drop-in trade.

Just as I was ready to admit defeat and ask a neighbor for directions, I saw something I recognized from the parking lot at Blues and Cues Roadhouse – it was Clive Holand's rusted-out old Firebird. The car was parked beside a large wooden outbuilding of some sort. Probably a barn. But I'm no expert. I pulled up to the fence gate.

The property was big, surprisingly prosperous and well-kept. A gleaming white, freshly-painted porch embraced three sides of a large, two-story yellow brick farm house. Gingerbread trim spiced the roofline, and an iron-railed widow's walk topped off the mansard roof. Behind this homestead stood several outbuildings that included that large barn, maybe dairy, and two long, low buildings which I guessed to be, maybe, chicken coops. But I'm no farmer. Beyond these buildings, large fields lay spread out on their backs, bare naked like they were waiting for some sort of action. Being the middle of November, I guessed they were in for a long wait. The entire property was edged with crisp, white, newly-painted wooden fences. Or maybe the fences were made of that composite stuff that doesn't need painting. I'm no carpenter either.

I stepped out of the car and discovered that the gate was locked. I could have hopped over it, of course, and walked up to the house, but I have too much respect for country dogs to do something that dumb.

A couple of little kids were playing on the front porch. They appeared to be pre-schoolers. They looked my way. I waved. They turned away.

To the left of the house two men on tractors were plowing or mowing or tilling or doing something, I'm sure, quite useful to the dirt. I waited, but they didn't look my way. So, I went back to my car, reached through the open window, and gave my horn a quick, tentative beep. Unobtrusive. Barely a sixteenth note.

The kids on the porch looked at me again. The men in the field did not. Somebody inside the house cracked open the front door and the youngsters promptly scurried into the open wedge of darkness. I turned my attention back to the men on tractors. Maybe they couldn't hear me over the sound of their engines.

I didn't want to seem rude, but I honked again, two quarter notes and a half note, and this time the men did look my way. But neither of them did anything to indicate that they were going to get off their machines. I got back into my car and picked up my cell phone.

Happily for me, my phone found a signal. So I dialed up the directory, searched Holand's name, and hit the call button.

"Yes." It was a woman's voice. In the background I could hear a baby crying.

"Hi, there, ma'am. This is Chief Tanager, Glen Echo Police Department. I wonder if Clive or Robbie Holand might be around?"

She paused – they usually do when they're told they're talking to a cop. Then they usually ask what I'm calling about. But this one didn't. "Just a moment," she said. And I heard a click as she put me on hold.

I kept my eye on the two tractors working the field. One of them slowed to a stop. Then my phone line popped to life again.

A man sighed, "Yeah?"

The sound of the tractor's engine now carried through the phone line. I grabbed my binoculars from my back seat. Yup, I was talking to the man on the tractor. Had to be Len Holand. His face was shaded by a cap, but I could tell he was too old to be either of the boys.

"Mr. Holand, this is Chief Tanager from the–"

"I know who you are," he stated.

The guy was clearly watching me from his tractor and could surely recognize my patrol car with the big Glen Echo Police Department logo on the side of it, but this didn't seem to impress him.

"It's about your sons, Robbie and Clive."

He paused, but he didn't budge off his Massey Ferguson. "Some sort of trouble?"

I couldn't believe it. This asshole was going to continue talking to me on the phone even though he could see I was sitting here in plain sight, just a couple of acres away. Or hectares. Or sections. Or furlongs.

For the sake of peace and civility I played along with his game. "Sir, I'm parked over here by your front gate." I waved, gave him a big friendly *yoohoo*. "If you could just come talk to me for a moment, maybe we could–"

"The boys okay?"

"Mr. Holand, I would prefer to speak with you in person if you don't mind. You see, I–"

"Supposed to rain this weekend."

"Uh, huh…"

"Roof on the chicken coop needs mending or I'm gonna have a lot of wet hens."

I guess that's a bad thing, but I'd had enough of this crap. "Sir," I said. "You ought to know that if it wasn't for the goodness of my big, kind heart your two sons would now be eating off tin plates and you'd be mortgaging that leaky chicken coop to raise bail."

He paused before saying, quietly but sternly, "Grant Hindle wouldn't talk to me in that manner."

"Well, unfortunately, Chief Hindle is somewhere on a Florida golf course sweet-talking alligators, and I'm afraid you're stuck dealing with me now. So, you have a decision to make: Would you care to mosey your ass on over to the gate and discuss this in a civilized manner with the handsome new Chief of Police, or shall I just go sober-up Judge Saperstein, get a warrant for your sons' arrests, and let some Lake Placid lawyers get rich off all of us?"

After a beat, I heard his tractor shift into gear. Meanwhile, the second man, the guy on the other tractor, looked over to see what was going on. I guess this guy decided it was nothing important because he went back to work spreading fertilizer on the field. I knew it was fertilizer because I'm a trained detective. And I have a nose. Plus, I could see a stack of large plastic bags near his tractor that were marked *Fertiliser.*

As Holand came closer I noticed he had a beard - not the usual Adirondack mountain-man weed-patch, but a neatly trimmed face-hedge.

When he got to the gate he stepped down off his tractor. But he left the engine running to let me know his time was precious and chicken coop roofs don't mend themselves. He walked to the fence, pulling off his leather work gloves as he strode.

Len Holand was an inch or two shorter than I – maybe five-eleven – and about twenty pounds more solid. When he got to the fence he thumbed his John Deere cap back so I could get the full effect of his dark piercing eyes. He said nothing, challenging me to blink first. So I did.

"Clive and Robbie assaulted a man in the Blues and Cues Roadhouse last night - a visitor to town."

"And now you're worried about a decline in tourism?"

"I'm worried about a decline in your sons' freedom to mend chicken coops."

"This tourist fellow… he pressing charges?"

"I don't believe so."

"Nice meeting you, Chief." Len Holand turned to go.

"But I might."

He turned back to me. "You going to?"

"I was there when it happened," I said. "Your sons jumped the man. The assault was unprovoked. Malicious. Plenty of witnesses besides me. I'll have no trouble gaining a conviction if I so wish."

"And do you *so* wish?"

"I'd rather not. Not if there's a viable alternative."

"I appreciate your restraint, Chief." He said the word *Chief* the same way I say *telemarketer*. "You were right to come to me with this." Holand put his work gloves back on. "If what you say is true I assure you the boys will be punished in a manner befitting the gravity of their transgression." His words were over the top but still sincere. Bitterly sincere.

"Mr. Holand, I'm all in favor of discipline starting in the home. There's nothing like a little spank on the butt to get a child's attention. But your boys aren't children. Clive is, what, in his early twenties? And Robbie can't be far behind. I don't know what they were like when they were growing up or how you dealt with them, but for some reason they've grown into big, nasty bullies. My experience tells me that bullying tends to be a learned trait. So, if you think you should continue to bully them the way you're now trying to bully me you're making a big mistake."

He paused to take a long look at me and a quick glance at the fence. I believe, for the first time since I'd arrived, he was sorry the fence was between us.

I continued, but with a little less hardness, more sincerity, "Look, Len. I really have to speak with Clive and Robbie myself. I need to tell them that this is both my only and my final warning. One more incident, no matter how trivial the infraction, I charge them."

"I'll pass along your message."

"Uh, uh. Not good enough. Those men, your sons, are going to hear this from me, not from their Daddy."

"Well, right now they aren't going to hear it from either of us. They aren't here."

"Sorry, but I don't believe you."

He turned his back to me and headed back to his waiting tractor. He mounted it like he was mounting a horse. The big rumbling machine seemed almost to cower and whimper when he laid his large hand on the gearshift and said to me, "I don't care what you believe, Chief. It doesn't change the fact that Clive and Robbie never came home last night."

Huh? I pointed toward the barn. "Robbie's car is here. The same car I saw at the club last night."

"What was that - around eleven? Midnight?"

"More or less."

"By that hour you no doubt had a beer or two yourself. Moretti, right?"

Now he was showing off. I was getting tired of his game. "Look," I said. "I don't know how you conned Chief Hindle into pussyfooting around you and your boys for this long, but he's gone now. And his problems are now my problems. Two of those problems – Clive and Robbie Holand – are still just minor problems. But as any dentist can tell you, minor problems, when ignored, can become major problems. And I plan to stop this decay right now."

"You worried about gum disease?"

I had to laugh. "Okay. Maybe I pushed the metaphor a little too far. But you know what I'm getting at."

"You're right, Chief, you have got yourself some problems. A murder and a suicide, all within twenty-four hours. More violence than this sleepy little community has seen in thirty-some-odd years."

I was surprised. "You… you know about Doctor Reesor?" Hell, Simon's body was discovered just a few hours ago.

"I do indeed. And if the Good Lord will forgive me, I can't say I'm terribly sad about it."

Now it was my turn to feel sorry the fence was between us. "You had a problem with Doctor Reesor?"

"Like I said, Chief, when I see Clive and Robbie I'll relay your message." Then Holand white-knuckled the gearshift lever as if he were choking the life out of it. But before he drove off he said, "By the way, you do know this is deer season, right?"

"You mean that's where the boys are?"

"Let's see… Clive's truck is gone. So are the ATV's. Two of our rifles are missing. And yesterday morning Charlotte loaded a couple of thermos containers with her Irish stew. Yes, deer hunting would be my guess." He then added, "'Course, I'm no hot-shot Buffalo homicide detective, so I could be mistaken." With that he slammed his tractor into gear. The transmission screamed in pain.

I gave him a big shit-eating grin and yelled, "Thanks for the chat, asshole." Yes, I knew the tractor engine was drowning me out. But it felt good anyway.

I got into my car and tried Manwaring's number again. This time I got through. He was still at Simon Reesor's house with his team. I gave him an early Christmas present.

"You found the letters yet?"

He hated to ask, but he had no choice. "Letters? You mean, like, love letters?"

"Hardly. Talk to the staff at Doctor Reesor's clinic. They'll fill you in. Probably lots of texts and emails, too. But I'd start with the letters." I hung up.

As I backed my car away from Len Holand's gate I glanced up at his house and noticed the drapes sway in the front window. Then the front door opened and the children rushed out to resume their activities. You can go outside now, children – the bad man in the uniform is leaving.

Turning onto the paved county road, I thought about Detective Manny Manwaring and how he probably wasn't going to look very long or hard at those threatening letters before passing them along to the feds. Manwaring was more interested in the *domestic* angle. And nine times out of ten, he'd be right. The vast majority of homicides are committed by someone close to the victim. That's why we usually start looking for our suspects in the bedroom and fan out from there. Usually, by the time we reach the kitchen liquor cabinet we have our perp nabbed. But in Evelyn Reesor's murder I knew this couldn't be true. I knew Simon loved his wife. Besides, and I don't want to be flip about this, but what kind of a husband would kill his wife by blowing up his own car? A brand new one, at that?

Of course, Manwaring would answer me: *a smart twat surgeon who wants to make a domestic homicide look like terrorism, that's what kind.*

CHAPTER SIX

I stopped by my house to get Stanley, and together we walked to the office. We both needed the exercise. And at least one of us needed some time to think. I needed a few minutes to consider my late pal Simon not as a victim, not as a suspect, not even as a prominent surgeon, but simply as a friend. I felt I owed him that much. So far I'd been referring to Simon constantly in the cold clinical jargon of criminal investigation, and it felt wrong. So I walked and took the time to feel sorry for myself and for everyone else who'd grown to know and love Simon and Evelyn.

The crisp autumn air smelled of wood smoke. And I like that. It's a smell you no longer get in the city. I didn't rush our walk – I let Stanley inspect and tag every lamp post along the way. My house was just a short stroll from the police station, a location I chose so I could easily come home for lunch and walk Stanley. At least, that was my original plan. Just like having the pooch sleep in another bed in another room was my original plan. Sometimes I feel original plans are highly overrated.

The offices of The Glen Echo Police Department are tucked away inside the Glen Echo Town Hall, an old stone building in the center of town that sits halfway up a hill. But then, everything in the Adirondacks sits halfway up a hill. As the pooch and I approached the building one of us, the shorter one, paused to baptize his favorite fire hydrant. While Stanley pissed on the cast iron fixture I prepared to do the same to the crowd of people I could see up ahead, waiting for me on the town hall steps, a scarved and mittened throng that included at least three television news crews – two from Watertown and one from Utica. To me, the news reporters seemed far too young to be real newspeople, but what do I know – I still read news I can fold.

As soon as the zygotes with microphones noticed my uniform they rushed me. Poor Stanley was only halfway through his squirt, so I stepped in front of him to give him some privacy. The poor guy has a shy bladder.

"Sorry, folks," I said. "You're wasting your time here. Both cases are being handled by New York State's finest. Your contact is Investigator Szczepan Manwaring. That first name is spelled… well, exactly as it sounds."

The pooch was finished peeing now, so we continued our climb up the steps while, behind us, the reporters shouted their usual inane questions. One young woman aimed her smart phone's voice recorder at me and asked, "How does it feel, like, to have two such horrible murders occur, like, you know, one right after the other like this?"

"Not good," I said. "I wish it were the other way round."

She actually nodded her approval at that one. I decided I owed them an official statement, so I turned and faced them full-frontal and let them have it. "The Glen Echo Police Department has nothing whatsoever to do with the investigation of last night's and this morning's tragic incidents. The events did not occur within our geographical jurisdiction and neither of the victims resided in the town of Glen Echo. If, on the other hand, you'd like to hear the grizzly details pertaining to the recent break-in at the Yarn Barn, I'd be happy to fill you in." I pulled my notepad from my breast pocket and flipped it open so as not to miss any pertinent details. "It seems the thief had a penchant for pre-shrunk, blue-green angora. I believe the color is sometimes referred to as *teal*, but don't quote me on that. I don't know how fast a knitter the perp is, but this winter my department will be keeping a close eye on any local pawn shops looking to fence new sweaters, scarves, or mittens knitted in said suspect hue. I do not know what prompted this latest crime-wave. Personally, I blame the Yarn Barn's knitting needle-exchange program."

En masse, the crowd groaned and turned off their cameras. And as they packed up their gear I made a more sincere and more confidential plea. I reminded them that Simon and Evelyn's family may still be awaiting notification, so please don't identify either victim by name until okayed to do so by the state investigating authorities. The kids seemed to understand me, although it's hard to tell with communications majors.

I turned and entered the town hall, one hand holding Stanley's leash, the other holding the tattered remnants of my chewed-up Chief of Police cap.

Inside the foyer, a frosted glass door proudly announced, in flaked gold lettering edged in black, *Glen Echo Police Department - Chief of Police, Grant Hindle.* The mayor has promised to get this sign updated any day now. In truth, though, he's waiting for my six-month probationary period to finish to see if my name is really the one he wants in gold leaf. With just two weeks left to go on that probation, I still haven't heard any news one way or the other. But I notice he hasn't called the sign painter yet.

I stepped inside the outer office and continued on past the four-foot-high security counter that effectively guards our inner sanctum from any three-foot-eleven-inch assassins wearing low heels.

The inner bullpen area is unnecessarily spacious, a holdover from a hundred years ago when this room coffee-and-donuted an eight-man police force, all of whom sported giant moustaches that needed plenty of turning space. Of course, that was before the town's feed mill ground to a halt, the furniture factory went legs-up, and the boot leather tannery marched south to a spot where it could pollute the mighty Hudson more directly.

In the basement we have four lockups. One, I still use for incarceration, mainly drunk and disorderlies. The other three jail cells provide safe and secure storage for my band's gear: a few guitar amps, a full P. A. system, and an old set of Ludwigs. My desk is up here on the main floor out in the bullpen area. I have an inner office which I don't use - that would just mean one more door for the mayor not to change the name on.

I said hello to my assistant Marlene and noticed the hands of the wall clock behind her head were pointing to one o'clock. That meant it was actually noon. A few days ago, when I had tried to change the thing from daylight saving to standard time, the little knob on the back fell off. The town council has promised to buy us a new clock, but until then we just subtract an hour from this one.

Marlene had saved a fresh donut from her breakfast for Stanley and a cup of warmed-over decaf for me. I don't like decaf, but Marlene does, and our budget allows only the one coffee maker. I poured myself a cup of the pointless brew and watched Marlene carefully split the donut in two. She popped one half in her own mouth and gave the other half to Stanley. The smaller half.

"Vet says we aren't supposed to feed him that junk," I reminded her. "He's getting fat."

"Donuts won't hurt," she mumbled, her mouth spraying a blizzard of powdered sugar over her breasts as if preparing the ski hills for an early season. "Look how svelte and sylphlike they've kept me."

When I first started working here and Marlene made one of these self-deprecating cracks about her size I would quickly respond with some hair-stroking cliché like, "You're not overweight, just under-height." But you can deny the obvious for only so long. Marlene is indeed a big girl. But I think she carries it well. In my eyes, she's quite sexy. Of course, my eyes aren't what they used to be. Ever since my divorce they've found themselves attracted to larger women. The lady shrink back in Buffalo told me this was because my ex-wife was slim, so now I'm overcompensating. I don't need to tell you what kind of figure the lady shrink had – only a skinny chick would think a guy has to be screwed up to like large women.

As she overfed my dog, Marlene stayed silent and tried to play it cool, but I knew she had to be curious about the two recent homicides, so I quickly brought her up to date on the deaths of Simon and Evelyn Reesor. I didn't particularly want to tell her about my own active participation in last night's action, but Marlene couldn't help noticing the bandages wrapped around my head and my left hand, so I got that business out of the way as quickly as possible. I didn't make myself out to be a big hero because some people don't like bullshit with their donuts. I did tell her that the whole thing was apparently on the Internet. As I was giving her this blow-by-blow, Marlene's A.M. radio was playing in the background. It was tuned to a local station up in Saranac Lake, and the announcer was just starting his noon news break. When I heard his lead headline, I stopped talking and hushed Marlene to do the same. I didn't want to miss a word.

The male newscaster reported that a prominent Adirondack area physician had died this morning. *By gunshot*, he said. That was okay, I thought. There are lots of doctors in the area. A whole hospital-full, actually. *The State Police aren't saying whether foul play was expected.* Fine too, I thought. The reporter went on, *The deceased man's wife had been murdered in her car late last night.* Still okay. I held my breath as the reporter leaked a few more details about the car bombing. Each time the reporter opened his mouth the leak flowed faster. Gushed harder. I could feel it coming. And I was right. The dam broke:

Dead... are... Doctor Simon Reesor and his wife Evelyn Reesor.

Aw, shit. I grabbed the phone.

*****

"You, uh… say you're a police officer?" The young lady on the other end of the line was understandably cautious.

"Chief of Police, actually. Town of Glen Echo. There's been a family emergency. Is Miss Reesor close by? I'd like to—"

An older woman's voice suddenly cut in on the line. She must have been monitoring the call. "I know what this is concerning," she said. "And you're about twenty minutes too late."

My heart sank. "So, she's heard the news then? About her parents?"

"Rebecca is currently in our infirmary. Nurse Alice has given her a sedative."

I was afraid to ask this next question, but I had to. "Could you tell me how Miss Reesor heard the news?"

There was a long pause. Then… "A friend texted her."

"Oh, no. I'm sorry."

"We immediately phoned the state police, of course."

"Of course."

"They wouldn't say much. Only that there's a trooper on the way."

"I'm sorry." I repeated, "I'm truly sorry that Rebecca had to hear it this way. There's no excuse for this."

"No, there isn't."

The woman had no more to say on the matter. And neither did I. Not to her, at least. I shouldn't have trusted Manwaring. The guy's a good investigator, but when it comes to the simple grunt work he leaves too many details to others.

I dialed Manwaring's cell number and got him at Simon's house where he was still working with his team. I informed him that I wanted to go up to the school and pick up Rebecca myself.

"But my trooper's almost there," Manwaring replied.

"A*lmost*?"

"Ten minutes. Just talked to her. According to her GPS she's three-point-two miles away from the college."

"I think I'd better go anyway."

Manwaring said, "I thought you weren't on this case."

"I owe it to Simon."

"And you feel guilty."

"That too."

"So what's my trooper supposed to do? Sit on her thumbs with the doctor's daughter for two hours waiting for you to join the party just so you can ease your fucking conscience?"

I thought this over. He had a point. "You're sure your trooper's almost there?"

"Satellites don't lie, sweetcheeks. By my reckoning Trooper Moira Lacroix will have your friend's daughter briefed, packed, and delivered to the loving arms of her aunt and uncle before dinner."

"Rebecca will be staying with Simon's brother?"

"You don't think we'd bring her back to her old man's house, do you? Shit, we haven't even wiped his brains off the toaster yet."

Manwaring seemed to have the matter well in hand, even if it was a rough hand. So, I told him to go ahead with his plans – I'd keep out of things for now. He seemed to like this idea just fine.

As I hung up the phone Marlene said, "If you're anxious to visit a school, may I suggest one closer to home?"

Damn. I knew what she was referring to. "The troll back at Cairnwood?" I asked.

"And the mayor's not too pleased about it."

"I'll bet he isn't." Cairnwood, an exclusive girls' school located just outside town, had recently been having trouble with a flasher. Because of the man's modus operandi – running out of the forest, dropping his pants, and promptly scurrying back into the trees – Marlene had christened him the Trouser Troll. And because my boss, Mayor Timothy Stinson, was an ordained minister who disapproved of any leisure activities that involved trousers, I'd been instructed to nab the creep, pronto. To add to the gravity of my mission, Mayor Stinson reminded me that he has influential friends on the school's board of directors, friends who could make or break a mayor's political aspirations faster than he could say *campaign contribution*.

I put on my official police jacket with the corduroy collar and my official Police Chief's cap with the bite marks in the peak, and I grabbed Stanley's leash. "C'mon, fella. We're off to catch ourselves a pervert."

I don't think Stanley was particularly impressed with the importance of our mission. But he's not running for office.

*****

The name plate on her desk read simply *Ms. Craven*. No first name. No initials. Such details would serve only to humanize.

I was sitting in the Cairnwood School for girls where I'd been sent to the principal's office not because I'd been a bad boy but because some other guy had been a bad boy. This creep had exposed himself on the soccer field. Again. He had done it a couple of times before, but this time one of the students has apparently drawn of sketch of the perp. That sketch was now in the iridescent white hands of the school principal.

"Sharla is one of our more gifted art students," Ms. Craven said as she handed me the sheet of stiff art paper, *stiff* being the operative word.

"She certainly is talented," I said as I examined the hand-drawn charcoal sketch of a semi-erect penis. "I like how she's shaded it. Almost three-dimensional." I was tempted to comment on how the testicles seem to turn and follow your eyes around the room, but I didn't want to make light of an obviously serious situation. So I just handed the drawing back to Ms. Craven and added, "But I don't think it's something we can pin up on the post office wall."

Ms. Craven laid the drawing on her desk face down. The drawing that is, not Mrs. Craven. She said, "This was the only feature Sharla really saw of the gentleman. Apparently, he wears a ski mask."

I took my pen and spiral memo pad from my pocket. "Did she happen to note the color of that mask?"

"Blue and green."

"Uh, huh…"

"Checked."

"Sounds like a tartan."

"I think so."

I pointed my pen at the young artist's sketch. "So we're looking for an uncircumcised Scotsman."

I smiled to let her know I was joking. I suspected that if she had smiled back it would be an attractive smile. But I'll probably never know – her auburn hair was pulled back too tightly to allow much facial expression. The bun in back was gripped in the hungry jaws of a tortoise shell clip. Her white polyester blouse was tied in a bow high at the neck and, I suspect, padlocked. Below that, a long tweed skirt kept her legs and ankles merely rumors.

"Security cameras?" I asked.

"I'm afraid he always picks the rare locations that are not covered."

"That can't be an accident. How about photos? Any of the girls ever catch this guy on their phone cameras?"

"You mean the *students*?"

Shit. I'd said *girls*. I should have said *students* or *ladies*. I replied, "Yes. Seems young ladies today always have a phone with them."

"Not at Cairnwood they don't." With this statement Mrs. Craven's eyes finally came to life. "During school hours students must leave their phones in their dorm rooms."

I asked a few more questions and ended the interview by promising to do everything I could to locate this perp, including once again interviewing the few known sex offenders in the area. I'd already spoken to most of these jerks at least once about these Cairnwood incidents, but it never hurts to let the men know I'm still watching them.

Our meeting over, Ms. Craven insisted on escorting me back to my car. Either she didn't trust me in a building full of young girls or she didn't trust me to find my way around the campus without getting lost in the woods. Smart woman.

When we reached my car I opened the passenger door and introduced Ms. Craven to Stanley. And this was where the lady finally lightened up. She gave the pooch a big, enthusiastic pat and, despite her tight hair do, managed to flash a warm juicy smile which won both of us over. She even bent down and let one of us lick her face. When Stanley finished slurping he left her and hurried to the edge of the woods to water a tree. Meanwhile, Ms. Craven sprinkled me with a brief history of the school and its more notable alumnae. This gave me the opening I'd been waiting for.

"You're obviously far too young to have been around here 'way back when, but didn't Nancy Briar attend Cairnwood?" I figured Ms. Craven would know Nancy Briar's name from the news reports last spring about the missing canoeist.

She immediately corrected me. "You mean Nancy Gaddsen. Yes. I knew Nancy. Not well, though. When I attended Cairnwood as a student she was a couple years behind me." Ms. Craven then added, "And please, call me Stephanie."

A couple of years behind? Ms. Stephanie Craven must be older than she looked. But now that I was seeing her in the daylight…

Stephanie continued, "So sad. Her poor husband…"

"Paul. He's come back to town."

"Right." She pointed towards the lake. "That's him out there."

Huh? I turned. And far out across the water I could see a small aluminum fishing boat chugging along the distant shore. I squinted for all I was worth, but frankly, my eyes couldn't tell if it was Paul Briar or Cap'n Crunch at the tiller. "Oh, yes," I lied, as if my long distance vision were as keen as Ms. Craven's. "Paul mentioned he was staying out here at the lake. That bed and breakfast, uh…" I fumbled for the name.

"Windermere," Stephanie said.

"Right, Windermere." We stood for a moment watching the sad little boat slowly putter along the line of bare naked maple trees. Or oak. Or aspen. "Seems rather late in the season for fishing," I offered.

"Oh, he's not fishing." She said this with certainty.

"No?" I recalled how Briar had told me that he and his wife had come up here last spring so she could visit her old alma mater, Cairnwood school, and how it was here, on this lake, that she had gone canoeing the day she disappeared. I said to Stephanie, "He isn't still searching for her is he?"

Stephanie smiled sweetly. "Hope burns eternal."

Yeah. So does denial, I thought.

We stood in silence, both pondering Paul Briar's quest for closure, and I reviewed the details of her disappearance.

Last May, Nancy Briar's canoe was found wrecked at the bottom of a set of rapids. Apparently, she'd gone out for an early morning paddle. Alone. Before breakfast while her husband was still in bed. She never returned. Her disappearance sparked one of the largest search efforts in the Adirondacks' history. No efforts were spared. Park rangers recruited an army of volunteers to march arm-in-arm through the woods along both sides of the river that flowed from this lake. The New York State Police brought down a Scuba Unit from troop B at Ray Brook to drag the lake and waterway below the rapids. Even a couple of K-9 teams from Cooperstown loaned their cold wet noses to the hunt. But no luck. After six weeks the lead state investigator officially terminated the search. By that time it was late June. The blackflies and mosquitoes must have been murder. Paul Briar, who had no family to worry about back home, stuck around for a few weeks longer, but finally, even he accepted the obvious conclusion. Or so everyone thought. Paul left the park and returned to New York City where he worked as some sort of television producer. Soon after that, in early July, I entered the picture. Glen Echo's previous Police Chief had recently retired and, in a final display of poor judgement, had recommended me for the gig. And here I am today, chasing unzipped perverts. Of course, the search for Nancy the missing canoeist never did have anything to do with Glen Echo's police department, as I've been trying to explain to Briar. That's why I'm not more up to speed on the case.

I pointed along the shore, to what I thought was upstream. "Far to the rapids?"

Stephanie indicated the opposite direction. "Down there. You enter the Khashe River. The falls are about two miles downstream."

"I don't get it," I said. "If she drowned going over the falls, wouldn't her body end up somewhere farther down river rather than back here in the lake?"

Stephanie was patient with me as she explained, "Nancy could have drowned here in the lake and the wind or current just carried her empty canoe into the river. It's a deep lake. For its size, it can get surprisingly rough." Almost on cue, a sudden offshore breeze gusted, catching the hem of Stephanie's long wool skirt. She was fast on the draw and preserved the modesty of her knees if not her ankles. Maybe that's why I saw this woman as being younger than she was. Not a lot of older women up here wear long, flowing skirts. Or any other kinds of skirts for that matter. Certainly not in November. Mountain women know better. The Adirondacks in autumn is strictly jeans, leggings, heavy slacks territory.

By this time, Stanley had finished watering the ferns and was now signing off his artwork by taking a dump. I fished into my pockets. "Damn," I said. "I forgot to bring a plastic bag." I started toward my cruiser. "I probably have some in my car."

But Stephanie grabbed my sleeve. "Leave it right where it is. We're fully organic."

"That's nice," I said while making a mental note to watch my step. I then looked back out across the lake one last time and asked her, "Windermere Inn… close by?"

Stephanie pointed to a clearing across the lake towards which Paul Briar's boat seemed to be heading. "When you turned off the highway, if you had taken the first right instead of left… You didn't see the sign?"

"Must've missed it." I didn't tell her that, for much of the drive here, I had been embroiled in a rescue struggle with a moth. The poor thing had gotten itself trapped in that little crevice between the dashboard and the windshield and was struggling to get out. I managed to catch and release it, but in the process almost put my car in the ditch.

Stephanie Craven and I stood for one last moment and watched Paul Briar chugging his slow, pointless way down lake towards Windermere Inn, struggling to get free of his own crevice, I guess. As I watched him I realized this would be a good opportunity for me to stop by and thank him for helping me pull Evelyn Reesor's body from the burning wreck last night. To be completely honest, though, for a while now I'd been looking for an excuse to visit Windermere Inn. And to be even more honest, my reasons for this visit involved a woman. A woman about whom I'd heard certain rumours.

I selfishly hoped those rumours were not true.

CHAPTER SEVEN

She was as attractive as I'd remembered. Maybe even attractiver. After all, the harsh fluorescent lighting in Pengilly's hardware store where'd I'd first laid eyes on her had washed out those high cheekbones, and the key cutter machine's screaming rasp had ground flat her rich sultry voice which, I now noticed, flowed as silky smooth as a sax solo by Stan Getz.

We'd already talked about the area's most recent tragedies – Simon and Evelyn's deaths last night – and were now on to more pleasant topics.

"Yes, I'm a 'Dacker," she said. "Third generation. Born in Saranac. Left for school. Got married. Saw the error of my ways. Came back. And with the help of some kind friends and a vicious divorce lawyer, bought this place. That was eight years ago."

"Naaann," drawled her lady friend, stretching the one-syllable word to the breaking point of soft taffy.

"Right, nine," Lindsay agreed. "It started out as a farm house, circa eighteen-eighty. We turned it into a B and B."

"Bed and Breakfast," explained Sharon just in case I'd rolled out of my patrol car head-first.

Lindsay placed her slim hand on the back of her young friend's neck and gave it a tender rub. "Then Sharon joined me. She brought a small infusion of capital and a large infusion of creativity."

"The kitchen needed just scads of work," added Sharon in a nasal banjo twang that sounded like Scarlett O'Hara if, instead of a grand estate, *Tara* had been the name of a double-wide trailer. "We enlarged the dining room, slapped on some individual baths, and made it into a raaat proper Inn."

"Or at least as proper as we care it to be," Lindsay added with a smile and a wink. It was a smile and a wink I could feel clear down to my toes.

Damn. If this Lindsay Porter woman had indeed "gone lesbo," as the fellas at Sam Pengilly's Hardware had warned me she had, somebody should be arrested. I don't know who but somebody. We're short enough on eligible women up here – we don't need to lose the hot ones to the other team. And Lindsay was indeed hot. I couldn't remember the last time I saw a woman with such easy, understated sex appeal.

In her late thirties, maybe early forties, Lindsay was wearing jeans and a thin jersey-knit sweater. No bra. She said I'd caught her running through some paperwork. Too bad I hadn't caught her running through the lawn sprinkler. But frankly, it wasn't what was happening below the neck that had me so enraptured. It was well above that. Her eyes. Dark and wide-set. And when they looked directly at me, which was most of the time, they seemed to bore holes through my skull like lasers doing brain surgery. Or heart surgery.

Her friend Sharon was attractive, too, but in a more obvious sort of way. Younger. Curvier. A bouncy castle in leggings.

We were sitting in the inn's Adirondack room – an electrically-heated glassed-in porch facing the lake – sipping herbal tea and watching Paul Briar's boat slowly chug and shiver its way against the cold autumn breeze toward the inn's dock. Lindsay had warned me that the little fishing craft would take a while to get here, having only six horses pushing it. But I didn't mind the delay. And neither did Stanley who was lying on a scatter rug with his head on Lindsay's foot. Every now and then I caught the pooch glancing up at her snug-fitting jeans and panting. Dogs are so obvious.

Outside, on the large lawn that separated us from the lake, a man on a garden tractor was vacuuming up dry leaves and pine needles. His name was Wilf, a gardener who, much to Lindsay's dismay, simply refused to stop using weed killer. Lindsay said she wanted to let the man go, but she couldn't bring herself to fire a man of Wilf's age. I thought how Mrs. Craven at Cairnwood would have dumped the guy in a New York minute if she'd learned about the weed killer.

Besides Wilf, Lindsay said she employed one other worker, a young part-timer named Ashley, who assisted whenever Windermere Inn was fully booked. The young woman wasn't needed today, though – Paul Briar being the inn's sole guest.

The Adirondack room faced east and the sun was low behind us, so Sharon decided to switch on a light. But when she clicked on the ceiling fixture the bulb popped and flashed out. I seized the opportunity to show off my manly mechanical skills and general manly tallness. "Here." I jumped to my size twelve feet. "Let me change that for you."

The ceiling was higher than I'd thought. Stretched fully, I could reach the fixture but not firmly enough to keep the antique art deco shade from slipping out of my hands after I'd unscrewed that little brass nipple do-hickey on the bottom. The heavy glass fixture crashed to the floor and shattered into a hundred colorful shards. Stanley jumped away and, I think, rolled his eyes.

Sharon hurried off to fetch a broom or stepladder or hard hat while I apologized for my clumsiness and assured Lindsay that I'd pay for the damage and keep my pistol holstered. She laughed and told me not to worry about it. The subject of firearms brought the conversation around again to what I did for a living and that, in turn, brought up the inevitable question: *So, What the hell is a clumsy ex-detective from the city doing working up here in Moose Fart Corners? And when are you leaving?*

Okay, Lindsay didn't put the words quite that bluntly, but I knew what she meant.

Now normally, when someone asks me why I left Buffalo I just shrug off the question with a lame joke. But something about Lindsay's interviewing technique – the way she looked deep into my eyes as if she could see the truth for herself so I might as well 'fess up – made me decide that honesty was my only option.

"I, uh... had some problems."

"I'm sorry." She immediately pulled back and added, with sincerity, "I didn't mean to pry."

I didn't want her to think she'd offended me, so I went on. I started my tale with a rhetorical question.

"You know the only thing worse than being told you're crazy?"

She shrugged, clearly reluctant to step further into the muck she'd stirred up.

"Being told you're sane when you know full well that you're batshit."

She nodded politely. She was anxious, I'm sure, to change the subject to something more comfortable. She found her wish in my half-empty cup. "More tea?"

"No, thanks. I'm fine."

"You sure?"

"Yes. It's delicious. Not too sweet. Chamomile?"

"Lemon grass."

I took a sip. "Mmmm, both lemony and grassy."

We sat. For a moment. Silent. I knew she wouldn't let me down, and she didn't.

"So, you, uh… you think you're crazy, do you?"

"Certainly too crazy to be carrying a loaded weapon."

Her eyes drifted to the sidearm holstered on my hip.

"Just for show," I explained.

"I see."

"Don't tell the bad guys."

"I won't."

"I haven't carried a loaded gun in a long time," I explained. "And the way I look at it, if you're going to start strutting around town with an empty gun, you'd best strut around a town like Glen Echo rather than a town like Buffalo."

"I see." Now that she knew my gun had no bullets in it she was starting to relax again. "So, tell me, why don't you load your gun anymore?"

"Because the last time I loaded it I accidentally shot someone."

"Oh."

"An innocent bystander."

"Oh, no."

"The board of inquiry determined it wasn't my fault. But still…"

She thought she understood. "Now you can't face the prospect of accidentally shooting another man."

"It wasn't a man."

"Oh, no." The turn of sadness in her eyes was as genuine as everything else about her.

I took a sip of my tea. I needed to wet my whistle for this next bit. "It was a domestic call. A man had shot his wife and was threatening to do the same to his daughter. I don't know what his problem was, but when my partner and I arrived on the scene the shooter was holding his little girl hostage. Four years old. She didn't have a clue what was going on."

"My God. The poor thing."

"The guy was standing in the open doorway of his house, on the porch, holding the child in front of him as a shield. She didn't squirm or try to escape or anything. Why would she? This was her Daddy. I'll never forget the look on that little girl's face. Pure innocence. No fear. Complete trust. The kind of trust a daughter has only in her father. Totally oblivious to the fact that Daddy was holding a loaded forty-five to the back of her sweet little skull."

Lindsay sat in rapt attention. Waiting. No longer bothering to search for a soothing word to urge me on.

"In her arms she held a puppy. A small black lab. At one point, while I was trying to talk some sense into her crazy old man, the puppy wiggled out of her grasp. The pooch hit the floor running and scampered back into the house. The little girl's reaction was to chase after her pup. Somehow she slipped free from her father's grasp. This left me with a good clear shot at her old man. He raised his weapon at me. But I beat him. Got a shot off."

"Of course. You had to." Lindsay was trying her best to help me out. "After all, you said he'd already shot his wife."

"Yeah, well… Seems I aimed a little low. The bullet just grazed the top of the man's inner thigh. But it did the job. He dropped his weapon, grabbed his leg, and collapsed."

"Good for you."

"And the bullet travelled on. Straight down the hallway. Right down to where the little girl had just run."

Lindsay covered her mouth in horror. "Oh, no! It didn't..."

"No, it didn't."

Lindsay relaxed. "Oh, good."

"It hit the puppy."

"Aww."

"Would you believe a lot of guys laugh when I get to that part?"

"They're probably just relieved the bullet didn't hit the little girl."

"I hope so." I reached down and patted Stanley. "The poor thing was dead before his furry little chin hit the floor. My heart still breaks when I think of that little girl picking up that limp fur-ball in her tiny arms and bringing it to her injured daddy for him to make better."

"So, is that what made you stop carrying a loaded gun? The fact that you'd accidentally shot the dog?"

"Not quite. It was more the fact that I felt so *bad* about shooting the dog."

Lindsay didn't say anything, so I leaned in and explained further.

"It's like this… I had shot a man once before. Dead. A drug dealer. A bust gone wrong. The details don't matter. Point was, he died on the way to the hospital. So, did I feel bad about that? No, I did not. Not one damn bit."

"That's understandable. Look at the lives he was ruining."

"But he was still a man. A living, breathing human being. And I took away his life. And I didn't feel one ounce of remorse. Then I shoot a dog, and I feel like shit on a bun. What's wrong with that picture? Did I really care more about the life of an animal than I did about the life of a human being? The simple answer was yes, I did. And should a person like that be carrying a gun? The simple answer is no, he shouldn't."

I leaned back in my chair. "See? Told you I was crazy."

Lindsay laughed, I think out of relief. "They say admitting you're crazy is the first sign you're sane."

"That's exactly what the department's psychiatrist said to me. So, I immediately amended my self-diagnosis and told her I was completely and without a doubt perfectly sane. She said it was too late – I'd already said I was crazy. Apparently, Freud doesn't allow take-backs."

Lindsay reached out and squeezed my forearm. Actually, it may not have been a squeeze, it may have been more of a caress. Anyway, she looked deep into my eyes and said, "Chief Tanager, if it means anything to you, I think you're one of the sanest men I've ever met."

"Really?" I said. "Maybe you should get out more."

This time she didn't laugh. Her face was now just inches away from mine. If this had been our third meeting, maybe even our second, I would have closed that gap. She seemed to be asking to be kissed. But I felt it was too soon. We'd just met. But on the other hand…

And just when I was about to weaken and plant a big wet one on her full juicy lips Sharon returned and probably saved me from a sexual harassment charge. The woman was carrying a lightbulb, a folding step stool, and a cordless drill. I had no idea what she had planned to do with the drill.

Lindsay and I immediately leaned back in our respective chairs as if we'd been caught doing something naughty. I know I certainly had.

As Sharon chose the correct bit for her power drill, I commented that she seemed to be very handy with mechanical things. Like a proud mother, Lindsay informed me that, back home in Tennessee, Sharon used to be an amateur stock car racer who could have easily turned pro. Although I know nothing about the sport, I made like I was suitably impressed. Meanwhile, I noticed out the window that Paul Briar's boat was nudging the dock.

I asked Lindsay, "Nancy Briar… her last morning here, she took the canoe out for an early morning paddle, right?"

"She told Wilf that she wanted to go visit her old school across the lake," Lindsay said.

"Cairnwood," Sharon piped in from atop her stepladder.

"Yes, I just came from there," I said. "Odd she didn't drive over. It's only ten minutes."

Lindsay looked out across the water as if she were looking back in time. "There's nothing like a canoe ride first thing in the morning. Mist rising from the glassy water. All alone. Just you and the loons."

As if *loons* was her cue, Sharon said, "I think Nancy had some pretty heavy shit on her plate."

I enquired, "Her frame of mind not the best?"

Lindsay was ahead of me. "If you're asking, Was she suicidal, I'd have to say no. She wasn't terribly thrilled with her life's direction at that moment, but I don't think she was looking to take any long walks off any short canoes."

Sharon chirped in, "She had some thinking to do - you know, about the baby an' all."

The baby? This was news to me. As far as I knew, Paul and Nancy were childless. Unless… "You mean, she was pregnant?" I said.

Lindsay shot Sharon a silent dagger that carried the message, *Maybe you should shut the fuck up now, grits-for-brains.* But aloud she just said, "It's really none of our business." Then she changed the subject by standing up and indicating the lake. "Looks like Paul has docked."

Paul was indeed tying up his boat, so the three of us went out to greet him.

The guy was bundled up in a puffy, designer-label bomber jacket and sporting a navy blue wool watch cap and matching gloves. Paul Briar skipped the hellos and immediately asked me if what he'd heard was true – had Doctor Reesor really shot himself? Like I say, the Adirondacks is a small community made even smaller by cell towers and smart phones. When I confirmed the sad news about my pal Simon, Briar said he was surprised that the doctor had been left alone at such a vulnerable time. I had no good answer to that. Never will.

I changed the subject by inviting Briar to join me for dinner in town. Okay, in truth I invited Paul and the two ladies to join me. It was a good opportunity to ask Lindsay out for a pseudo date without putting my meaty self-esteem on the chopping block. But alas, Lindsay ground my suggestion into minced male ego by claiming that she and Sharon had work to do here at the inn in preparation for a large party that was checking in tomorrow. Paul Briar, on the other hand, accepted my invitation, agreeing to meet me in town after he freshened up. I warned him that the joint I was planning on taking him to didn't require freshening up. He thought I was kidding. I wasn't.

I'm sure Paul thought, since we were stuck here in the back woods, that a boys' night out had to be just that – strictly us fellers. And for most of the year, he'd be right. But right now, for these few weeks of hunting season, the Albion Hotel in Glen Echo heats up the frigid autumn nights by bringing in warmed-over strippers from Utica and Syracuse thereby giving the Elmer Fudds something to drool over besides each other's pump-action big-bores.

Briar and I closed the bar at two. Since I had picked up the tab for the food and drinks, Briar paid for the cab to get us both home. Good guy, but then I knew he was worth my time and concern when he'd helped me pull Evelyn's body out of that burning vehicle last night. Now I wanted to return the favor. I wanted to talk him out of doing something stupid like hiking into the mountains alone to look for his missing wife, if that was indeed his plan. Trouble was, even with a few drinks in him Briar still wouldn't tell me the truth about his plans and why he had come back to Windermere Inn. He insisted that the only thing he was hoping to find in these mountains was *closure.*

Now I must say, as a musician, I'm fortunate enough to have something called relative pitch. This means I can identify any note relative to the last note played. It's a handy skill to develop. Among other uses, it helps a musician identify a change in key signature, and so far, the only key I'd heard Paul Briar singing in was the key of B for bullshit. He definitely had something planned. A man just doesn't spend all day freezing his ass off in a leaky little fishing boat unless he's looking for something a bit more concrete than closure.

Yes, saving Briar's ass was a definite concern of mine that night. But by morning, the tables had turned. It wasn't Paul Briar's ass that was on the chopping block. It was my own.

CHAPTER EIGHT

As soon as Stanley and I stepped into the office, Marlene gave me the bad news: His Worship wanted to see me. Upstairs.

As is common in most small towns, the mayor's gig in Glen Echo doesn't pay a full living wage. My boss, His Worship The Honorable and Most Reverend Tim Stinson, must still preach at his evangelical church as well as run his evangelical sideline, The Wondrous Cross Motor Court. I'm not kidding. It's advertised as a Christian motel. This means when you drop a quarter into the bed the bible vibrates. Okay, now I'm kidding.

I rapped on the Mayor's office door and opened it, but not necessarily in that order. "How ya doin', Timmy?"

He held up an index finger indicating he was in the middle of something highly important and should not be interrupted under any circumstance no-way, no-how.

"You wanted to see me?" I interrupted.

He was busy adding up a long list of figures, probably his weekly liquor bill. This guy's office always smells like last call.

While I waited for His Honorable Reverend Worship's upstretched finger to lower to half-mast, I pondered the reasons why he'd likely summoned me here. It had to be one of two things: First, that His Worship wanted to talk to me about the Evelyn Reesor homicide and remind me that it's a matter for the state police and that I should not get involved. If this was the case, he wouldn't get any argument from me. I'd just go ahead and investigate the case on my own time. After all, with my pal Simon gone, the band wouldn't be working for a while, so I'd have some time free.

The other reason the Mayor may have requested my presence here today could be regarding my community liaison work with Paul Briar last night. The Mayor has probably heard about our visit to the peeler bar and now he wants to let me know that getting lap dances, especially while in uniform, does not reflect well on the good citizens of Glen Echo who buy my hats.

Without looking up from his desk, Mayor Stinson used his handy upstretched finger to motion me toward a chair. I complied. He continued writing. Or adding up.

Mayor Tim Stinson, a tall thin man in his early sixties, seems at first glance to have a tiny head until you realize it's an illusion created by his enormous ears.

I looked around the office and whistled a tune just to let him know I was still on hold.

After those ears, the third largest thing in the room was Mayor Stinson's desk. Made of burled walnut with rosewood inlays, it matched the fourth-largest thing in the room - his liquor cabinet. On top of this vital piece of furniture sat the tools of the mayor's trade – a bible, a computer printer, a Wi-Fi router, a hot-air popcorn machine, another bible but this one with crayons and coloring pages, and a large silver ice bucket which Marlene fills every morning from our fridge downstairs. Mayor Stinson would have a fridge of his own, of course, but his office doesn't have room for one, what with those ears and all.

When the mayor finally looked my way his red eyes opened wide as if his doctor had just snapped on the rubber glove. "What the hell is that?" he asked.

"What… oh, you mean my chapeau?" I took my tattered police cap off, but I did it carefully. The peak was barely attached. Stanley's tooth marks filigreed the edge.

Stinson quipped, "Marlene try to eat it for breakfast?"

Now, it's one thing when Marlene, herself, jokes about her hearty appetites, but it's quite another thing when big-eared, self-righteous, elected drunks do it. I fingered the busted brim. "Just one of those 'line-of-duty' things, Tim-bo." He hated *Tim-bo* almost as much as he hated *Timmy*.

"That item cost the town sixty-five dollars and eighty-nine cents. We expected you'd take better care of it."

"Don't you worry. I'll have it fixed." I added, "At my own expense, of course." I smiled.

This didn't seem to cool him down much, so he stood up to give his brain some fresh air. Then he walked to the front of his desk and sat on the corner of it. Time for a little heart-to-heart. All that was missing was the gooseneck lamp directed into my eyes.

"I understand you paid a visit to Len Holand yesterday afternoon."

Wow. I hadn't seen that one coming.

"Yes. Nice fellow," I said. "I think we bonded."

"That's not what I heard."

"Then I guess just *I* bonded."

I went on to explain how I'd visited the Holand farm hoping to talk with Len's two sons.

Mayor Stinson said, "I hear Robbie and Clive have been stirring up a bit of mischief again."

"I'd hardly call aggravated assault and uttered threats *a bit of mischief.*"

"I'm told the offended party didn't choose to press charges."

I wasn't surprised that he knew about Paul Briar's incident. Mayor Stinson doesn't miss much. It must be those giant ears. I said, "The victim, a Mr. Paul Briar, has bigger problems to deal with right now."

"We all do, Chief Tanager. That's why I don't want you bothering Len Holand."

"I didn't go out there to bother Len Holand. I went out there to bother his two bullying sons."

"Let me rephrase that: I don't want you bothering Len Holand's *family.*"

"I don't get it, Tim." I was sincere now. "What's the problem?"

"The problem is that Len Holand is a very successful, hard-working, God-fearing dairyman. He's a valued citizen of this community. He built that place up from nothing with the sweat of his own two hands. Toughed out some bad times on that farm. He doesn't need the grief. He's worked hard to get where he is."

I wasn't swallowing any of this. "I don't care if he put his first Guernsey together from a kit. Something's got to be done about his sons."

Mayor Tim Stinson got up off his desk again and walked around behind my chair where I guess it was easier for him to change the subject. "I understand that pervert has been exposing himself to those little girls at Cairnwood again."

I twisted around to try and look him face-to-face. But he turned away so I ended up talking into his ass, which was pretty much the same thing. "None of the young ladies can identify him," I said. "Not with anything we can use in a lineup, at least."

Tim continued around his desk until he was in front of me again. "So let me get this straight. We've got a dangerous pervert loose at a girl's school, yet you're wasting your time harassing a couple of harmless farm boys because they let off a little steam in a local saloon."

"In my opinion, the flasher at Cairnwood poses no immediate threat to life or limb. Some emotional trauma, yes. He's given those young women a hell of a scare. And for that reason I intend to do everything I can to apprehend him as quickly as possible. But a flasher incident hardly takes precedence over an aggravated assault."

"And then there's the Yarn Barn."

"Shit, Tim, she had five skeins of wool lifted. I can't exactly set up roadblocks."

The mayor, having finished his grand intimidation tour, sat down again. It was now time for him to play Good Mayor. "Tanager, I know this sort of stuff is small potatoes to a man with your background in criminal investigation. I'm sure you'd rather be working on something more substantial. But that's not what this town needs. As I told you when I hired you, we need someone to keep the toughs from spitting on the sidewalks. Someone to catch the hooligans who've been batting the mailboxes off their posts. And yes, someone to keep the perverts out of our school yards. What we don't need is someone trying to make a name for himself on the Internet."

"The Internet? What are you–"

"That stunt in the parking lot, pulling that woman free from her car."

"Stunt?"

"What you did was very courageous and probably sincere, I'm sure, but geez, Tanager, it's all over the YouTube."

"YouTube…" I suddenly realized what this meant. "Holy shit!" The thought of Evelyn's friends and loved ones seeing her charred remains like that… Goddamn, I hate the Internet.

"All this time you're spending with the media…"

"What are you talking about? I've been doing all I can to avoid the media. I've been sending them all up to Ray Brook." The village of Ray Brook is the nearest headquarters of the New York State Police.

"If you're trying to keep such a low profile then why are you spending so much time with this Paul Briar fellow?"

Now he really had me puzzled. I asked. "What's wrong with my hanging with Paul?"

"I'll tell you what's wrong. He draws attention, that's what's wrong. People see you two together they start asking questions: '*What's that man doing back in town? Have they still not found his wife's body?*'"

"You mean, it reminds them that not everything in those dark woods is marshmallows and hot chocolate."

"Tanager, this town depends on tourism. It's all we've got. Camping, skiing, hunting, fishing… we're selling outdoor adventure. We don't need any reminders about young women canoeists drowning in our beautiful lakes."

"I couldn't agree more, Tim. And the last thing we need is for another tourist to go missing. That's why I'm keeping an eye on Briar. I'm afraid he might be thinking about searching on his own. So I'm sticking close."

But the mayor held fast. "The Briar woman's drowning is a matter for the state police. Same for that bombing of the doctor's car. You're a town cop, Tanager. A constable. I want you to do the job you were hired to do. Nothing more, nothing less. And leave the detective work to the state boys. Do you think you can live with that? Because if you can't, it's best we both know now."

I had nothing more to say. Nothing that wouldn't get me fired on the spot, that is. I liked this gig. I liked this town. I liked working with Marlene. I liked the roadhouse I was playing in every weekend and the band I was playing it with, even if we were now playing it with one less musician. Since moving to these mountains I'd been happier than I had been in years. I certainly didn't want to move back to the city.

I had been hired by the good people of Glen Echo on a two-year contract, but that agreement had a six-month probationary period. And that period was almost up. If the mayor wants to fire me he'll have to do so within the next week. And we both knew it. So I bit my well-chewed tongue and put on my well-chewed hat, its mangled brim dangling limp over my eyes like a forgotten price tag.

I stood up and walked to the door. But before I made my escape Stinson had one more order for me. He cleared his throat and held out the empty ice bucket to me as if it were one of his church collection plates, "Would you mind? Please?"

With a smile I retrieved the silver container from my master's soft, freshly-manicured fingers.

After all, he had said *please.*

*****

For the next few days I was a good boy. Mayor Timothy Stinson's good boy. Yes, I did let the state police update me regularly on their investigation of the Evelyn Reesor homicide, but that was all. Manwaring was even kind enough to email me the lab reports on the car bomb. Apparently, the explosive was standard stuff – ammonium nitrate and nitromethane, both easily available from local hardware stores, garden centers, or the Internet. The primary explosive had been detonated by a home-made electrically-fused blasting cap made from mercury fulminate and the spent .223 shell we had found at the scene. The carpet tacks inside the pipe appeared to be a house-brand from a nation-wide hardware chain whose nearest outlets were in Plattsburgh and Utica.

While on the subject of geography, special agent Yasuda at the F.B.I. told me something about my deceased pal that I did not know: Apparently, Simon used to fly down to a little town in Louisiana near the Mississippi border to perform abortions at a nominal fee. I've heard that this is common practice among OBGYN's in the northern states. It gives them a chance to help out in places where local doctors feel too intimidated and frightened to perform terminations themselves. Yasuda said that, because of Dr. Reesor's connection to Louisiana, the Bureau was pursuing leads from that part of the country as well as leads from up here.

I was glad to see that the feds were working nationally while Manwaring, still thinking mainly about the cuckholded husband angle, was working locally. Meanwhile, I kept myself busy curbing jay-walkers, chasing graffiti taggers, sweeping litterbugs from the sidewalks, and kicking skateboarders off the courthouse steps. Punk bastards, the lot of them. Pretty soon, the local gangstas knew who was running this town. I even managed to nab the suspect who was ripping off the Yarn Barn. I'd borrowed a motion camcorder and set it up on a shelf behind a loose-weave afghan. Next thing I knew, I had an HD video of the masked perp running off with a skein of chenille. Sure, the masked perp turned out to be a mother raccoon who was using the comfy material to insulate her new nursery up in the attic, but hey, it was one more perp taken off the mean streets.

Yes, for a couple of days I was indeed a good boy. I was determined, for the last week of my probationary period, to stay away from any crime more serious than failure to stoop and scoop. For two days I kept myself as clean as the sidewalks, unsullied by the effluent of human as well as animal transgression. And then one day I found myself in the shit once again. And this time I couldn't bag it for takeout.

It happened the night we held a wake for our dear deceased pal Doctor Simon Reesor. His and his wife, Evelyn's, families had already held a dual private funeral service, and Simon's medical associates had held some sort of memorial event at the hospital. Now it was time for his musician friends to bid him a proper goodbye.

Our wake/jam session, a musical celebration of a life lived to the fullest, was held at The Blues 'N' Cues Roadhouse. Jack and Vanessa, the owners of the bar, donated the evening's proceeds to Simon's private clinic, the Glen Echo Women's Medical Center. We had posted a notice in the local paper announcing this fact. We also publicised the event on Facebook. At the time, we thought this to be a fairly innocuous gesture.

Silly us.

Mentioning the Women's Health Center publicly like this was like filling a bird feeder with fresh sunflower seeds. While it brought many species of grateful bird from close by, it also attracted a few brightly-feathered opportunists from farther afield, birds who had their own agenda.

The local print pigeons landed first. They were eager to swallow and then regurgitate their stories into the local papers. These birds were closely followed by a flock of television crews who migrated up here from down state. At first, I found all this media attention neither surprising nor threatening. After all, Doctor Simon Reesor was a prominent citizen in our little community, so why shouldn't his send-off garner a little ink and camera time.

Silly me.

Next, a pair of plain-feathered State police investigators found perches on the sidewalk. No surprise there. After all, Simon and Evelyn were the victims of at least one homicide. And then, because of the possible link to abortion terrorism, several federal agents from the Bureau in Albany flitted by. These birds tried to blend in with the local plumage but without much luck. Granted, for once, these feds showed enough smarts to leave their dark suits and sunglasses at home, but they had stupidly insisted on all using the same department-sanctioned barber which, in a crowd full of jazz and blues musicians, made them stand out like black-capped chickadees in a field of a blue jays.

Finally, to complete the aviary, the peacocks and cockatoos with picket signs showed up. These protesters arrived in separate cars, but they proceeded to then go fetch their signs from out of the same van, indicating that they were one well-organized flock. Their placards chirped such catchy slogans as CHOOSE LIFE, SUPPORT THE UNBORN, and A WOMB IS NOT A TRASH CAN. While I respected the passion and sincerity of their message, and even understood the moral direction in which their internal compasses were guiding them, I didn't think much of the method and timing of their migration. This was a damn wake, for crying out Pete's sake. Two innocent people were dead – at least, from my point of view they were innocent. Hadn't some maniac with a bomb already made his point perfectly clear? Did these people really have to capitalize on the insanity?

Yeah, I know. One person's murdering zealot is another person's brave freedom fighter. But this was still my pal's funeral.

Anyway, while the protestors marched around the parking lot and chanted their hymns appropriately off-key, and while my investigative colleagues shot videos and recorded vehicle plate numbers, I went into the club to organize the evening's more festive activities. Despite the bird shit and feathers threatening to hit the fan outside, I was determined to give Simon a decent send off.

Happily, inside the bar, I discovered the party was developing into quite a respectful shindig. I wasn't surprised to see that musicians were arriving from across the North Country, and by eight o'clock we had more than enough revellers to start making some joyful noise. I rounded up our guitarist, Roger, our drummer, Earl, and our guest lead vocalist, Lance. I also added Nita, a young talented female sax player who'd come down from Lake Placid. This would be our core section for the jam. I'd like to have added a keyboard player, of course, but for the first few tunes it felt right to leave Simon's synth stool unoccupied like an empty chair at a family dinner table.

Things started smoothly. The five of us stepped onto the stage and were discussing the opening song when I heard a ruckus behind me – a couple of shouts of profanity. Then we all heard a chair hit the dance floor.

"Great," Earl sighed without bothering to look up over his crash cymbals. "The bottles are flying and we haven't even started *Mustang fucking Sally* yet."

Of course, when I turned around to check out what was going on I expected to see a couple of dudes circling each other. But nope. It was two women. One screaming. The other not screaming, just silently taking the verbal abuse. The screamer had her back to me. No idea who she was. But the screamee, the quiet one taking the abuse, was turned towards me. And I appreciated the effort. Man, did she look good. Even better than yesterday. It was probably the nighttime makeup. Or the freshly coiffed coif. Or the big loop earrings. Or maybe the high heels. Whatever it was, Lindsay Porter from Windermere Inn added a lot of class to this bar.

Now, as I've mentioned before, when heated situations fire up at Blues 'N' Cues I usually stay away from the early flickers and let the bar's staff cool things down. But tonight, considering the dry tinder of plucked feathers and cardboard picket signs swirling in the wind outside, I didn't want any sparks flying around in here as well. So, I unstrapped my bass guitar and stepped off the stage..

As I walked along the dance floor I heard an angry shout, "Liar. You killed her. You killed them *both*."

I circled round and got a look at her face. She was in her early twenties. Pretty. I'd seen her before, but I couldn't remember exactly where. It wasn't here in the club. I didn't even think it was here in this town. But I'd seen her somewhere before. And recently. Then it hit me.

She had been standing on top of Simon's grand piano. Well, not actually in person, but that's where her framed photo stood. She was Simon's daughter, Rebecca. Her stepmother, Evelyn, had called her Becky, but Simon always used her full name. That photo had been taken a few years ago at her high school graduation, but it was this girl all right. Man, it's amazing what a few years will do to a girl at that age. Her face had lost the baby fat, and her figure had… well, not lost the baby fat. And it didn't lose it in all the right places. Oh, and there was one other difference between her photograph on the piano and this picture I was now staring at.

In the photo she wasn't holding a gun.

A crowd had already gathered round the perimeter of the dance floor, forming a horseshoe behind the shooter so that nobody was in her direct line of fire – nobody, that is, except Lindsay Porter, the woman at whom Rebecca was pointing the weapon and hurling accusations at the top of her healthy young lungs.

Lindsay stayed surprisingly calm as she said, "I have no earthly idea what you are talking about nor what makes you think I would be involved."

Wow. You have to admire a woman who keeps firm hold of her grammar under heat like this. I mean, even at the best of times who the hell uses the word *nor*?

"Like shit you don't," was Rebecca's less-grammatical retort. "You've been trying to close down my father's clinic for, like, years. When that didn't work you decided to kill him. Only you fucked up. You fucked up big. You ended up killing my mother instead."

I wasn't surprised Rebecca referred to Evelyn as her mother rather than as her stepmother. According to Simon, Rebecca and Evelyn were very close. But calling Lindsay a terrorist? A car-bomber? That, I didn't get.

I edged my way forward towards the action and finally stepped into the open ring. Rebecca noticed the idiot who was suddenly putting himself in her line of fire, but she didn't recognize him. So I helped her out.

"Hi, Rebecca." I spoke as if nothing were amiss, like women waved guns at my chest every night. "Nice to finally meet you. I was a friend of your dad's. Your stepmom's, too." I then added, "I'm sorry. Truly sorry. I'd like to help you if you'll let me."

She lowered the gun, but not far enough to be a real improvement. "Just keep away. Okay?"

"Hey, no problem. I just wanted to let you know that I played in your Dad's band. Name's Tanager." I edged closer to her. "I play bass. Sing a bit, too. But not very well. Hey, your dad told me you sing."

"Please," she said. "This has nothing to do with you."

"I'm sorry, Rebecca," I said. "But I'm afraid you're wrong. This has everything to do with me. You see, when I'm not playing here with your dad's band, I'm keeping the streets safe and nabbing bad guys."

A glimmer of understanding. "You… you're the cop?"

"Chief of police, actually. That's why I know who planted that bomb that killed your stepmom."

She looked doubtful, but she didn't say anything.

I kept talking. I nodded toward Lindsay. "And I can tell you, it wasn't this lady."

"Bullshit," Rebecca answered. "She's been hounding Daddy for, like, forever. Trying to make him stop his work."

By now I had closed the gap to an arm's length, so I slowly extended my hand for her to give me the weapon. Of course, I could have just dived in and made a quick grab for the gun, but with all these bystanders hovering around such a move would be a little foolhardy. So I held my hand out and kept on talking. "Believe me, Rebecca, Lindsay Porter, here, had nothing to do with your mother's death. Honest. I know. We all do."

"You… you *all*?"

"I work closely with Detective Manwaring of the state police. You've probably met him. Large fellow. Long teeth. Round, ruddy face. Looks like a Vermont cheddar." As I babbled, I watched Rebecca's eyes closely and could see that she was on something. Her eyelids drooped but did not blink. Her pupils were dilated to the size of pajama buttons. Her gun hand was shaking like an old man reaching for the bannister. One involuntary twitch and someone near and dear to me might be dead. Or at least have his balls shot off.

Rebecca said, "Who was it then? Who killed Evelyn?"

"Give me the gun, Rebecca. We'll talk. I'll tell you the whole story. But you'll have to give me the gun first. Okay?"

My words only served to bring the weapon back to her attention. She raised it up toward my chest. "You said you know who killed her. Who? Tell me."

Of course, I had no idea who killed Evelyn Reesor. I was bluffing. I was also sweating. The small gun pointed at me was not heavy, but the small hand holding it was weak and trembling. Meanwhile, Lindsay had edged her way forward to stand closer me. Dangerous move. Dumb move. But considerate just the same.

Very slowly, with my left arm, I urged Lindsay to back off away from me. Meanwhile, I stretched out my right hand to Rebecca. "Give me the gun, honey. It's the smart thing to do. You have every right to be upset. But not with this lady."

And that's when a smart lady did something stupid. Lindsay lurched and grabbed hold of Rebecca's gun hand.

I dove in and quickly added my big hairy mitt to the mix. I guided the weapon skyward, away from the screaming crowd. Happily, young Rebecca's drug-marinated body did not have a drop of fight left in it. She released her grip on the weapon and collapsed into my arms. Frankly, I think she was glad to call the whole crazy stunt quits.

Gently, as if I were placing the grocery bag containing the eggs into my trunk, I lowered Rebecca into a chair. I then turned my attention to the gun. I flipped the safety on and popped the clip.

Turns out the weapon was as empty as its pretty young owner's threats.

* * * * *

I emptied Rebecca's purse out onto the table. She protested as I rummaged through the pile of lip balms, tampons, thumb drives, and sugar-free breath mints, but I found the bottle of pills. A common sedative. According to the label they had been prescribed recently by one of our local physicians, probably to help Rebecca cope with her grief. I could also smell rum on her breath.

Rebecca was a little dazed and queasy, but in my judgement, she didn't need any medical attention. Her pulse felt strong and steady, and her color was good. All she needed was some rest and rehydration.

Lindsay, who obviously didn't seem to hold a grudge, brought Rebecca a glass of water and then offered to stick around and talk things out with her young assailant. But I suggested that this might not be the best idea. I wanted some time with Rebecca alone.

Rebecca confessed that she had absolutely no intention of harming anyone including Lindsay Porter. The desperate young woman just hoped to scare a confession out of her stepmother's killer. It was a spur of the moment thing. Rebecca had cooked up the whole scheme just a half-hour ago, out in the parking lot, when she had noticed a handgun in the glove compartment of a male friend's car. I didn't ask who this male friend was and if he had a permit to carry. Right now, I was more interested in why Rebecca was so sure Lindsay was the bomber.

At first, Rebecca was reluctant to talk any further. She feared that I was going to haul her ass off to jail. Usually I use this fear as a bargaining chip in an interview, but not this time. This girl had been through enough. So I played it soft and easy, told her she wasn't in any serious trouble as long as she cooperates. I mean, what else could I do – she was looking up at me with those big brown eyes – the eyes of her father, a man who'd be alive today if I'd done the right thing and stayed with him after his wife's tragic death. So I made a deal with Rebecca: if Lindsay Porter agreed not to press charges, I might be persuaded to forget this whole incident ever happened on the condition that Rebecca stay clear of alcohol for the next month. Otherwise, the deal's off.

I expected her to grab my generous offer with both hands like it was the last pair of shoes in her size in the store, but Rebecca played it cooler than that. She took a deep dramatic let-me-think-about-it sigh before finally agreeing to my conditions. This was clearly a young lady who was used to getting her own way, especially from men. And I wasn't surprised.

Rebecca Reesor was a pretty girl. *Woman*, I should say, but I'd always heard Simon refer to her as his *little girl*. Flawless skin. Almost translucent. And a moon-shaped face that was haloed by a golden cloud of soft blonde curls that floated gently to her shoulders. Quite an angelic look when she doesn't have a gun in her hand.

It was now time to turn on just a few drops of bad cop. Or at least, stern cop: "So what the hell makes you think that Lindsay Porter is the maniac who planted that bomb?"

"I have my reasons."

"Name one."

"The clinic."

"Lindsay had a problem with your dad's medical practice?"

Rebecca rolled her eyes. "Like, duh… You are a cop, right?"

Funny how often I get asked that question.

Rebecca continued, "Don't you know that she's been trying to close Daddy down for, like, eons?"

"You mean, Lindsay is one of those letter writers?"

"Letters. Emails. Texts. Protests. Marches. She's pulled every stunt in the book. She's blocked his driveway with her truck. Thrown eggs at patients trying to use the clinic. I mean, shit, that skinny bitch has got all sorts of tricks up her designer sleeves."

At this point Earl came over to tell me he'd found a couple of harmonica players and did I want to get the party going while they were still sober enough to blow. I knew there was at least one other bass player in the house who would be happy to sit in, so I told him to grab one of them and start the show without me.

After Earl left, Rebecca asked me, "So, why isn't he in jail?"

"Huh? Who? Earl?"

She rolled her eyes again. "The bomber. The guy who blew up Evelyn."

"Right… the perp. Yeah, well, you see, I, uh…"

Rebecca understood I was bluffing. She turned away from me in disgust. "Asshole."

I needed a quick change of subject, and happily, at this very moment, I saw one enter the front door of the club.

I hadn't seen Paul Briar since we closed the Albion strip club together, four nights ago. I gave him a big wave. He saw me and started to thread his way through the crowd. When he arrived, I introduced him to Rebecca, and instantly, the sparks flew.

As the young girl gazed up into Briar's tanned countenance the stale air in the darkened room shimmered aglow like someone on high had switched on the Northern Lights. I suppose he was good-looking in a boyish sort of way. Briar was about ten years younger than I, which put him about half-way between me and Rebecca. A little old for her, I thought. But Rebecca obviously didn't agree.

"I'm very sorry for your loss," he offered her.

"Thank you," she cooed. Then she actually fluttered her eye lashes at him. I've had young girls do this at me but only during fly season.

I said, "Paul is a TV producer."

"Yes, I know," Rebecca said.

Briar's smile blossomed to full bloom as he pointed a trimmed, buffed, and polished fingernail at her. "Now, I remember. Windermere."

Softly, delicately, Rebecca laid her hand on his arm. Her smile fell from her face. "I'm sorry."

Briar understood. "Thank you. I'm sure she's in a better place."

Well, you don't have to hit me with a brick. I'm a professional detective. So I turned to Rebecca. "You worked at Windermere Inn?"

"College intern, *they* called it." She rolled her eyes once again. "Plantation slave, I called it."

"So how's school going?" Briar enquired.

"Fine, thank you," she demurred.

"Hotel management, right?" he showed off.

"You remembered," Rebecca gushed.

I was obviously a third wheel on a bike that was rolling along just fine on two, so I excused myself and went and joined Lindsay and her pal Sharon who were seated at a nearby table. I doubt either Briar or Rebecca noticed I left.

Lindsay, on the other hand, welcomed my company but not for the reason I had hoped. She was anxious to give me her side of this whole sordid story.

Yes, it was true that Lindsay had regularly and publicly voiced her objections to the medical procedures Simon Reesor, Rebecca's late father, had carried out at his clinic, although not in any violent way. But this was not the real reason, Lindsay suspected, that the young woman was angry with her.

"She's never forgiven me for letting her go."

"You fired her?"

"I hated to, but…" Lindsay's words trailed off. She seemed reluctant to speak ill of a young woman who'd just lost both her parents. Sharon, on the other hand, felt no such reservations.

"The chick's a slut."

"No, no," Lindsay protested. "I wouldn't go *that* far."

"*She* would," Sharon tipped the neck of her beer bottle toward Rebecca. "That chick's easier to make than Kraft Dinner."

Lindsay decided to clear things up for me. "We didn't like some of the young men she was bringing around. I don't want to sound like a snob, but we cater to a certain level of clientele. I know, in retrospect, it sounds rather tight-ass of me, but–"

And just then my own ass went off. As always when I'm playing with my band, I had my phone set to *vibrate*. I pulled my phone out of my pants pocket and checked the display. It was a Glen Echo 911 call. I answered and, through the wonders of satellite technology and off-shore 911 service, a woman in Mumbai sing-sang me the particulars of an emergency situation that was happening just outside of Glen Echo. I thanked the nice South Asian lady and hung up.

The band was on stage, just firing up the opening horn line of *Midnight Hour*, so I had to shout out my quick apologies and goodbyes to Lindsay and Sharon. On my way out of the club I dropped by the storage room and grabbed my official police chief's cap and jacket. I also popped an official breath mint into my mouth to cover the smell of beer.

Curious thing: As I climbed into my cold, dark car that evening, I noticed that I felt much better than I had when I'd first arrived at the club. I didn't know exactly why. It wasn't the booze – after all, I'd downed barely one beer. Maybe I felt good because I had done something to help out my friend Simon's daughter. After all, her stunt in that bar could easily have gotten out of hand, and if a more hard-nosed cop had handled it, someone like Manwaring, say, she'd now be in serious trouble. Or maybe I just felt good because I was now answering a real call, something that was a little more important than ticketing a senior citizen for parking his Buick in the loading zone beside the denture clinic.

Whatever the reason, my exhilaration didn't last long – only about ten minutes. That's how long it took me to drive to the scene of a homicide. And that's how long it took me to recognize the bashed-in skull and mortal remains of Robbie Holand, Len Holand's youngest son.

CHAPTER NINE

Poor Carl Tatum. The old guy seemed to be more upset about getting nabbed with an open bottle of Wild Turkey in his fishing skiff than he was about hooking his line onto a dead body.

I walked him down shore to get him out of earshot of Mr. and Mrs. Baumeister, the couple whose river-side property the beached, deceased body of Robbie Holand presently rested upon.

"I told you, Carl, I don't care about the open booze in the boat. I don't even give a shit about the regulation personal flotation device you don't have on board, an infraction for which I could nail you with a hefty fine if I were so inclined. I just want you to tell me about finding that body."

"Ain't much to tell."

Right. I thought about all the free beers this man would soon be tossing down while relating his tale in a local pub. I bet he won't be saying, *There ain't much to tell* then.

"I was trollin' low and slow 'long the south bank, here, don't you know. Cold nights like this the small-mouth come upriver. All of a sudden, my line starts playin' out. She don't jerk or nothin', so I say, 'God damn, done it again - snagged a log.' See, that's the problem with night fishin'. Can't see them dead heads. Do you wanna know I've lost three lures along this stretch since September? Expensive ones, too. Them battery ones what glow in the–" Carl suddenly realized he was talking about illegal lures.

"So you thought you'd hooked bottom, but you'd actually hooked a body."

"No, no. I'd hooked bottom all right. But when I backed up to see where I was snagged, this white thing catches my eye. It was lyin' under them branches by the undercut over yonder." He pointed to the far bank of the river. "I shone my flashlight on 'er, and well..." He shuddered, then licked his lips as if he needed a drink.

"What did you do then? Did you poke it? Move it?"

"Hell, no! Think I'd touch somethin' like that? I wouldn't touch nothing like that. No, sir. No how, no way. Not me. I'd touch a lot of things, but somethin' like that–"

"Well, somebody touched it. It didn't wash up on shore with the tide."

"Her." He pointed towards the woman and the man who owned the property, both of whom were standing downstream by the river's edge. Carl continued, "Saw the house here. Pulled up to the dock. Told 'em what was lyin' off their doorstep. The old woman, uh..." He tried to remember her name.

"Mrs. Baumeister."

"Right. Baumeister… Sounds German, don't it."

I nudged him back on topic. "You told Mrs. Baumeister about the body."

"And didn't she get her leather knickers all twisted up. Said we had to yank him out quick on account of he might still be alive. I took one look at the back of his head and tol' her, 'Fuck, lady, if that thing's still alive I don't want to know about it.'"

"So I take it you and Mr. Baumeister then dragged the body out of the water?"

"You could, but you'd take it wrong. She done it herself. Them German women, they're strong." He added, "It's all the pork. Krauts is horny for pork."

I walked Carl back toward the scene, to the two property owners standing on the lawn by the water. An ambulance was already parked in their driveway – it had beaten me here – and the two attendants were now inside the house waiting for my further instructions. As we walked, I explained to old Carl Tatum, "Some of my colleagues are on their way. They'll want to speak with you."

"Geez, I dunno… it's getting kind cold. And I'm gettin' awful thirsty."

We had reached the Baumeisters now, so I asked them if they would please take Carl inside to warm him up. They were happy to do so. As Mrs. Baumeister walked her thirsty guest up to the house, I heard her say to him, "I make you nice hot drink. Do you like German hot chocolate?"

"Never eat German," Carl said. "No offense, ma'am, but my daddy lost a testicle flyin' over Bremen."

Mrs. Baumeister was duly sympathetic. She shook her head in sadness. "The war was an awful thing. Just terrible."

"Oh, Daddy wasn't in no war."

I was sorry I couldn't hear the rest of that conversation, but I had to go have a look at the body. It was dark, so I drove my car across the lawn, parked close to the river's edge, and aimed my headlights at the deceased.

The first responders had left Robbie Holand lying spread out on his back, his clouded eyes staring up at the moonless sky as if he were searching the heavens to see if there was room for one more tortured soul. Robbie, the younger of Len Holand's two adult sons, was the better one. Not good, just better. I think if he could have stayed clear of his brother, Clive, he might have had a chance at a useful life.

I snapped on my latex gloves and kneeled down.

The deceased was dressed in faded blue jeans, a gray wool flannel work shirt over a dingy white t-shirt, and a fleece-lined denim bomber jacket. As far as I could recall, this was a similar outfit to the one I'd seen him wearing four nights ago in the bar when he and his brother hassled Paul Briar.

Robbie's short dark hair almost, but not quite, covered the deep crimson gash behind his right ear. I poked around the body a bit, but pretty soon I saw three sets of headlights coming down the road. Only the lead car had its red cherry light flashing. I had called the New York State Police on my way here. Sure, many reasonably sized municipal police departments up here – like Tupper or Saranac or Placid – will often handle situations like this alone. But my department is not reasonably sized. It's ridiculously sized.

The first man to get out of the lead NYSPD car was wearing a bulky winter jacket thrown over what appeared to be a loose cotton track suit. He hadn't shaved for twenty-four hours and his breath smelled of beer, much like mine. But that's okay. Remember, this was November. The summer tourists had long gone. The winter tourists were still in the city waxing their skis. Not much going on these days besides hunting. Even on a Saturday night, things tend to be quiet. I offered the detective a peppermint breath lozenge, but he waved it away as being unnecessary. Clearly, his job was more secure than mine.

He introduced himself as Lieutenant Giles Rykert, an investigator with the New York State Violent Crimes Unit, recently transferred from down state. He was the same level as Manwaring who, apparently, was not on call tonight. Unlike Manwaring, this guy gave me no grief about jurisdiction. From the moment he arrived Rykert deferred all authority to me, making it clear that this was my turf and that he was here only to assist. This was nice, but I suspected he was really just glad to be passing along the extra workload.

More troopers joined us, some in uniform, some sporting the standard black jackets with Crime Scene Unit lettered in white across their backs. A couple of civilian cars also arrived. One of these, an Infiniti, was driven by a man dressed in a full length camel's hair coat and silk scarf. He was carrying the traditional black bag. Lieutenant Rykert introduced him as Doctor Norman Jacobs.

The doctor didn't bother shaking my latex-gloved hand. Nor did he bother to look at me and make small talk. Instead, he just stared at the body lying in the tall wet, muddy grass. And he sighed. I got the feeling the sigh wasn't for the poor dear departed but for the poor inconvenienced physician who was about to get his expensive English oxfords dirty. He took a large green plastic garbage bag from his coat pocket and carefully laid it out on the wet ground so he could kneel.

While the doc started his examination, I explained to Lieutenant Rykert the circumstances under which the body had been found. When the doctor stood up to stretch his back and legs, I confirmed a couple of things with him.

"Twenty-four hours?"

The doc answered with the usual noncommittal medical maybe: "Depends on how active the vic was immediately before death. Rigor seems fairly complete. Sure, could be twenty-four. Could be forty-eight. Let's go with thirty-six, shall we?" He grinned. The doctor, too, smelled like happy hour. On weekends up here there's not a lot else to do but drink.

"Dead before he hit the water?" was my next question.

"You said he was floating?"

"According to the finder he was a few inches below the surface."

"Doesn't look like he drowned," said the doc. "But don't quote me. Not yet."

I turned to Rykert and pointed out the wound on the back of Robbie's head. "Right-handed hitter?"

Rykert knelt down for a closer look and said, "Whichever side he hit from, I'd say he used his slap shot. With something big."

"How about a freshly-cut log?' I suggested. "Hardwood. Probably maple."

Rykert's lips said nothing, but his eyebrows screamed, *Huh*?

I pointed to a spot on the wound where the hair was glued to the broken skin with something the color of amber. "Take a sniff. Makes me want pancakes." Ever since the bars went non-smoking, my nose works like a bloodhound's in heat.

While Rykert took a sniff, the doctor opened his black bag and took out a digital thermometer. "Okay if I pull down his pants?"

"Hey," I said, "It's your party."

While the doctor went to work, and Rykert and I looked the other way, we were joined by Gordon MacIntyre, Glen Echo's leading portrait and wedding photographer. He was dressed even more formally than the doctor.

"Your cummerbund is upside-down," I said.

"Last time I looked, so was the bride." He glanced down at the body. "Shit, that's Robbie Holand."

"You know him?"

"Took his high school graduation photo couple years back." MacIntyre cocked his head to study Robbie's dull, fish-eyed stare from a better angle. "Must say, he looks a lot better now."

Lieutenant Rykert was impressed by the doctor. "You remember the name of every kid you've snapped a picture of?"

"I'm a people person." With that said, Gordon focused his camera on the pale, blue eyes of the young high school graduate who was now having a thermometer shoved up his cold, blue ass.

Leaving Gordon to digitally capture the grim analogue details of death I walked Lieutenant Rykert up to the house so I could introduce him to our finder, Carl Tatum, and to the two homeowners. As we walked up the hill, we passed troopers going down to the river carrying floodlights and a portable generator.

"Don't think we'll find much," I suggested to Rykert. "I doubt he was killed here. Or even dumped here."

"You think the current carried him down?"

"Makes no sense otherwise." I pointed toward the highway. "Look how far the road is from the water here. Why risk carrying a body across these lawns, past all these residences? The closest this road comes to the river round here is up at the dam. There's public parking up there. Wouldn't take very long for a floater dropped in up there to reach this point. I think you should send someone up now and secure the area."

"Me?" asked Rykert.

I turned to the Lieutenant. I wanted to get this settled now. "Look, I know the puck is behind my blue line, but I'm a one-man police force. I'm sorry. I'll do all I can, but I'm going to have to hit you pretty hard for resources and personnel."

"You know this is the cold and flu season."

"I'll try to do as much as I can on my own."

By now Rykert and I were at the Baumeister's porch. I surprised him by proceeding to split away from him and continue on to my car. As I departed, I called back to him, "You got my cell number?"

Rykert didn't like this at all. "Where the hell you going?"

I pointed toward the parked ambulance. "Don't let them transport the body yet, okay?"

He understood. "You think you can get us a spot I.D.?"

"Give me an hour."

Rykert blew warm breath into his cold, clasped hands and mumbled something toward the mud. I don't think he was thanking his high school for advising him on his career choice.

* * * * *

The soft glow of the speedometer whispered that I was doing seventy-eight miles an hour. At times like this, I wished my siren were working. But hey, at least I have the hat.

I don't like driving fast through the mountains at night. Too many nocturnal critters roaming around. Skunks. Foxes. Deer. Cops. Musicians.

The voice on the other end of my cell call asked me, "This about my boys again?"

"I really can't discuss it over the phone. I'll be at your place in five minutes."

It was almost midnight. Len Holand must have guessed that whatever news I was bringing did not involve balloons and a giant cheque. So he simply said, "The gate will be open."

"Thank you, sir. And I–"

But he'd already hung up.

The inky black nothingness ahead of me swallowed my car without chewing, like a giant hungry squid with a taste for Fords. Luckily, I'd been to the Holand farm recently, so I knew approximately where his mailbox should pop into view.

True to his word, Len Holand had left the gate open, so I drove up the dirt driveway and parked at his front porch. Out of respect, I had switched off my CD player as I'd neared the place. Now, as I stepped out of my car, the dead quiet seemed to scream at me. I guess the crickets were showing respect too. I'm still not used to the absence of city hum up here. Still makes me uneasy. That's why, as I approached the house, I was happy to hear a soft breeze pick up a whirl of dry leaves and scratch them against Holand's cinder block foundation. I also enjoyed the creaking of the wooden steps as I climbed up onto the big porch that horse-shoed around three sides of the old brick building.

I wasn't thrilled with the next sound, though.

Just as I opened the screen door and was about to knock, two huge dogs came thundering around the corner of the porch barking their giant slobbering heads off. Until this moment I'd heard nothing from them. Not a peep. The monsters must have been trained to stay still until their prey had boxed himself in on the porch, his one avenue of escape blocked. I made a mental note to check under the porch later for chewed remains of Jehovah's Witnesses.

The dogs didn't actually attack – they were too well trained for that. They just growled, bared their teeth, and waited for me to have a coronary. So I tried something. I faced them down and commanded in my most stern Dr. Phil voice, "Sit!"

And sure enough, they sat. I'd guessed right. Len Holand had trained the pooches well. The barking stopped dead as if I'd lifted the needle off the turntable. I then reached into my pocket and took out a couple of biscuits I carry for Stanley. I gave them each a treat and a pat. They were beautiful dogs, both sporting the shaggy bad haircuts and Santa Claus eyebrows that identified them as Irish wolfhounds.

By the time Len Holand answered the door I had made two good furry friends. But I doubt I was going to make a third. Len looked at the dogs. Then, as a form of weak apology, said to me, "Don't usually get visitors this late."

I peered past him and saw two women standing in the hallway. One was in her early thirties. The other, just past forty. I wished I were wearing my full uniform. News like this is easier to deliver when you have a costume to hide behind.

Holand didn't actually invite me in, but he did step aside, which for him was the same thing. The dogs started to follow me into the house but then looked up at Holand and thought better of the idea. Smart animals.

As I brushed past him, Holand said, with his big hand still clutching the doorknob, "This about the boys?"

"It's Robbie." I said. "I'm very sorry, sir." I paused just a moment – a quick verbal air bag to cushion the blow. I looked straight at the two women then back at Holand. "We found his body in the river."

A gasp.

"Robbie is dead."

The older woman buried her face in the younger woman's shoulder. Len Holand didn't say anything. His knuckles just whitened on that doorknob. I turned back to the women and urged them toward the living room, "Maybe we could sit down."

But nobody moved. Len Holand asked, "And Clive?"

I finished my report, "Robbie's body was found floating in the Rosseau River near the mouth of the lake, just past the dam. He appears to have suffered a blow to the head." I paused to let my simple statements penetrate what must be three spinning minds. Then I finally answered Len's question. "No, we haven't seen any sign of Clive."

The older woman was sobbing openly now. The younger one guided her to a large couch in the living room. I presumed the older one was Robbie's mother. I reached to take Len Holand's elbow, saying, "Please, Mr. Holand. If we could all sit down..."

But Len Holand had other plans. He opened a closet door and took out a windbreaker. "Where is Robbie now?"

"Robbie will be taken to Syracuse."

"Syracuse?" He didn't seem to like this idea.

"Yes," I tried to address my comments to the two women as well as to Len Holand. "The University there has a forensic lab."

Holand spoke coldly, almost to himself, like he was going over a checklist. "No, no, no. No scientists are going to pick through my boy's bones. He's going to be laid to rest at the church. Whole and intact. As soon as possible. Where he was baptized."

"That's fine, sir. Wherever you wish. But first we have to take him to Syracuse for an autopsy. We need to determine a few details about his death."

"Details?" Holand stayed calm but firm. "You want details? I'll give you details." Holand slipped his jacket on. "Robbie and his brother were out in the boat. They got to fooling around, probably hit a rock or something. Maybe tried to shoot the rapids. I told them to be extra cautious this year. We've had a dry autumn. Water's low. Charts can't be trusted." He grabbed my shoulders - not with anger, but with desperation. "Don't you see? The only detail we have to determine now is where my *other* son is. Where is Clive."

"This boat," I said. "Where do you keep it?"

"It's just a canoe. Most of this summer it's been in the back of the pickup."

I knew the craft he was talking about. It was yellow with black detailing. I'd seen it often in their truck parked in the lot at Blues and Cues.

Holand kicked off his house slippers and slipped his stockinged feet into a pair of boots. "We're wasting time." He was anxious to find Clive, and frankly, so was I. But I didn't want to leave without getting at least a few words out of the two women. I needed to know what shape they were in. "Ladies, is there a friend I can phone? Someone who can come over and–"

Len Holand answered for them, "They're strong. They'll be all right. They love Robbie very much. We all love Robbie very much." The log-jam started to break behind Holand's eyes; tears started to well up. "He's a good boy. A little rambunctious at times, but he... he's a good boy." The shock was finally started to hit him. With one hand he covered his eyes. With the other he grabbed hold of the oak newel post on his stair banister.

Worried his knees might buckle, I took hold of his elbow and urged him into the front parlor. Len Holand lowered himself into the nearest seat, a large wingback chair. I then proceeded to the kitchen where I opened a couple of cupboards. Over the refrigerator I found a bottle of port wine and some tumblers. I brought them back and poured a shot for Holand which he seemed to welcome. I poured a second glass, but neither of the women accepted it, so I put it on the coffee table and sat myself down in a chair. While I waited for Len to pull himself together, I took the opportunity to glance around the room.

The place seemed nicely furnished - nothing terribly new or modern, but nothing old or worn out either. All in all, inviting and comfortable. The dark oak floor and gumwood trim bordered light-green walls which were adorned with framed oil paintings, mostly landscapes. I noticed one of them was signed by C. Holand. I'm no art expert, but it seemed pretty good to me. In one corner of the room a wooden toy box, neatly filled with dolls, trucks, and preschooler distractions napped silently, waiting for morning play time. The young children I had seen on the porch on my last visit, must now be in bed.

I turned to the two women and said as softly and gently as I could, "I take it one of you is Robbie's mother?"

At first, nobody answered. Not even Len Holand. Finally, "We're all his family," was the younger one's cryptic reply. "My name's Carol. This is Charlotte."

I asked, "Does Robbie have any other brothers or sisters? Besides Clive, that is?"

"There's Jess and Claudia," Carol said. "They're asleep."

"And Gloria," said Charlotte, speaking for the first time. "She's not here."

I still needed an answer to my first question, so I tried again, "And one of you is Robbie's mother?"

The two women looked to Len, and he offered, "Robbie's mother died in childbirth."

Carol added, "A frail woman. Bless her."

Len stood up. "I've got to go find Clive." I noticed he'd used the singular first-person pronoun, showing that even when stressed to the emotional limit like this he didn't welcome assistance from outsiders.

"Sir," I said. "If you're up to it there's something I'd like you to do first."

Len hurried toward the door, and I followed after him, explaining, "I'm afraid somebody has to officially identify the… your son. It's purely a formality, mind you, and it could certainly wait until tomorrow if you're not up to it. But I thought if you were able to attend to the matter tonight…"

Now in the front hallway, Len started to reach for the set of car keys that he'd left hanging on a hook by the door, but I lunged forward and beat him to the prize.

"Why don't we take my car," I suggested.

He looked at me, at my hand. I held my fingers closed tight around the keys. I braced myself, thinking I might have to wrestle.

Len Holand just turned and continued out the door. I put his keys back on the hook and followed him into the night.

From their guard stations, lying on the floor of the front porch, the two Irish wolfhounds looked upwards through bushy eyebrows at Holand's legs passing them by. Neither of the dogs moved a muscle to follow their master, proving once again that dogs are smarter than humans.

*****

We drove in silence, which was understandable considering our mission. I don't like to intrude on a man's grief at a time like this, but after ten or fifteen minutes I thought the time might be right to try a word or two. Something about Len told me he was up to answering a few questions and this might be my only opportunity. Both literally and figuratively a man like Len Holand doesn't leave gates open for long.

I kept both hands on the wheel as I turned and asked, "Mind talking a bit?"

He turned away, stared out at the passing night. I pressed on, knowing I was doing so at my own risk. I started with a question I was sure he'd been anticipating. "Robbie and Clive… they get along okay?"

"You've seen them, haven't you?"

"Sometimes guys act differently when they're in a bar."

"The boys have their differences, sure. What can I tell you? They're brothers. Brothers fight. But in the end Clive always looks out for his younger brother. That's the way it is out here. We look out for each other."

"Do the boys often take off like this? All of a sudden? Without telling you? No note? No phone calls?"

"It's hunting season."

"Do they have a favorite spot to go? Like, a cabin or something?"

He looked at me as if I were an idiot. "You don't hunt." It was an accusation not a question.

"No. I don't."

He looked back out at the passing forest again. "Not enough game up here to wait for the deer to come to you. You have to go to them."

I nudged up to my next question rather awkwardly. "So, you're sure that's where they went. Hunting. Deer. There's nowhere else they might want to spend some time. No other kind of game they might have gone after. I mean, they *are* healthy young men."

Holand understood my not-too-subtle suggestion. "Clive's got a girl. Tupper Lake."

"Do you happen to know what her–?"

"Arden."

"Any idea how I can get in touch with–?"

"None whatsoever."

He let me get the next one out completely. "Do you know where she works?"

"Work? This girl?" He grunted a half-laugh. "Single mother. Lives off the state – welfare, social assistance, food stamps, state child support, whatever she and the baby can suck off the public teat. Sometimes Clive stays at her place. But like I say, I have no idea where that is."

"You say she has a baby?"

He was ahead of me again. "Not Clive's. Couldn't be. Far as I know, he hasn't known her long enough." Holand rolled down his window to let some fresh air into the conversation.

"And Robbie?" I asked. "He have a girlfriend?"

"Robbie's a quiet boy. Shy. Keeps to himself. He's been spending a lot of time with Clive and this Arden woman, though. I guess he's getting to that age where he needs a little distance from the old man." Len turned away from me, probably to hide his moistening eyes. He must have suddenly realized he'd been speaking of his son in the present tense again. Something he'll have to stop doing.

I asked, "You know Arden's last name?"

"Davis… Davidson… something like that. Check the county welfare rolls. There can't be many Ardens."

I decided I'd intruded enough on this man's private sorrow for now, so I shut up and drove on silently, focusing my attention on the white tunnel my headlight beams were carving out of the blackness. Suddenly, to my right, on the road's shoulder just ahead, two pinpoints of light sparkled like tiny diamonds. They moved.

I hit the brakes. But it was too late. I felt a soul-sickening bump and thud.

We came to a stop. I didn't want to look. But I had to. I adjusted the rear-view mirror. Couldn't see anything. It was too dark back there. So, I put the car into park, reached over past Holand and opened the glove compartment. I removed the flashlight. Opened my car door. I shone the beam down the roadway behind us.

It was a fox. Big ears like satellite dishes and a white-tipped tail. His large nocturnal eyes shone in the flashlight's beam. He wasn't dead yet, but he wished he were. So did I. His hind quarters were mashed to the asphalt. His front quarters writhed in agony.

I went to reach again into the glove compartment, this time to get my service revolver. Lately, I've been keeping it loaded. But the gun was no longer there. It was in Len Holand's hand.

I had no idea what he was trying to pull. "I'll take that," I said.

"I'm a farmer," was his simple explanation to me as he opened his door.

I said, "I can't let you…"

But he was already out of the car as he said, "I'm used to it."

I guess he was right.

He fired the gun. A moment later he was back in the car, putting the weapon back where he'd found it. "I tossed it into the bushes," he said.

"Thanks." I shifted the car into gear. "That sorta thing… it isn't easy for me."

"Shouldn't be," he replied.

*****

I thanked the ambulance driver for waiting. He didn't mind – apparently Mrs. Baumeister's hot chocolate was delicious.

Lieutenant Rykert escorted Len Holand into the vehicle to make the official identification while I talked with one of Rykert's sergeants and got caught up. I learned that Rykert had already sent a couple of troopers up to the dam to secure the area. At first light more troopers will start searching the area for signs of suspicious activity. I instructed the sergeant to alert all police units throughout the state to keep an eye out for an old green Chev pickup truck that might, or might not, have a yellow canoe in back. I included the truck's license plate number that Len Holand had given me.

After a short time, Holand crawled out of the ambulance with Rykert following close behind. The two men conferred for a moment. Then Holand walked over toward the trees, probably for a quiet moment alone. Meanwhile, Rykert strolled over to join me. He looked stunned, as if he were the father who had just identified his son's remains, not the other way around.

Rykert shook his head in wonderment as he spoke. "Never saw anything like that before," He paused to grab a plastic cup of coffee from a passing trooper, then continued, "I had the body all prepped for him, laid out flat on its back, everything carefully covered except the face. I made sure no trauma was showing. No wound. No blood, no gore. Wanted to make it as easy as possible on the next of kin. So, what does the old man do? Cool as ice, Daddy unzips the whole bag. Top to bottom. Then, before I can stop him, he lifts up his deceased kid's head and turns it around so he can have a nice look-see at the wound. Meanwhile, I'm shouting, 'Shit, don't touch that. You're contaminating evidence.' But what can I do, there isn't room in there to swing a cat let alone wrestle with Paul Bunyan. When he's finished with the kid's head, Daddy proceeds to examine the rest of the body, shoulders to toe. Tanager, you should have seen him. I wish Doc Jacobs had been that thorough. I finally grabbed him, but the old guy's strong as an ox. Anyway, by that time the postmortem is over. He zips up the bag."

I told Rykert I wasn't surprised by any of this. Frankly, I don't think anything about Holand would surprise me.

Len Holand was now walking toward my car, so I excused myself from Rykert and went over to him.

I asked Holand if he'd like a coffee. He ignored my question. Instead, he asked one of his own. "So, who's this tourist Robbie and Clive had the fight with the other night?"

I was wondering when he'd think of this angle. "Nobody," I said. "Just a gentleman who's staying in town for a few days."

"What's this gentleman's name? And where is this gentleman staying?"

"Len," I said, feeling we'd been through enough together by now for me to call him by his first name, "Take my word for it - the guy had nothing to do with Robbie's death. I know him. The guy's all right. Like I said, he didn't even want to press charges."

"Name?"

I knew that Holand could find out easily enough on his own. It's a small community. The bar was full of witnesses to the fight. So I said, "Name's Briar."

"*Paul* Briar?" Holand asked.

I wasn't surprised he recognized the name. The story of Briar's missing wife had been big news. So I added, "If you know his name you know what the guy's been through. Take my word for it – Paul had nothing to do with Robbie's death. The poor man's got his own problems to deal with."

Len Holand said no more. He didn't have to. The look in his eyes sang choruses. I made a mental note to warn Paul Briar to watch his back. And to think seriously about finishing up whatever he came here to do. And then leave town.

Soon.

CHAPTER TEN

I sat and I watched the doorknob turn. I watched the door creak open. Slowly. Just a crack. Marlene was obviously puzzled. She didn't know what to make of finding the office door unlocked at this early hour. She was always first one here.

I imagined her standing on the other side of that door, frozen, cautious, trying to decide what to do next. Should she enter? Was someone inside waiting to jump her? Or had she just forgotten to lock it yesterday when she last left?

Come on in, Stanley barked. *And bring those vanilla donuts with you.*

Recognizing the bark, Marlene pushed the door open wide to find me sitting at my desk. "What the hell happen?" she asked. "Your bed catch fire?"

"Good morning. I've been here for hours." Truth was, after taking Len Holand back to his farm last night I'd gotten home too late to bother going to bed.

As Marlene placed the box of donuts on her desk the phone rang.

"Let's hope it's the mayor." I said. And I wasn't kidding. It would be nice to impress him with my early morning attendance. So I answered the phone.

But it wasn't His Worship. It was a Mrs. Ferris from New York State Welfare Services down in Albany returning my call. I'd phoned her earlier and left a message on her voicemail asking her to check if she had anyone named Arden Davis or Arden Davison listed on her welfare rolls. By the tone of the woman's voice you'd think I had asked her to find me a spare kidney.

"I've checked everywhere," she grumbled. "I can find no such individual."

"Are you sure? Like I say, I don't know if I have that last name right. It could be Davis or Davison, or Dav–"

"I find no Arden of any surname of any age of any sex on our family or child services lists in either Hamilton or Franklin or St. Lawrence counties." She added, "And let me tell you, Chief Tanager, that this new C.C.S. software didn't make the search easy."

"I'll bet it didn't." I had no idea what software she was talking about, but I felt she needed my moral support.

"I don't know what they were thinking of when they designed it."

"Sometimes you just gotta shake your head."

"Search function covers only one county at a time."

I pounded my desk with my fist. "Son of a bitch."

The woman from welfare paused. I guess I'd gone too far. Then she asked, "So tell me, Chief Tanager, does this have anything to do with that murder you had up there last night?"

"We don't know if last night's incident was actually a murder."

"The man on the radio says it was." By the challenging tone of her voice she obviously thought I take great delight in lying to officious bureaucrats. I do, but I'm surprised it showed.

I thanked Mrs. Ferris for her trouble and hung up.

Marlene asked me, "Another murder?"

"Looks like." But before I had a chance to explain further to her about Robbie Holand, the phone rang again. This time Marlene picked it up. She listened for a moment then handed it to me. "The Banner. Something about a body? In the river?"

I took it. "Chief Tanager here... Oh, hi, Troy, so how the Muskrats look for next season?" Troy Lascombe is the Glen Echo Banner's crime, entertainment, and sports reporter. I believe he also handles wedding coverage, but Marlene always grabs that section before I can get to it.

Troy asked, "So what's this I hear about a floater washing up down river?" Troy adjusts his jargon to fit his reportage. Happily, he rarely uses the word *floater* when covering weddings.

I explained most of what I knew about Robbie's death, including the Who, Where, What, and When – I couldn't help with the Why yet. I assured him the next of kin has been notified. As I spoke, Marlene listened. I was sorry she had to get it second-hand this way. Even though she's a civilian I like to show her the respect I'd show a fellow officer. When I got through with Troy, Marlene was pretty much up to date on the facts of the affair.

"Robbie Holand..." Marlene opened her box of donuts. "That's too bad. Nice kid. Not like his useless turd of a brother at all. Any suspects?"

"His brother hasn't been seen for a couple of nights," I said. "By the way, do you know who that other woman at the Holand house is? The younger one? Name's Carol?"

"Word has it she's Mrs. Holand number two."

"I thought the older one is Mrs. Holand number two."

"No. Technically, I believe she's number three. Apparently, Mrs. Holand Number One was so good it took two to replace her."

"You mean Holand now has two wives?"

"More or less. Nobody seems to know for certain. I don't think they all live at the farm."

"I take it no one has told Len Holand that bigamy is slightly illegal."

Marlene shrugged. "This is the North Country. People don't come up here because they like mosquitoes the size of Cessnas. They come here because they want to live life their own way, yet still be within a day's drive of a good dentist. Think of the Adirondacks as sort of a *Montana Light*." Marlene sipped her coffee. "You make better coffee than I do."

"I used a new filter."

"Oh, well… if you're going to blow the year's budget…"

The phone rang. Marlene's mouth was full, so I answered it. Turned out to be a news producer from a radio station in Glens Falls. This guy wanted to interview me live on air about the Robbie Holand murder. I corrected him, "Suspicious death."

"So can we?"

"Can you what?"

"Interview you."

"Sure," I said. "What would you like to interview me about?"

"The murder."

"There was a murder?"

"Okay, 'suspicious death.'"

"Oh, you must mean the murder."

The reporter paused. Then, "Is there someone else I can speak with?"

"Would you like to speak with our public relations director ?"

"Sounds like a good idea."

"Hi, there. Glen Echo Police Department public relations. How may I help you?"

He was finally onto me. "You don't want to be interviewed."

"Bingo. But thank you for your concern." I hung up but immediately lifted the phone back off the hook and left it that way. I said to Marlene, "We'll use our cells today." With the landline off the hook, any 911 emergency calls are automatically routed through our cells.

Just then I heard a knock on the open doorjamb behind me. I expected to turn around and find another reporter waiting to annoy me. I was wrong.

"Good morning, Chief Tanager." The young woman looked a whole lot better than when I'd last seen her. Less tired. Less drunk. Less lethally-armed.

Rebecca Reesor was wearing jeans and an oversized, bulky sweatshirt that sported the well-known logo of some shoe company or rock band or wine cooler – I don't follow pop culture very closely. She wore no coat, and in my opinion the weather this morning was too cold for just a sweatshirt, but Rebecca was raised up here and therefore more acclimated than I. Or maybe just tougher. And younger. I started to introduce her to Marlene, but turns out they already knew each other. I invited Rebecca to take a seat.

"Can't stay. I, like, uh, kinda just wanted to apologize for last night."

"The person you should be apologizing to is Lindsay Porter."

"She isn't going to press charges, is she?"

"Lindsay knows you've been through a lot. We all do." I waited to see what was next. What was on her mind.

Rebecca looked out the window, smiled again at Marlene. Then she noticed Stanley. Gave him a good pat. Dogs are a great ice breaker. Rebecca made a little small talk about various pooches she had known and loved. Finally, she said, "Well, I guess that's all I wanted to say. Just, uh… thanks."

"Rebecca, would you like to go for a coffee?"

She did.

*****

One could say that the Golden Dragon Restaurant has changed hands more often than a masseuse with a hangnail. I wouldn't say it, but one could.

The original owners, a Chinese couple, sold it to a Greek man. I'm told that the Greek then scratched out the word Dragon and changed it to Calf. Eventually, he sold The Golden Calf to an East Indian who scratched out the word Calf and changed it to Goat. The East Indian guy's exotic cuisine didn't go down too well with a Yankee population whose favorite spice is gravy, so he sold the business to a retired hippie from Vermont who changed the word from Goat to Stream. For some reason this hippie thought The Golden Stream sounded rustic and bucolic, befitting a quaint country eatery. Of course, most passersby assumed the place had been sold to a urologist. After the Golden Stream slowly piddled itself into bankruptcy, the current owner bought the place. His name is Ken Tamori. He's of Japanese ancestry, but he suspects that the older folks in town might remember Pearl Harbour too well and that the younger folks might remember Detroit, so he passes himself off as Chinese. Ken was at the cash register when Rebecca and I came in. One sight of me and he immediately looked at his wristwatch. "Is it noon already?"

"I thought I'd try one of your breakfast omelettes in the morning for a change,' I said. "See if they taste any fresher." Actually, Ken makes the best Denver omelette this side of... well, I guess Denver.

Rebecca and I took a seat. I started to introduce her to Ken, but it turned out they already knew each other. Ken offered Rebecca his sympathies for her two recent and tragic losses. He then steered the subject toward the latest news everybody was talking about. "Shame about Robbie Holand," Ken handed us our menus. "Accident?"

"Still to be determined." I glanced at the menu. "How's the blueberry pancakes?"

"Still to be determined." He then added, "Robbie and Clive were in here just a couple nights ago."

"Monday?"

Ken thought before answering. "Yeah. Smorgasbord night."

"You have smorgasbord night?" Rebecca asked.

"My wife's Swedish."

I said, "I thought she was Danish."

"Not on smorgasbord night."

"Was Robbie with his brother?" I asked.

"Unfortunately."

"What time?"

"Early. Around six."

"Just the two of them?"

"Three. Clive's new chick."

"Arden?" I asked.

"Don't know her name," Ken said. "Long, dirty brown hair, usually wears it in a ponytail. Short girl. Compact. Good shape. What my honorable ancestors used to refer to as a *spinner*."

I thanked him for the news update and then ordered my usual omelette. Rebecca ordered just tea, no food. I don't imagine the alcohol and drugs had done any favors to her stomach. After Ken left, Rebecca mentioned that she'd heard about Robbie Holand's death from some friends this morning. I asked her how well she knew Robbie and Clive. She said that, although she went to grammar school with Clive, she and the Holand brothers travelled in different circles. When she had hit high school age her father shipped her off to a private school in Albany. So, no, she didn't really know the boys.

At this point I let the conversation lag to give her an opening for what was really on her mind. She eventually filled the verbal void.

"Your friend Manwaring is a moron."

"You two not hitting it off?"

"He thinks Daddy killed my stepmom. That's so ridiculous."

"You have to understand, an investigator has to cover all bases."

"While the real murderer gets away?" Rebecca leaned in closer and said, "Chief Tanager, how do I get Manwaring off the case and you on it?"

"I'm afraid that's not possible."

"Why not? You were there when it happened. You knew Daddy. You know how much he adored Evelyn. What a loving husband Daddy was. You know this whole thing happened because of the kind of work Daddy was in."

"Has the F.B.I. been in touch with you?"

"Some guy came to the house. Took away Daddy's files. His laptop. Tablet. Phones."

"Then there you go. They're on the right track."

"But I haven't heard a word from them since then. Meanwhile, this Manwaring idiot is poking his big nose into all Mom and Daddy's personal stuff. Making all sorts of insinuations. Going through their bank statements, credit card receipts. Asking everybody in town if my father had any girlfriends. If my stepmom screwed around. Do you know how disrespectful that is to, like, their memory and stuff?" Rebecca sat back in her chair for her next revelation. "He's even talking to people about how my *own* mother died."

Rebecca was now referring to her biological mother, and I'd been waiting for Manwaring to latch onto this juicy little tidbit. I, of course, already knew all about it.

About fifteen years ago Rebecca's biological mother, Jacqueline, had taken her own life. By gunshot, just like Simon ended up doing. I got this story from the other guys in the band, not from Simon. For obvious reasons, Simon was never anxious to talk about it. To this day I have no idea what troubles led Rebecca's mother to make such a decision. I can imagine, however, that Rebecca might now be wondering if the suicide gene runs in her own DNA. Or worse, she might be wondering if she, herself, is somehow responsible for the two tragedies. Sounds crazy, but suicide is like that. A selfish act. When a person blows his or her brains out, a lot more mess is left behind than can be handled with a mop and sponge.

I felt terribly sorry for Rebecca. I started to tell her that I was here to help and that anything she might need, she should come to me, but I was interrupted when Ken came by with a tea for her and a grapefruit juice for me. He laid out a couple of paper placemats on which were printed street maps that pointed out local points of interest. Upon closer examination of the maps, I noticed a few anomalies. "Hey, Ken, since when did we get all the wax museums?"

"Got a deal from a buddy. Runs an Italian joint in Niagara Falls. Be right back with your omelette." Ken returned to the kitchen, and I returned my attention back to Rebecca.

"Your aunt and uncle at the house with you?"

"Aunt Margaret is. Uncle Frank had to go back to Baltimore."

"I don't suppose you feel like returning to school yet."

Rebecca was clearly impatient with my attempt to change the subject away from the investigations. "Chief Tanager, you and I both know that bomb was planted by a terrorist."

"It seems a logical assumption."

"A right-to-lifer."

"I wouldn't go that far."

Rebecca straightened herself upright in her chair. "I know you think I'm crazy for what I did last night, but somebody has to confront those women. Somebody has to look into what's going on at Windermere."

Now it was my turn to stay quiet. I took a sip of my grapefruit juice.

Rebecca continued, "I know those women. I worked there. They're heavy-duty Pro-Lifers. They think doctors like my father are murderers. Ask them. They'll admit it."

I finished my juice. Tart, not too sweet. I said, "I'm not going to bother those ladies, and neither are you. Lindsay and Sharon may not sanction abortion, I don't know. But that doesn't mean they're running around blowing up cars. Most Pro-Lifers are reasonable, law-abiding folk who wouldn't harm a fly. That's kinda what their whole movement is all about, isn't it?"

"Yes. And I totally respect that. Just like my father did. I really do. But every political group has it's nut cases."

"You think Lindsay and Sharon are extremists?"

"Chief Tanager, you should have seen them the night Nancy Briar told them she was going to terminate her pregnancy. Sharon went ballistic. She started–"

I interrupted. This was a hell of a news flash. "Nancy Briar was going to get an abortion?"

"Didn't you know?"

"I knew she was pregnant, but I didn't know she planned to terminate it. Was she going to have your father perform the procedure?"

"I doubt it. She was from New York. There's, like, loads of abortion providers in the city. No need to come all the way up here."

"And you say Paul and Nancy Briar talked about all this at Windermere? With perfect strangers?"

"They weren't exactly strangers. Not by that point. I was in the kitchen. The wine was flowing pretty free. They all got a little buzzed, especially Mrs. Briar. It was a small house that night – just the four of them. Next thing Mr. Briar knows, his drunk wife is confessing to her new very best friends in the world about how a baby is the last thing she and her husband need, what with their careers and all. So they've decided to terminate."

"Did Paul and Nancy know how their hosts felt about the matter?"

"I don't think so. Not right at first, anyway. But as the evening wore on and they switched from wine to brandy, things got pretty loose. Lindsay and Sharon finally let their true feelings come out. Got all worked up. They started spouting about how lucky Nancy was to be pregnant. How blessed from heaven. How giving birth was a woman's main purpose in life. All that shit. Lindsay and Sharon talked about how they'd both love to have children, but adoption agencies don't exactly put same-sex couples at the top of their lists. Then they started talking about how killing a fetus was the same as killing a person. How doctors who perform abortions should be thrown in jail for murder."

"Did they know you were there, within hearing distance?"

"Maybe. Maybe not. Or else they'd just forgotten what the kitchen help's father did for a living."

I took a moment to digest all this. So Lindsay and Sharon were indeed a same-sex couple. This was not the sort of news I wanted to hear. We have few enough eligible, youngish single women up here. And by *youngish,* I mean able to chew their own food without planning ahead.

At this point Ken arrived with my Denver omelette and fries. I ripped open a packet of ketchup as I said to Rebecca, "Funny, Paul never mentioned any of this to me."

"Why would he? Abortion is like gun control. People don't talk about it. Not unless they're drunk. You never know how the other people might feel about the subject." Rebecca snatched a fry from my plate. I asked her again if she wanted to order something to eat. She didn't.

I dug into my omelette. Beside it, on the Niagara Falls placemat, was an advertisement for *Ripley's Believe It Or Not Museum.* I turned my attention back to my table companion. "Have you mentioned your concerns about these two women to Lieutenant Manwaring?"

Rebecca leaned into her own placemat, mashing her right breast squarely into The Maid of the Mist. "Yes, I did. And you know what the good Lieutenant told me? He said women don't do things like that. He said – and I quote – 'Men plant bombs. Women plant petunias.' Can you believe that? Typical man. Typical cop. Sexist pigs the whole fucking–" She suddenly realized to whom she was speaking and what this particular whom did for a living. "Well maybe not all." She took another fry and leaned back.

"Sure you don't want something to eat? A muffin?"

"Chief Tanager, can't you take over? I heard you used to be a big homicide detective back in Buffalo."

I was getting tired of hearing what I used to be. I wiped my mouth with a paper napkin that, I noticed, advertised The Niagara Butterfly Conservatory. It reminded me that Evelyn Reesor once told me that she had always wanted to visit that place.

Rebecca sat back to let me chew over what she'd just fed me. The poor kid was going through a rough time. But the worst was yet to come. I'd dealt before with kids who'd lost both their parents suddenly. Usually from vehicle accidents. The initial shock usually leaves kids numb.

I looked into Rebecca's eyes. She didn't look numb. And she didn't look away. She stared straight back at me, not pleading, but daring me to tell her how crazy her theory was about her step-mother's murder. For the first time I noticed that this young woman had her father's mouth. Same full lips with a slight downturn at the corners. Except, the last time I saw her father's lips they were speckled with powder burn.

Carefully, delicately, I tip-toed. "Rebecca, I'll take your word for it that Lindsay Porter may have given your dad a hard time – written some letters, organized some demonstrations. But frankly, that's a long, long way from…"

That was enough. She sat back and said, "So you're not going to help me."

Until now I had hesitated to mention her being fired from her summer gig, but the subject had to be approached. "Rebecca, I know Lindsay let you go from your job at the inn."

Her eyes widened. "You think I'm pissed because… because she fired me?"

"I just thought that maybe since you didn't get along with her terribly well, your judgement might be—"

That did it. "I'm sorry." Rebecca stood up. "I thought you were different. Being a friend of Daddy's and all. I thought you'd understand. I guess I was wrong." Then she tried some reverse Psych 101 on me. "I'm sure you're right, Chief Tanager. I'm sure Lindsay Porter and Sharon what's-her-name are a couple of saints who wouldn't hurt a fly. Never mind that Lindsay once threw eggs at my dad's window."

"His window? Where? Your house?"

"The clinic. But I'm sure it was an accident. It must have slipped from her hand. Just like the pie."

"She threw a pie? At your dad?"

"At Evelyn. They caught her coming out of the hairdresser's. The pie was full of ketchup so it would look real gross. Cute, huh? But you're right. I'm sure they were all just accidents. I'm being silly. A silly young girl. What do I know? Too emotional. Nice talking with you, Chief Tanager. Thank you for the tea."

And with that said, the young woman left.

After showing a moment of due respect, Ken Tamori, who'd been watching the whole show from the wings, felt it was time to casually drift by. "Lady not staying for dessert?"

"I believe she's had her fill."

Ken said, "I heard her mention pie."

I considered the matter for a moment. "Got any lemon meringue?"

He did.

*****

"Mind if I just eat the filling?"

"You don't like meringue?" I dropped the second piece of pie, still in its triangular takeout container, onto my own desk.

Marlene wrenched her plastic fork into the lemon curd filling sideways, like a miner following a horizontal vein of gold. "Doctor says I'm supposed to watch my cholesterol."

"Meringue is just egg whites. No yolks."

"Really?" And with that good news, she attacked her tart treat with more of a clear-cut, open-pit mining technique.

Between bites I asked Marlene about the history of Doctor Simon Reesor's medical clinic in the years before I came to town. Could she recall any trouble at the place? Any demonstrations?

"Couple of incidents, I think. Some marching. Picket signs. Horns honking in both support and opposition. Couldn't tell which. Nobody could. But that was years ago."

"Any violence?"

"Nothing I can recall." She pushed a newspaper toward me and added, "But that might change. Looks like things are heating up a bit."

The newspaper was the Albany Post, one of several dailies we receive here at the station. A small headline below the fold read:

PROTESTORS EGG CONGRESSMAN'S CAR.

The story started with a backgrounder explaining that New York's abortion laws were among the most liberal in the country. But a bill was currently being tabled in Albany that might change that. Called a parental consent law, the new legislation would prevent any young woman under the age of sixteen from obtaining an abortion without her parents' permission. Opposition to this newly proposed law was strong and, in the writer's opinion, the bill was not expected to pass. This, of course, was upsetting a lot of anti-abortionists, one of whom yesterday made her feelings clear by tossing unfertilized chicken embryos at a state representative's Mercedes.

Marlene watched me read and waited for my comment. Getting none, she tried to scrape one off me like she was scraping the meringue off the lid of the pie container. "Pretty dumb, huh?"

"It sure is," I said with exaggerated passion. "Imagine – a United States congresswoman, during volatile times like this, driving a foreign-made car."

Marlene gestured to the newspaper. "I meant that bill, the one the pro-lifers are trying to push. What right does a parent have, especially a father, to tell his daughter she can't have an abortion? He isn't the one who's going to be throwing up his Pop-Tarts every morning. He isn't the one who's going to have to quit school and get a job flipping burgers or swinging from a stripper pole to raise the kid. He isn't the one whose dates will never call her back because no guy wants to get involved with a chick who comes with an instant family."

Marlene paused again, waiting for me to comment.

So I did, "How come you can say *chick*, but I have to say *woman*?"

"Cause you're not a chick." She dug her plastic fork back into her pie.

I was happy to deflect this conversation away from abortion. Maybe it's my police training, but I'm very uncomfortable when it comes to taking sides on social issues. My job has always been to break up fights, not judge which combatant is right or wrong. Besides, on some issues I really do see the merits of both sides, and the abortion debate was one of those issues.

I picked up my landline phone and called Lieutenant Manny Manwaring at Ray Brook to see how the Evelyn Reesor investigation was progressing. He informed me that he had been reviewing Evelyn's cell phone records, and apparently, her last few calls had been mostly to and from her husband, Simon, and her step-daughter, Rebecca. No surprise there. But mixed in with these calls, were a couple of outgoing calls to a number up in Lake Placid – a number, curiously enough, that was not in any of Evelyn's stored address books. Manwaring said he traced the number to a male ski instructor who apparently had a reputation as a hound. This implied, in Manwaring's words, that "Evelyn was waxing the guy's ski pole." Manwaring went on to tell me how ski instructors, like golf pros and tennis instructors, grab more tail than the tank cleaner at Red Lobster. I informed Manwaring that, at Simon's request, Evelyn had plans to learn how to ski this upcoming season so she could join her loving hubby on the slopes. But Manny was not impressed with my rationale.

When I asked Manny if he'd heard about the anti-abortion demonstrations in Albany yesterday, he said he indeed had but that he was leaving the whole terrorism angle to the Feds. I thought he was right to do this – it was within their purview. After I finished with Manwaring, I called Lieutenant Rykert for an update regarding Robbie Holand's death, a case that was clearly within my own purview.

I reached Rykert on his cell. He was on his way to Albany. He told me that the medical examiner in Ray Brook had not yet released an official report on Robbie Holand but unofficially the cause of death was blunt force trauma to the head, and by the way, Robbie's last meal consisted of corn, potatoes, and lamb – in other words, his mom's Irish stew. The M.E. also said he found no traces of alcohol or drugs in Robbie Holand's system, but added that the body hadn't been fresh enough for that determination to be terribly conclusive. The doc confirmed that Robbie had been dead for eighteen to thirty-six hours and in the water for most of that time. Rykert currently had a couple of scuba divers combing through the weeds and muck where the body had been found. As far as the most likely spot where the body had been dumped, the dam upstream from the Baumeister's cottage, Rykert said his troopers had taken impressions of several fresh tire tracks and the resultant plaster molds were now part of a forensics package he was currently transporting to Albany. I told him that I would contact Len Holand and find out what brand of tires was on the boys' missing truck.

Regarding our number one Person of Interest, Rykert said that nobody has yet seen any sign of Clive Holand. I wasn't surprised at this. Last night, when we first found Robbie, Lieutenant Rykert had asked me if I wanted to set up roadblocks, but I decided not to waste his manpower. Considering the length of time the victim had been in the water, the perp was surely long-gone by then. So, I just had Rykert issue an inter-state bulletin to watch out for Robbie's missing green Chev pickup.

Our update complete, I signed off, telling Rykert I was currently following a couple of leads locally that might help us find Clive. Rykert wished me luck on my search, but truthfully, I don't think he cared much one way or the other. He was just relieved not to be lead investigator on this case. Or any case, for that matter.

I hung up, put on my jacket, and asked Stanley if he wanted to go for a ride and watch Daddy do a little old-fashioned detective work. Stanley was about as enthusiastic about the idea as Lieutenant Rykert had been. The pooch was clearly happy right where he was, warm and comfy, waiting for his next donut.

Older dogs can get like that if they aren't careful.

CHAPTER ELEVEN

Bar rooms always smell worse in the daytime. It's probably a matter of context. Or maybe in the daytime my nose is just wider awake. For whatever reason, when I stepped into the bar of the Albion hotel the stink hit me like a sour blat from a high school trombone section. As my nostrils contracted and my pupils dilated, I carefully shuffled blindly into the heavy gloom. Three small steps later, a voice called out from somewhere in the bowels of the cave, "You're early, Chief. Girls ain't on 'til five."

I recognized the voice of Garth, the Albion's bartender. Last time I'd talked to him was last week, the night I had brought Paul Briar in here.

My pupils had now expanded their f-stops wide enough to make out actual furnishings, so I pulled a stool up to the bar and squinted at my wristwatch. "It's almost noon. Where's your lunch crowd?"

"Still throwing up breakfast." Garth poked his head up from beneath the counter where he'd been loading beer into the fridge. A roach crawled across the bar. He bashed it with an empty beer bottle that had a cigarette butt in it. "I told the exterminator to skip a week." Garth reached below the countertop for something. "Damn roach spray makes my nuts taste bitter." Garth plunked a bowl of peanuts and a cold bottle of beer in front of me.

I nudged them both away. "On duty."

A wiry little man in his mid-thirties, Garth opened the beer and took a swallow. "No booze… No girls on yet… I know you didn't come for the food… You must be here for educational purposes."

"Got a question about one of your ladies."

He leaned one elbow on the bar as if preparing for a long, heart-to-heart. "Like I told you the other night, Tanager – a man like you, new to town, you gotta mix. You gotta join. Community service clubs. Elks, Masons, Kiwanis, Rotarians, Knights of Columbus, model railroading, duplicate bridge…" He suddenly got a brilliant idea. "Hey! You like to curl?"

"Nobody likes to curl."

"Single babes do." He winked. "Cougars love a little ice time."

"I don't like to date women with cold feet."

He went back to refilling his fridge. "Face it, Tanager, you and I are a lot alike."

"You're selling yourself short, pal."

"Our career situations. Neither of us is in a position conducive to meeting women of our own social ilk."

"Would we really want to?" I asked.

"Guys like us, we gotta get out. We gotta circulate. We gotta join." He straightened up and pounded his fist on the bar. "We gotta join 'til it fucking hurts."

"You certainly make it sound attractive, Garth," I said. "And talking about attractive... do you by any chance have a girl working here by the name of Arden?"

"How would I know? Don't have them here long enough to learn any names. Three, four weeks, tops. Just for hunting season. After that they go back to Albany and we go back to karaoke. Sure wish the state would extend moose season."

"Arden," I repeated.

He thought the name over. "Arden… Sounds familiar…" Then the light bulb flashed on. "Oh, yeah. You mean, Tara."

"No… I think I mean Arden."

"Short chick? Nice rack? Kind of chunky. Dirty blonde hair. Wears it in a ponytail?"

"Sounds right."

"Arden Dawes. Stage name – Tara."

"So, she does work here, then."

"Damn it, Tanager, how could I know she was underage? You know how it is. I.D.'s are like tits - I can only make sure they got 'em. I can't vouch for their authenticity."

"Relax. This girl is not underage. At least, I don't think she is."

"That's good to hear." Garth squatted down and went back to loading his fridge. "'Cause I certainly wouldn't want to lose a little cash machine like Tara."

"Tell me about her."

"Not much to tell. Like I said, wears a ponytail. Dresses very preppy, you know, like a schoolgirl. Guys love that shit, especially the guys from the high school."

"High school? Are you telling me–"

"Settle down, officer. Not the students - the teachers. It's the sensible shoes and the plaid kilt. They eat her up like cafeteria meatloaf."

"Will Tara be here tonight?"

"Doubt it. Couple days ago she called in sick. Sounded like hell. Said she won't be in all week. Flu or something."

"Got an address?"

Garth paused for a moment's thought, then said, "This got something to do with Robbie Holand's murder?"

"Why do you ask?"

"Tara... Clive... Robbie... It ain't exactly six degrees of fucking separation."

"Does Clive hang around here?"

"Hey, I'd start charging the guy rent 'cept he drinks like a politician and he drops close to a C-note every night on dances."

"Dances? Why's the guy buying dances? He's her boyfriend, isn't he?"

"There are boyfriends and there are boyfriends."

"You mean, she's hustling him?"

"Well... there's hustling and there's hustling."

"Garth, you ever think of running for public office?"

"Well, there's running and there's running."

"Garth, Arden's address?"

He went to the cash register. Beside it, wedged between some plastic menus and a pile of Anthony Robbins inspirational DVD's, was an address book. He thumbed through it, then announced, "Sixteen-and-a-half, Florence."

"Tannery Bay?"

"Where else? Not a lot of legit landlords like getting paid in soggy singles that smell like Flipper's laundry hamper."

I bid good-bye to Garth and headed out. When I reached the door, I thought of one last question. "Garth, you ever get any lesbians in here? You know, girls who like watching girls?"

"Not that I've noticed. But hey, if that's what floats your kayak, Tanager, I'm telling you… curling. Dykes love tossing rocks."

As I opened the door to leave, one of Garth's strippers walked in, probably coming to drink her breakfast. She wore a loose-fitting jogging suit, and she was carrying a gym bag, but nobody would mistake her for a physical fitness devotee. Her dull eyes had all the sparkle of a week-dead trout, and her skin had the pallor of the cheese in one of Garth's rat traps.

Her smile revealed yellow teeth and receding gums that testified to a host of dietary deficiencies. I'd say she'd been riding the horse for a couple of years or using meth for half that time. Whatever her drug of choice, I could only hope she had brought her supply with her. As far as I knew we didn't have any hard dealers in town these days. Lots of weed, but that's all.

Acknowledging my uniform and official hat, the stripper gave me a little wink much the same way a boater gives a fellow sailor a wave when they pass on the river. Cops get this a lot from sex trade workers. It's a professional's acknowledgement of common interests and backgrounds.

I tipped my cap at her and thought about how Garth might be right. Maybe it was time I joined a new club.

*****

Sixteen-and-a-half Florence turned out to be a two-story clapboard semi-detached house, one of six identical semis that backed onto a herniated bulge of river water called Tannery Bay. The area was so-named because, back at the turn of the century, leather was cured here. These modest homes, originally built to house the workers of the long-defunct tannery, were now rented to seasonal employees of the local resorts – college kids during the summer, ski pros during the winter, and a handful of the Albion Hotel's strippers during fall hunting season.

The homes had no driveways, so I parked my car at the curb and walked up to Arden's door. I tried ringing the bell, but either I'd gone deaf or it wasn't connected. So I knocked.

A woman's voice tumbled down from above, "Leave her the fuck alone."

I looked up to see a thirty-something woman leaning out the upstairs window of the adjoining unit. "Afternoon," I offered.

She didn't answer. She was too busy chewing her gum. She pulled a dirty terrycloth bathrobe back up over a bare shoulder. No makeup. Her hair was still dripping wet. I couldn't help wondering to myself, who chews gum in the shower?

The air temperature out here was barely above freezing, so I called up, "You're going to catch your death of cold."

"It won't be all I've caught in this dump," she said, scratching herself somewhere below the windowsill.

"Arden here?"

"Who wants to know?"

I found this an odd question considering I was wearing my uniform and driving a marked patrol car. But I played along. "Glen Echo Police."

"No shit?" The woman squinted toward my patrol car. "Can't see fuck-all without my lenses. Sierra call you?"

"Yeah, right. Sierra. She called me." I remembered that name from last week. Sierra was a Ukrainian stripper whom Paul Briar and I had met at the Albion. Nice woman.

The neighbor lady stopped scratching herself long enough to point an accusing finger at some unseen entity. "You tell Sierra to mind her own fuckin' business."

I tried the doorknob. It was locked. I asked the itchy lady next door, "You got a key?"

"You got a warrant?"

I leaned against the door. "Oh, I see it's open." The century-old rotting wooden jamb didn't need much of a kick.

I stepped inside the house. "Arden?" I called. Then I tried, "Tara? You in here?" Finally, "Arden Dawes? This is the police. Are you all right?"

A yard sale's worth of household crap clogged the cluttered hallway – a rusty bicycle, a small hibachi barbecue, some folding lawn chairs, a pile of overcoats – some of them infant-sized – and several cases of empty beer bottles. As I edged my way past a baby carriage, I peeked inside it. The carriage cradled a clean blanket but no baby. I stepped over a pile of winter boots and poked my head into the living room.

The small space looked, and smelled, like Sunday morning at a college dorm. The TV was turned on, but the volume had been muted. A large bag of corn chips lay strewn on the coffee table, its contents spilling out like an MSG-laden horn of plenty.

Again I called out, "Arden? I'm a policeman. Hello?"

I heard the floorboards creak. Close by. To my left. I turned to find a young woman standing in the kitchen doorway. Garth had been right - she looked like a high school kid – a short, pug-nosed, baby-faced Lolita.

She shuffled into the room, her small feet half-digested in big furry slippers. Her dirty blonde hair had been loosely tied back but was gradually freeing itself from the elastic shackle. Her matted bangs swept low across her forehead but were too thin and mangy to cover her strong, dark eyebrows. I couldn't tell what her body looked like – she'd wrapped it deep inside an oversized fuzzy pink dressing gown. With bunnies. All-in-all, I'd say little Arden Dawes looked like she should be sucking her thumb and clutching a teddy bear instead of what she was clutching - a bottle of bourbon.

As she shuffled closer, I discovered a splash of facial features Garth had failed to tell me about. Big, bloody, facial features. Her bruised left eye was almost closed shut. Her sex-kitten, pouty lips were clawed and swollen. And a deep red gash canyoned across her forehead. She stared at me through her one still-pretty unswollen but watery blue eye.

"Tol' Sierra not to call nobody." Her speech was slurred by the combination of bourbon and swollen lips. She continued walking past me, swaying, stumbling. The tail of her housecoat swept a pile of glamour magazines off the coffee table. When I reached down to pick them up, I noticed a box of disposable diapers lying beside the sofa.

"Arden, where's your baby?"

The young mother collapsed backwards onto the lumpy, stained couch.

"Is he upstairs?" I asked. "Arden? Is your baby upstairs?"

"I don't know why people just won't mind their own fuckin' business."

I left her and hurried up the stairs, dodging empty bottles to take two steps at a time.

The top floor held three small bedrooms. One was filled with big plush stuffed animals and overflowing ashtrays. I assumed this one belonged to Arden. The other was a lot neater, more grown-up. I figured this one housed her roommate, Sierra. The closet doors in both these bedrooms were full of the usual glitzy stripper gear - bikinis, teddies, peignoirs, and glow-in-the-dark spike-heeled shoes. The third bedroom was almost empty. No ashtrays. No beer bottles. No fuck-me shoes.

Just a crib.

I carefully pulled back the blanket. And there, staring back at me, was a fat little baby with big blue eyes and a plastic dummy stuck in his yap.

"What's your name, pal?"

He didn't answer, of course. I'm no expert on these matters, but I'd say he was about a year old.

I gave him a little koochie-koo under his spittle-glazed chin and slowly peeled the blanket back for a good look-see. Carefully, I loosened his diaper. He must have welcomed the cool, fresh air on his little pink parts because he immediately spit out the pacifier to give me a great big smile. The kid's diaper smelled clean, but that's not what I was inspecting him for.

I lifted him up to check his suspension and undercarriage. As far as I could see his chubby little bum, back, and legs looked delightfully free of burns and bruises. I popped the rubber cheater back into his mouth and gently pulled the blanket back up to his shiny chin. There's something nice about tucking in a baby. I bet it lowers your blood pressure just like when you pat a dog. Mind you, I wouldn't relate this cozy baby/puppy comparison to any mothers.

I stood watching the kid suck on his latex soother and thought about how most babies of stripper mothers probably spend their whole infanthood sucking on plastic without knowing it. Not this guy, though. Judging from what little I'd seen of Arden's short but compact figure I don't imagine she needed any space-age polymers to keep her dance schedule or her bikini top full.

I went back downstairs, stepping carefully to avoid hitting a beer bottle and flying on my ass. When I got to the living room, I found Arden stretched out on the couch, fast asleep. Her right hand, which hung loosely over the edge of the sofa, was still clutching the neck of the liquor bottle. For the time-being, I left it that way and went back to the front hall.

I had seen an infant's car carrier here, so I quickly grabbed it and installed it into my patrol car. I should have one of these with me all the time, but then I should also have a working siren. I went back inside and retrieved the baby. Finally, after I got him strapped into the car, I went back into the house and carried out his Mommy who was still out cold. I had considered calling an EMS unit for this transport, but decided that this wasn't an emergency. More important, I had reasons for wanting to keep full control of this situation myself.

I dropped the baby off at Miriam Coates' place. I knew Miriam because, when she's not singing lullabies to slobbering children at her private day care center, she's singing blues standards to slobbering drunks at one of our local watering holes. I assured her I'd be back for the baby before the day was finished. Then I continued on with the still-unconscious mommy, Arden, to our next stop.

* * * * *

Doctor Libby Liao was new to Glen Echo Samaritan, but that, in itself, is nothing new. Our little hospital changes staff often. Despite the many advantages the North Country has to offer prospective professionals –clean air, a low crime rate, and no rush-hour traffic – it's not easy to keep doctors up here for long. One struggle through our ridiculous six-month winter or one attempt at a golf game during black fly season, and family physicians tend to hop the next bobsled south. But Doctor Liao told me she hated golf and loved to snowboard, so I figure she might have a chance.

Doctor Liao, who knew Arden from previous visits, told me that the young woman's wounds were not serious, but the patient should stay for the rest of the afternoon for observation. Fine. I'll check back for her later.

As the doctor walked me to the door, she mentioned in passing that during her examination she'd noticed that Arden had recently terminated a pregnancy.

"An abortion?" I said. "When? How long ago?"

The doctor hesitated to answer. "I've probably said too much already."

"I understand," I said. "But you should know that a close friend of hers was murdered last night."

"The drowning?"

"Robbie Holand. His brother was Arden's boyfriend."

"And you think she might be in danger?"

"I don't know, but…"

Doctor Liao got my message and continued, "I last saw her four weeks ago. That's when I told her she was pregnant. She was not very happy about it. Neither was I, frankly."

"She didn't want a second baby?"

"Not if it meant changing her lifestyle. I told her in no uncertain terms, 'Young lady, you have a serious decision to make: the baby or the booze.'"

"Seems she made her choice."

"Can't say I'm sorry," Doctor Liao said. "I've seen the ravages of fetal alcohol syndrome."

By now we'd reached the front door of the hospital. It was raining pretty hard, and I was in no hurry to get soaked, so I took the opportunity to ask my escort a couple more questions. "Doctor, can you tell me how many physicians in your hospital do terminations?"

"As of two weeks ago, none."

"You mean Doctor Reesor was the only one?"

"Yes. And he hadn't been doing them for long. From what my colleagues tell me, he's been doing the procedure for only six years."

"Six?" I didn't understand. "But Simon's been practising up here for a lot longer than that. Twenty years, at least."

"Apparently, he didn't always do terminations."

"Do you know why not?"

Dr. Liao shrugged. "I wouldn't know. It was before my time. All I know is, he'll be missed."

I thanked the doctor for her help then pulled my collar up, hurried across the slippery parking lot, and jumped into my car. The rain was now mixed with wet snow, and my windows were fogging up, so I turned on the defroster and waited for the mist to clear. While waiting I watched a group of boys playing soccer in a sports field down the street. The air was bitter cold and the icy rain had to be soaking those kids clear through to the bone, but they refused to call their game. I've seen this sort of thing a lot up here. Bad weather doesn't faze these kids. City kids would have scurried for cover at the first drop. But these Adirondack kids tend to tough it out.

As I watched the intrepid players slip and slide in the mud, I thought about another Adirondack kid, now grown up. Clive Holand didn't strike me as the type to tough anything out. If he discovered he was about to become a father, I doubt he would be anxious to stay in the game for long. Like many young men, I expect Clive would have no objection to his girlfriend terminating her pregnancy. His old man, on the other hand, would be another matter. As proud grandfather of the impending child, Len Holand would not want to deny the world a successful shot between the posts by the Holand team. Len Holand would never call a game on account of bad weather.

My car's windows were clear now, but before driving out of the hospital parking lot I checked my texts then called Marlene at the office. She said that a couple of small matters could use my attention, but she insisted they could both wait until later. I could tell she wanted me to keep my attention focused exclusively on the Robbie Holand investigation. She liked it when I had something important to do, but I reminded her that I was still the town's one and only law enforcement officer. Besides, I didn't want to give the mayor any more ammunition to load into his *let's-fire-Tanager-for-dereliction-of-duty* shotgun. So, off I went on my appointed rounds.

My first call took me to the Dollar Store, the scene of a reported smash and grab early this morning. Although the only thing taken was a display of kites, the store's owner was quite upset. So I invited him, next windy day, to accompany me to the town park and together we'd nab the shiftless, good-for-nothing, string-tugging bastard. The shop owner said he liked my way of thinking. I told him I'd appreciate it if he'd pass along his kind compliments to his town councillor.

Next, I dropped by the Glen Echo Public Library where, according to the report, the full-figure statue of our town's founding father had been abused in a lewd manner through an inappropriate application of root vegetables. I removed the offending rutabaga and continued on to my next urgent matter – a domestic scrap between the man and woman who ran our local scrapbooking and stationery shop. By the time I showed up at the store, things had quietened down. Neither of the combatants wanted to file charges. According to the wife, her husband has been cheating on her. The hubby tried to deny the affair, but he didn't have a chance. I saw the evidence, myself. The scrapbooking wife had all the incriminating photos, phone records, and illicit motel receipts neatly pasted and mounted in a lovely leatherette album. I suggested they might work things out with help from their church minister, my boss The Reverend Mayor Tim. I thought he'd appreciate the referral.

After a quick early dinner at Blues and Cues I phoned the hospital to check on Arden. The nurse said the young patient was sobered up, cleaned up, hydrated up, and juiced up with a shot of vitamin B complex, ready to be released. I said I'd be there as soon as I fetched Arden's baby from the daycare center.

As the kid and I drove together to the hospital to pick up his Mommy, I was prepared for the usual rug-rat fountain of fluids from him, but the little squirt pleasantly surprised me. He was a dream. No crying. No puking. In fact, no trouble at all. Just good company who, when he did piss and shit himself, was kind enough to keep the mess confined to his plastic shorts, a consideration I wish more of my squad car passengers would show.

The kid's name turned out to be Sean, and Arden was both thrilled and surprised I'd brought him back to her. This young woman was no fool. She knew that a mother in her situation was not generally reunited with her baby until the authorities conduct a lengthy investigation into the parent's fitness to care for the child. I told her that this was exactly why I had not taken little Sean to a government-run agency or let the EMS people get involved. After all, I could see with my own eyes that, although Arden wasn't worth squat when it came to watching out for herself, she obviously took damn fine care of her baby. I explained this to Arden as I drove her home from the hospital. She seemed duly but crudely appreciative.

"So what d'ya want – a medal or a blowjob?"

"Well, I've already got a drawer full of medals…"

"You fuckin' cops are all alike."

"Arden, all I want you to give me are a few straight answers." I looked her in the eye. "Deal?"

She didn't answer, so I pressed on, "Arden, do you have any idea where Clive went this morning after he did this to you?"

I'd obviously thrown her off balance. She wondered how much she'd told me earlier, when she was drunk. Had she admitted to me that it was Clive who had assaulted her? She didn't know. So she finally just shrugged and said, "How should I know where he went? Ask his old man. Or ask Robbie."

This answered my next question: *Had Arden seen any local TV newscasts, social media reports, or read the newspapers this morning?* I pulled the car over to the side of the road and shifted it into park. I undid my shoulder belt so I could turn and face her.

"Arden, I have some bad news."

She turned and looked at her son who was firmly strapped into the rear car seat. She then turned back to me. "No, no. They can't. Nobody's taking him away. I don't care what they think of me. I don't give a fuck what they think about what I do for a living. Sean is mine. Nobody's taking him. Nobody's taking my baby. You can't–"

"Arden, Robbie is dead."

She looked at me. She didn't make a sound. She didn't blink. She just looked at me.

"Last night. We found his body in the river."

Arden turned and faced front again. Then she looked out the side window.

"I'm very sorry, Arden. I know you cared very much for Robbie."

I didn't know for certain that she loved Robbie, of course. But the stunned look in her eyes told me she had strong feelings for him. Certainly stronger than she had for his violent older brother, Clive, who was still paying her for lap dances.

I was still waiting for her to do something. Cry, fall apart, get angry. She'd had a rough afternoon. First, she'd thought somebody was going to take her baby away. Now she's been told her friend is dead.

But it was Sean who started crying. His soother had fallen out, so I reached back and picked it up from where it had fallen. I twisted round, started to stick it back in his mouth, but Arden grabbed it from my hands.

"Fucking idiot. You can't do that!" Using the tail of her shirt she wiped the plastic dummy free of any lint and hair that it had picked up from my back seat. "Don't you know? Kids are delicate. Any little thing can hurt them. They aren't like you and me. They got no immune system worth fuck-all yet. They get sick real easy. You can't just treat them like... like… You can't just..."

Now it was her turn to cry. I didn't reach out to soothe her, though. I didn't put my hand on her arm, pat her shoulder. In Arden's line of work she was used to older men using any excuse to touch her. So I just left my hands in my lap and said, "I'm sorry. If there's anything I can do…"

She sniffed. "To start with you can find me a fucking Kleenex."

I opened the glove compartment where I keep a pack of tissues. She snatched a handful out and blew her nose. Then she said, "And you know what else you can do for me?"

"What?"

"You can find the man who killed Robbie." She wiped the tears from her eyes. "You can find fucking Clive fucking Holand."

CHAPTER TWELVE

I unstrapped the baby and carefully hoisted him out of the back seat. I was going to carry him up to the door of Arden's house for her, but she grabbed him for herself. According to her, I had almost conked his wee noggin on the door frame as I'd lifted him out of the car. Not true, of course. She also gave me hell for not dressing him warmly enough for the November wind. She may have had a point with that one.

As we walked to her front door, I asked Arden what made her so sure that Clive was the one who had killed Robbie.

"'Cause he found out."

I thought I understood. "You mean about the new baby you're expecting? He found out that Robbie was the father?"

"Oh, no, Clive didn't give a shit about that. He knew it was a toss-up."

"I see…" I said this casually, as if two brothers sharing the same girlfriend was as normal as two brothers riding the same bicycle. "So what was it that set Clive off?"

"The money."

"Money?"

"You think strippers have a medical plan?"

"You asked Clive to pay for your abortion?"

"Clive wouldn't help me. Not for something like that."

"But he had enough to pay for lap dances."

She laughed. "Funny huh? He's got plenty of bucks to spend on his own lap but not a cent to spend on mine."

I didn't understand. I had to clear this up once and for all. "Arden, what did Clive do when you told him you were going to get an abortion. How did he react?"

"Fuckin' ballistic, that's how he reacted."

"Clive doesn't believe in abortion?"

"Clive doesn't give a fuck one way or the other. He was just scared his old man might find out. The old man thinks we're all fucking breeding stock."

I now led the witness. "But not Robbie. He wasn't like that."

"If he was, you think he'd have stolen the money for me?"

I led her again. "The money that Clive was pissed about."

"Clive was saving it for new struts for his car." She laughed again. "Boy, if Robbie's old man ever finds out, huh? His own sons helpin' get his very own grandchild aborted. Talk about goin' ballistic." She pushed the door open and walked in. I stayed outside on the porch.

Before Arden shut the door, I gave her baby a little tickle goodbye. We'd sort of bonded in the car. The kid sure was a sweetie. I tweaked his wet little chin and gave him a koochie-koo. He looked at me and smiled. I remarked to Arden, "He's a real cutie-pie. It must have been tough."

"What do you mean?"

"You know. When you found out you were pregnant again. Deciding to abort it. That must have been a tough decision." I touched the baby's tiny perfect hand and added, "Especially after seeing what good work you turn out."

Yes, I know it was a terribly cruel thing of me to say. But now that I knew all the possible fathers' and/or grandfather's feelings on the subject, I wanted to get the mother's thoughts.

My nasty ploy worked. Arden's face turned ice cold. Frighteningly cold. Cold like the liquid nitrogen in science class that instantly turns soft rose petals to brittle glass.

She looked up at me. And with a gaze that froze my soul brittle she said, "You know why I had that abortion?"

I fudged around with, "Well it's not really any of my—"

"Hunting season's almost finished, then I gotta go back on the road. Syracuse, Utica, Rochester, Buffalo." She poked my stomach like I had been poking her baby's tummy. "How many fuckin' club owners you think gonna hire a fat stripper?"

She didn't wait for me to answer. She just shut the door.

I walked back to my car. But I didn't drive off yet. I paused to do some thinking. Thinking about two children. One was her little boy, Sean. And the other would have been his younger brother. Or sister. We'll never know which, because Sean's brother or sister never made it out of the gate. His or her life never got started. And why? Because Mommy had to pay the rent by shaking her naked ass in some horny idiot's drunken face.

Men, huh? You gotta love us. But what the hell, it was Arden's decision. And I honestly believed it should stay her decision. Not some man's. Not even the father's. Nor the grandfather's. And certainly not the government's, which is run mostly by horny old men, anyway.

And then I thought about my ex-wife. I often suspect that a baby might have held us together. But on the other hand, it might not have, and in that case the little tyke would now be caught in the middle of an ugly custody battle. Either way, it's all just a moot point. We were both too busy to have children. But whenever I see a sweet kid like little Sean I can't help wondering what I'd missed out on. Selfish of me, I know. Or maybe not. After all, if we bass players don't have little bass players what are we going to be left with? A world full of drummers and guitarists. And that can't be good.

I put my keys in the ignition and looked back at Arden's house. But I didn't start the engine. Not yet. Something was bothering me. Scratching away in the dusty corners of my empty attic. I had no idea what, but it was something Arden had done.

Or something she hadn't done.

Yeah, that was it. She hadn't unlocked the door before going inside. She didn't have to, of course. I'd busted the latch this morning when I kicked my way inside. I'd forgotten about that. And here she was strolling into an empty, unlocked house by herself. Alone. With a crazy boyfriend still on the loose.

I jumped out of the car. As I hurried up to the door, I kept telling myself I was worrying needlessly. I didn't even know if Clive was still alive. And if he was, would he really be dumb enough to come back here, with every cop in the state looking for him?

The door was still ajar. I didn't knock.

The first thing I saw was little Sean. He was crawling toward me down the front hall, smiling and gurgling like nothing had happened. Like everything was fine. Like it was an everyday occurrence for his mother to be lying on the floor behind him like that. On her back. Coughing. Gagging. Choking on her own blood.

I knelt down. She was conscious. But barely. Her nose was broken, mashed to a pulp. And her mouth was badly cut. She'd lost some teeth and was having trouble breathing. I rolled her onto her side, stuck my fingers down her throat, and gave her a hard slap on the back.

Nothing. She was still choking. I didn't want to give her CPR. Not yet. With that broken nose and busted teeth, who knows what obstruction I might be forcing deeper down her windpipe.

She had stopped coughing and seemed to be getting air. I felt her wrist for a pulse. Too weak to detect. I tore off her sneaker and felt the top of her foot. I thought I got a pulse there, but it was still very faint. I gave her another, harder, slap on the back, this time with the heel of my hand. She sputtered a bit. Then she coughed a little stronger. I turned her face-down to let the blood flow more freely from her mouth and nostrils instead of back down her throat.

Meanwhile, from somewhere at the back of the house, I heard a screen door slam shut. My natural instinct was to chase the perp, but right now that was not an option. I grabbed my cell from my belt and hit the emergency call button.

While waiting for a 911 operator to answer I ran to the living room window. I watched Clive Holand jump into his brother's green Chev pickup truck. Every cell in my dim-witted cranium screamed at me *Chase the bastard, you idiot. This may be your only chance.* But I couldn't. Somebody had to stay with Arden and the baby until the paramedics arrived.

Then I noticed a woman standing on a front lawn down the way. It was the itchy lady from upstairs. She too was watching Clive hop into the truck.

I knocked on the window. She saw me. She sauntered towards the open door. But not too fast. She wanted to make it clear she didn't rush for any man.

With the phone held tight to my ear I ran to the open door. "Come here," I yelled to her. "She needs your help."

Her eyes went to the dark hallway behind me, and the moment she saw Arden lying on the floor she got the idea. She ran inside and kneeled down to her bleeding, convulsing neighbor. "I knew he'd be back," she said.

The operator finally came on the line. I gave her the pertinent info and told her to get an ambulance out here, stat. And while I had her on the line, would she please call the state troopers for me? Tell them the green Chev pickup we're all looking for is now on Highway Three near Glen Echo, probably headed west.

I hung up the phone and asked the neighbor lady, "Think you can handle her 'til the paramedics get here?"

The neighbor lady looked to Sean, "The kid okay?"

"Yes." I looked out the door and watched Clive's truck speed away.

"Then why the fuck you wasting your time here?"

I ran out and jumped into my patrol car.

As I turned onto Highway Three, I could see the Chev truck heading west, away from town, toward Cranberry Lake. With one hand on the wheel I called the State Police and requested backup and a roadblock if they had the manpower. But I didn't hold out much hope. Troopers are spread pretty thin in this area.

The first stretch of the chase, straight down the highway, was a quick sprint, but with oncoming traffic and a couple of intersections to worry about I couldn't stomp the gas full out. I wished my car's siren were working. The horn helps but it doesn't clear the road nearly as well.

Clive's truck was fast, but my old Ford Crown Vic was faster. Within a minute I had caught up to him and was just starting to pass his truck, readying to edge it off onto the shoulder, when we came to an intersection. He pulled a quick turn north onto Highway Fifty-six, but I missed the turn and overshot. I braked, skidded around a quick one-eighty, then continued the chase.

Highway Fifty-six follows a river valley and ribbons through some tight curves and blind hills. I soon lost sight of him. My problem wasn't that my car was less manoeuvrable than his truck – it was just that he took chances I wasn't willing to take. I couldn't risk endangering other drivers. As a result, after a mile or so, I had completely lost him.

When I came to a straightaway that climbed up a long upward slope, I spotted him again. He was stuck behind a slow-moving Winnebago, a giant Motel Six on wheels that was wheezing to get its wide, barbecue-and-bicycle-laden ass up the hill. Of course, Clive could do the smart thing and wait for a safe place to pass the aluminum behemoth. But no, the moron stepped on the gas and pulled out blindly as he crested the top of the rise, trusting the Gods of Idiots to look after him. Unfortunately, the Gods were otherwise occupied. A big shiny new black Nissan pickup popped over the rise just in time for the Nissan's surprised driver to find himself face-to-face with Clive's oncoming truck.

Now, although Clive was headed uphill, the road he was on was cut into the rocky shelf of a river valley which meant that the shoulder to his immediate left butted against a steep hillside and the shoulder to his immediate right dropped off straight down a cliff and into the river.

The driver of the on-coming Nissan pickup hit his brakes. And the Winnebago captain did the same, but the giant RV's high center of gravity had its own plans: Its big boxy ass started swinging like the tail of a killer whale, first left, into Clive's truck, which was now directly beside it, and then right, onto the narrow soft shoulder. The first meaty slap knocked Clive's green rust-bucket truck onto the far left side and the second bounce left an opening, a momentary cleft in the wall of vehicles, through which the driver of the black Nissan pickup was able to thread his vehicle. His pickup's rear bumper, however, caught the back of the Winnebago. This sent the Nissan pickup's right rear wheel off the asphalt and onto the shoulder. Luckily, he didn't roll, but as I passed him, in my rear view mirror, I watched the Nissan's tailgate fall open. His cargo – a three-wheel ATV, a case of beer, and a dead deer – bounced out onto the dirt. As the Nissan pickup slowed to a stop, the driver extended his arm out the window and gave us all the finger. By this time, on the other side of the road, the Winnebago had also come to a halt. I felt sorry for the Winnebago guy. For the guy with the dead deer, not so much. Meanwhile, with the roadway now clear again, Clive zoomed ahead.

I decided this madness couldn't continue – we would end up killing an innocent passerby. So I eased off my accelerator and grabbed my cell, ready to phone the state police again. And this is when fate and after-market auto parts stepped in and gave me a hand.

In the far distance, a few wispy clouds of steam started seeping out from under Clive's old battered hood. He was slowing down. Pretty soon the thin cirrus cloud blossomed into full-blown cumulonimbus, leaving a jet contrail that was suitable for skywriting. His radiator had obviously blown a hose. Clive didn't stop, but that didn't matter. Any moment now his engine would. I kept following him.

We were now winding our way through a series of tight S-curves that occasionally caused me to lose sight of him, but I wasn't worried. He wasn't going far.

But when I reached a straightaway again, he was nowhere in sight. Where had he gone? What had he done? I hadn't noticed any side roads. Could I have missed a little logging trail or something?

I slowed down to a crawl and kept my eyes glued to the passing forest. And that's when I saw it – a quarter mile up ahead – steam billowing from a pink dinosaur's rectum.

No, I wasn't hallucinating. I was coming up to a cheapie roadside zoo where, on the front lawn, a huge twenty-foot-tall pink plaster Tyrannosaurus Rex stood beckoning tourists to stop and visit. The creature's stubby little forearms held a sign, *Reptiles of the Adirondacks.* His lips were curled to reveal mammoth sharp teeth which would have looked quite ferocious if he hadn't had one eyebrow raised which, instead, just made him look sarcastic, like he was daring some jerk to ask why he was painted pink and why he had steam coming out of his ass. I soon knew the answer to the second question. Parked behind the creature sat Clive's truck belching vaporized coolant like Old Faithful.

But the truck's cab was empty.

I pulled into the parking lot just in time to see Clive vaulting over a tall chain-link fence. I rammed my gear shift into park, jumped out and continued my pursuit on foot.

As I passed the main office, a man in a brown uniform came out to see what was going on. I yelled to him to stay inside and lock the door – if Clive was armed, the last thing I needed was a hostage situation.

I climbed over the fence that Clive had just negotiated. I didn't stop to question why such a big, sturdy chain-link enclosure was erected around a reptile zoo that supposedly housed snakes and lizards. In hindsight, I should have.

Clive was now a hundred yards ahead of me, climbing over another fence.. He scurried through tall grass, lumbered past a storage shed, and scampered up a steep hill into a stand of hardwood trees. I didn't pull my gun yet. I knew I'd need both hands free to climb that next fence. Certainly seemed like a lot of tall fences for a reptile zoo.

By the time I was over the second chain link barrier I'd temporarily lost sight of Clive over a small rise. I hurried around a storage shed and was just passing the open door of that shed, when an answer to my fence concerns suddenly hit me.

I'd seen the story on the local TV news just a couple weeks ago. The owners of some roadside attraction in the park had revamped their business plan. Realizing the name *Reptiles of the Adirondacks* did not hold the same promise of danger and excitement as, say, *Giant Omnivores of the Adirondacks*, they expanded their inventory to include a couple of grizzly bears. Never mind that these new arrivals weren't any more indigenous to the area than were the turtles, lizards, and snakes they had previously been exhibiting. The zoo just needed an attraction that made some fuss and noise. According to the news story the local ASPCA had objected to the grizzly bears' adoption, saying that the zoo was too small to house such substantial animals. The zoo's owners had countered this argument by saying they were only looking out for the animals' best interests. These bears had been rescued from a mob-affiliated Russian circus that was facing bankruptcy after its top aerial act had left for Las Vegas to join *Cirque du Soleil*, all of which wouldn't have happened if Russia had stayed with communism and Vegas had stayed with comedians and lounge acts.

Anyway, all this backstage showbiz aside, I now realized why, when I reached the shed, I suddenly found myself face-to-face with a pissed-off giant brown Soviet refugee.

I froze. From somewhere behind me, I heard the zookeeper call out, somewhat redundantly, "Don't move."

But I did move. Ever so slowly, I lowered my hand down to my holster. Gently, I popped the clasp and carefully withdrew my service revolver.

"Please, don't shoot." That was the zookeeper pleading, not the grizzly bear.

I kept the gun in my hand, but I didn't fire it. Not yet.

The zookeeper suggested, "Make yourself look big."

I thought about this for a moment. I didn't do anything about it. Just thought about it.

"If he mouths you, play dead," was his next survival tip.

The bear grumbled a bit – probably wondering, like me, what the verb *mouths* actually meant. The giant animal was close enough for me to pat. But I didn't. I stood still while he sniffed around my ankles. Meanwhile, out of the corner of my eye I watched Clive climb the farthest fence. He then ran a large circle around the perimeter and doubled back toward the parking lot.

"Don't make eye contact," was the zookeeper's next helpful tip.

I didn't. My eyes were otherwise occupied watching Clive get into, not his dead truck, but my still-running patrol car.

The bear's nose started sliding up my leg, following my inseam like a near-sighted tailor that had just eaten a seamstress. When his cinder-block head reached my crotch he snorted, his hot breath both warming and moisturizing my frightened, shrivelled bits. He then bared his large yellow teeth and growled. Or maybe it was more of a laugh.

I had to do something. Clive Holand was getting away while a large hairy Russian with bad breath and a grudge against Las Vegas circus acts was about to turn my balls into borscht.

I looked the bear straight in the eye and sternly commanded, "Sit."

Nothing. Okay, so the animal hadn't been trained as well as Len Holand's hounds. Or, if he had, he didn't understand English. So, I tried the zookeeper's first suggestion. I stepped back. I slowly unzipped my jacket. I held it open wide between my arms like bat wings. Then I puffed out my chest, wondering, did this make me look bigger, or was it like showing him the dessert cart?

"That's good," whispered the zookeeper from somewhere safe behind me. "You're making him think twice."

And believe it or not, the guy was right. The bear did look indecisive. He backed away, stood on his hind legs, and sniffed the air. I too backed farther away, toward the gate.

And that's when the second bear came out of the shed.

This bear, which was shorter than the first bear, but wider, stood up on its hind legs, and started sniffing. For no reason whatsoever, I noticed this animal was a female. A *sow*, I believe it would be called by someone who cared. I continued waving my arms high above my head and slowly sidled backwards toward the gate.

"You're doing great," encouraged the zookeeper who had entered the pen and was now beside me. As a shield, he held one of those wooden Adirondack chairs, the kind that everyone up here puts on their porches but nobody over the age of fifty ever actually sits in.

The lady bear took one look at the annoying piece of furniture and gave it a vicious swipe with her huge paw, proving that she, too, must have once tried hefting herself up out of one of these silly things.

The zookeeper tossed what was left of his chair at the male grizzly who promptly started chewing on it. A fight between the two bears ensued over who gets to kill the dumb chair. With the bears now occupied, the zookeeper and I bolted for the exit.

The zoo guy latched the gate closed behind us while I continued down the driveway to watch my patrol car disappear over the hill.

I searched the parking lot for alternate transportation to continue the chase. But there was no hope. The only other car in the lot besides Clive's overheated Chev pickup was the zookeeper's rusted out Lada which he said had starting problems.

Turns out he'd bought that thing from a Russian circus as well.

CHAPTER THIRTEEN

"Your fucking car? He took your fucking car?" The guy was screaming so loud his voice almost rattled the phone out of my hand.

"And would you believe it," I said, "I'd just filled the tank." Everyone here in the room with me laughed at that one. Not the guy on the phone.

"A whole God-damned car... a whole cock-sucking, motherfucking *police* car, right out from under your shit-for-brains nose?"

Okay. At this point I truly considered telling His Worship The Reverend Mayor Tim Stinson that, at this end of the phone line, here in the office of the reptile zoo, he was being broadcast on a speaker phone to six New York State Police troopers, two of them female, plus Troy Lascombe, the kid reporter from the Glen Echo Banner, who was taking copious notes. But I figured Mayor Tim had already received enough bad news for one day. So I just said goodbye and assured Mayor Tim that I'd meet with him first thing tomorrow morning as he'd requested. I assumed the meeting would not be to announce my pay raise.

Marlene arrived to pick me up. One of the troopers had kindly offered to give me a lift back to town, but I had a stop to make and I didn't want to make it with a uniformed officer in a state police car.

As Marlene and I left the zoo's parking lot, I apologized to her for having called her away at dinner time. I then asked her if there was any news on Arden.

"Hospital called an hour ago. Doctor says she'll be okay. Says you probably saved her life."

I didn't take any curtain calls for this. I knew that if I'd just used my brain Arden would never have gotten hurt in the first place and her assailant would now be in police custody instead of racing around God-knows-where in a stolen police car. So, I changed the subject to something more immediate, "Sure you don't mind making this stop with me?"

"Is it far?" Marlene glanced down through her steering wheel to check her fuel gage. "I don't have a whole lot of gas."

"Not far. Just stay on this road until you reach the end of civilization. Then make a left."

*****

Len Holand and his wife Charlotte were so happy to learn that their darling son Clive was still alive, they seemed to forget that the mischievous little scamp was now wanted for the aggravated assault of his girlfriend, the theft of a police vehicle, and possibly the homicide of his younger brother.

After I'd filled in Len on my day's adventures with the young rascal, I asked Len if he was aware that Arden Dawes, had recently become pregnant.

Len seemed genuinely surprised as he asked, "And the father is…?"

"She wasn't too clear on that detail."

I watched his face closely. In my opinion, Len Holand honestly didn't know about Arden getting pregnant. I didn't mention about her subsequently getting herself *un*pregnant. I decided to leave that touchy subject until later.

I asked him if I could have a look at Robbie's and Clive's bedrooms. To my surprise, Len readily agreed to my request, cautioning me that Lieutenant Rykert's people had already searched the entire place this morning in connection with Robbie's murder. Rykert had the proper warrants, of course. I knew this because I'd been the one who'd pulled Judge Marjorie Saperstein away from her game of duplicate bridge to sign the papers. During their search, Rykert's investigators had confiscated the family's computers, thumb drives, cell phones, and a tablet to examine. But there were still a couple of things I wanted to see with my very own analogue eyes.

Len Holand led me down to the finished basement where the two boys had their rooms. Marlene remained up in the living room with Charlotte. Len's other wife or mistress or whatever, Carol, was apparently busy upstairs tucking the younger children into bed.

Clive and Robbie's living quarters were originally the family's recreation room that Len had partitioned into two rooms. These bedsitting rooms were cleaner than I had expected, but then, the boys did have at least two mothers in the house to pick up after them. Clive's furnishings included a bed, TV, sofa, a couple of chairs, plus a recently emptied desk that had previously held a computer. Judging by the magazines in the drawers, Clive's hobbies included souped-up cars and hunting. There were no girlie magazines, but what guy needs those if he's connected to the Internet? There was an electric guitar and amplifier sitting in a corner, but there always is. Just once I'd like to search a young perp's room and find a tenor sax lying under his bed.

When I opened the closet, I noticed a large empty space on the top shelf that was clear of dust.

"Knapsack's gone," said Len Holand, anxious to prove he was a step ahead of me.

In the rear of the closet, a rifle leaned into a corner. It was a .223 Remington – the same cartridge that had been used to make the blasting cap for the improvised pipe bomb – but I didn't get too excited about this bulletin. That particular calibre is a popular size for hunting barnyard pests and small game. I asked Len what other guns he had on site. He said he owned a .270 Winchester rifle, and a twelve gauge shotgun – both of which were presently missing – taken, he assumed, by his sons for their hunting trip.

Robbie's room was a little smaller than Clive's. Len Holand didn't volunteer to come inside his late son's room with me. The wound was obviously still too fresh even for this hardened man to poke into. This room held just a bed, a chair, and a small desk. Robbie's tastes in reading leaned towards science fiction in the form of graphic novels – what we used to call comic books back when Betty and Veronica were virgins. I saw no evidence of a desktop computer having been here, so I presumed Robbie must have just used his cell or tablet. I had noticed a wireless router upstairs.

The only other room downstairs was a small workshop, and the only item of interest in it was a box full of cannibalized electronic parts from old radios, VCR's, and computers. I supposed they could be used to fashion a homemade triggering device for a pipe bomb, so I made a note to tell Yasuda at the F.B.I. about them. I doubted, though, that the feds would get a warrant the way I had, seeing as how there were no real leads to tie these premises to Evelyn and Simon's car bombing.

As I was leaving the basement, I passed a bulletin board which held, among other items, a small photograph of Clive. I thought the wallet-sized picture might come in handy but I wasn't sure Len would voluntarily give it up. Behind me, Len was busy fishing around for something in a desk drawer, so I quickly turned and surreptitiously reached for the photo. But just as I was removing the thumb tack, I felt a tap on my shoulder.

"Here." Len handed me a four-by-six photo of Clive. "It's more recent."

I sheepishly thanked him and replaced the tack in the unneeded photo. We headed back upstairs.

As we approached the living room, I could hear the voices of three women: Marlene and Len's wife Charlotte had been joined by Carol, wife number two. The voices were increasing in both volume and pitch.

"But shouldn't it be a woman's prerogative? I mean, shouldn't she have the final say in what happens to her own body?" Marlene's normally deep, calm voice had risen an excited octave.

"Not when that final say means the murder of an unborn child." That was Charlotte, I think.

"Murder?" Marlene squeaked like a mouse caught in a trap. "How can it be murder? The fetus isn't even a person yet. It's not fully-formed. It can't survive on its own. It's still an integral part of the woman's body."

Carol entered the fray. "The way I see it, murder is murder whether it happens to a ninety-year-old person or a ninety-minute-old fetus."

"That's pure, unadulterated, grade A horse shi–"

"Whoa, there Nelly…" I said, now realizing why I rarely took Marlene on domestic calls. Chuckling, I turned back toward Len, "We leave the rink for five minutes and there's a bench-clearing brawl." I was smiling as big and as hard as I could, but it wasn't helping. I said to Marlene, through clenched teeth, "What in the world brought this particular subject up?"

Marlene picked up a newspaper from the coffee table and waved the headline at me. I recognized it as last week's edition of the Adirondack Times, the one with the front-page story about the bombing of Doctor Simon Reesor's car. I took the paper from Marlene with the intention of changing the subject to something less volatile. But I changed my mind. This was too good an opportunity to pass up.

I turned to Len and indicated the newspaper. "So, what do you think of this pro-life-terrorist angle, Len? What would you think if, say, one of your sons had a wife or a girlfriend who wanted an abortion?" Yeah, I know. Sometimes I'm as subtle as bagpipes.

"Would never happen," he replied. "The boys would never allow it."

"Allow?" Marlene jumped in. "*Allow*? How is it their decision to allow? They aren't the ones carrying the—"

I delicately placed my hand over my associate's high-octane mouth and continued to Len, "You don't think they would, huh?"

"Not a chance."

I said as casually as I could. "How can you be so sure?"

Len exchanged looks with Charlotte. Should he say anything? Or maybe it was a warning. He wasn't a man to wait for input from the womenfolk. "Three years ago my eldest daughter got herself into some trouble."

Marlene said, "Got *herself*?"

It was my own fault – I had loosened my grip.

Len continued, "Ellie didn't see fit to share her burden with us. Nor did she consult any of us when she went to some butcher to have the matter taken care of." Len walked to the fireplace. He looked into the unlit firebox as if somewhere in those cold ashes some memories still burned. He continued, "I guess the procedure went smoothly enough. Ellie survived the ordeal, if not in holy spirit, at least in earthly body." Len looked back at me. "That baby would have been my first grandchild – who knows, maybe my only grandchild. We shall see." He turned his body away from the fireplace. The heat that had long since died in the fireplace now burned bright in his eyes. "But that's not important. What's important is, she had no right to deny that child his or her rightful place in Heaven with Our Lord. She had no right to condemn that child to purgatory by taking its life it before it was Baptized."

I said nothing. I learned long ago not to argue religion. Your side will use logic. Their side will use faith. And as any casino dealer can tell you, faith beats the piss out of logic every time. So instead I just suggested to Marlene that it was time for us to hit the road. Frankly, I don't think she wanted to leave – she was all geared up for a fight. But I reminded her that it was late and we had to get up early tomorrow. And I was telling the truth.

After all, one of us had to get into the office bright and early tomorrow morning to get his sorry ass fired for losing his patrol car.

*****

"Did you see it? Did you see his stupid car?" That was all she said. Marlene shut the door behind her and stomped into the office without asking me why I was here, seated at my desk, at such an early hour. No, *Good morning, Tanager.* No, *What are you doing here before noon? Did your pyjamas catch fire?* She didn't even pause to give Stanley a donut. She just dumped her box of sweet treats on her desk and marched to the window where she parted the vertical blinds to look out once again at the monstrosity that was parked by the curb. "A Hummer," she announced. "A fucking Hummer. Only *he* would drive a fucking Hummer. I remember when he bought it."

I looked out the window. Yup, a Hummer, all right. Not a full-sized, Arab-loving, camel-humping Hummer, but a Hummer nonetheless. I turned to Marlene. "You know the owner?" I can be a veritable fireball of deduction.

She stomped back to her desk and opened her box of donuts. "Pencil-dick Darcy. Darcy Grenfeld. That little suck-up drives a Hummer." She bit into her donut as if she were biting off someone's balls. Darcy's I presume.

It made sense that Darcy Grenfeld would be here today. He had been runner-up for my job as Chief of Police in Glen Echo, and if it had been up to Mayor Tim Stinson, Darcy would have taken the first prize ribbon. Luckily for me, the town council decided to go with the older, more experienced candidate. Although, I'm not that much older. And truth be told, Darcy did have some experience. He had been second-in-command to the previous chief, Grant Hindle. Back then the Glen Echo Police Department had a budget big enough to pay two trained lawmen. But when Grant Hindle announced his retirement, the town council decided that the community, which was getting older and therefore less troublesome, could get by with only one cop. Catch was, in order to take on the extra workload, that lone lawman would have to know his dick from his nightstick, and that prerequisite excluded Darcy Grenfeld. Mayor Tim Stinson wasn't happy with the council's decision, though, and I could understand why. According to Marlene, Darcy was a world-class kiss-up and brown-noser, the exact kind of compound modifiers any mayor, especially a slightly corrupt one, would be thrilled to have heading up his police department.

And now it looked like Mayor Tim was finally going to get his wish, because that was obviously why Darcy Grenfeld's big silly car was parked out front. Mayor Stinson was probably, right this very minute, upstairs giving him the good news: *Congratulations, Darcy. You're in and Tanager's out. Chief Tanager is a proven fuck-up, and his dog smells funny. I'm going to see that his contract is not picked up. And this time the town council can have no objection. After all, look at what has happened since the bass-playing moron's been on the job: Our homicide rate has skyrocketed. Our women-folk are getting' blowed up, and our fine young men are getting bashed in their heads and dumped into the river. Innocent upstanding citizens like Len Holand are being harassed. And now the idiot cop has lost our one and only police cruiser. It'll cost us a fortune, all at a time when the town's municipal parking revenues have nose-dived because, it is rumoured that, Chief Tanager doesn't give out parking tickets to any car that has a dealer sticker signifying the vehicle was purchased here in town.* Actually, this last accusation was a wee bit true. It's a little initiative I'd taken to help out Earl Gautier, the drummer in my band who, coincidentally, owns the local Chevrolet dealership. So, hang me for supporting local business and the American auto industry.

I put on my Chief's cap and walked toward the door. "If you need me I'll be at Cairnwood."

"Cairnwood?" Marlene asked.

"Message was on the machine. Trouser Troll's back."

"You're chasing a pervert?" Marlene was visibly taken aback. "But what about Robbie Holand? We *are* lead agency in the investigation."

"We *were* lead agency."

"Were?"

"I had a meeting with Mayor Tim this morning. His Worship thinks the case is best left to a department that still has a squad car."

"He's busting your balls."

"And doing a darn fine job of it. Call Rykert, will you. Give him the good news. It's his baby now. Tell him I'll email him an official sign-off. Fax, if he prefers that." I put on my jacket, scarf, and gloves and fished my car keys out of my pocket. I'd driven my own vehicle to work this morning.

"So that's it? That's all you're going to do? You're just giving up? You're going to chase down perverts? Hand out parking tickets? Check that car doors are locked and somehow hope the town council doesn't go along with Mayor Numbnuts and hand your job over to Darcy Grenfeld?"

I shrugged a silent, *what else can I do?* then started for the door. But Marlene's voice hooked me back before I'd made my full escape.

"Tanager, can I ask you one thing?"

I leaned on the doorjamb. "Is this one thing going to be personally demeaning and professionally insulting?"

"Kind of."

"Shoot. I'm on a roll."

"Do you ever get angry?"

"Yeah, sure. I guess I get angry. Who doesn't?"

"No, I mean *angry*," she growled. "Pissed off. So pissed off you want to hit something. So pissed you want to tell a guy like Mayor Tim to go fuck himself and the horse he rode in on. So angry you just have to… you just have to do something. I don't know what but *something*."

"Yeah, sure. Occasionally."

"You do, huh?" She didn't sound convinced. "So, what happens when you get that angry?"

I thought long and hard about this one. And finally I had my answer: "The band sounds really, really good."

She looked at me blankly. So I explained further, "Nothing locks in the groove like when the bass player gets really pissed off. Or the drummer. When either the bass player or the drummer gets charged up and hot under the collar the band kicks serious ass." I smiled at her and waited for her understanding. I had a long wait ahead of me.

I looked down at Stanley. "You want to come for a ride, fella?"

He didn't answer me either. Or maybe he did. He stayed right where he was, lying under my desk, like he didn't want to be seen with me.

Smart dog.

CHAPTER FOURTEEN

Given time, almost every criminal makes a grand and final mistake. The flasher's fatal goof-up had involved a change in venue and curtain time. He premiered his latest purple puppet show in broad daylight. And with more than just one talented young artist as witness. This time half the soccer team saw him.

The girls had a good look and all agreed he wore a ski mask. One of the girls told me it was green while another testified that it was dark blue. The goalie insisted it was black, like my hat. Two of the young ladies said he was of medium height. The third swore he was tall, like me. The goalie said he had a regular-sized nose. The two others claimed he had a big nose, again like me. They all laughed at that one. Ms. Craven apologized and said the students were just kidding and in no way did I have a large nose. I like Mrs. Craven.

The only thing the witnesses all agreed upon was that he was old and that, when he ran away into the woods, he ran with a limp which slowed his escape so much that they could easily have caught him but they didn't. Ms. Craven had warned them not to do things like that. They just wished they had their phone cameras with them. So did I.

I thanked the girls and told them they'd done good. After Ms. Craven corrected my colloquial grammar, one of the girls added one more note: "Chief Tanager, the man we saw this morning, I think I recognized him."

I wasn't surprised.

She continued, "But for the life of me, I can't remember where from."

"That's okay," I said before Ms. Craven could correct the young woman's sentence-ending preposition. "I think I know from where he came."

Mrs. Craven smiled at me.

*****

The game was over, and he knew it. But he wasn't quite ready to admit it.

So I played my final card. "Can I put you in a lineup then? Let the little girls have a good long look at you?" I added, "Of course, this time you'll have to leave your pants on."

The old fellow in overalls stood at the planting bench and pondered his hand trowel, examining the dirty tool as if it might come in handy for a dig into his past. "You know, I used to work for them kids. Kept their petunia beds nice and clean. Never a weed."

I patted the tired old pervert on his bony shoulder. "If it's any consolation, I noticed the place is overrun with dandelions now."

"That's on account of that new principal," he said. "She's organic."

I had come across Wilfred Pritchard's name during my very first visit to Cairnwood School when I was going through their personnel files. I'd noticed that he had been caretaker at the school for twenty-seven years but was dismissed four years ago – the same year Mrs. Craven had been hired as principal. No reason had been given for Wilf's dismissal, but it was now obvious he hadn't seen eye-to-eye with his new boss about her organic gardening philosophies. At the time, I gave the fellow no more thought. But today, when I interviewed the young girls, I realized their eyewitness descriptions perfectly matched Wilf, the handyman I'd met here at Windermere Inn. As the young girls had attested, Wilf Pritchard did indeed have a nose that would appear large even under a ski mask. And he was certainly elderly. And judging by the scarf he had worn around his neck when I was introduced to him, the man does have a fondness for green and black tartans. And finally, there was his limp. Like the girls had said, he truly would have been easy to catch. In total, this was not a whole lot to hang the old pervert with. But certainly enough to call his bluff on.

"You shouldn't have been doing something like that," I said. "You know that, don't you. You gave those little girls a hell of a fright."

We were in his greenhouse at Windermere. Wilf looked away from me, twisted his hand trowel down deep into a pot of soil as if he were trying to bury his guilt. "Ain't my fault."

"No?" I'd heard that one before. "Whose fault is it?"

"Doc Holman's fault."

"Doc Holman's?" I hadn't heard this one before.

"He's the man give me them pills, didn't he."

"Pills? You mean E.D. medication?"

"Them pills work a treat. And let me tell you, young man, if you sprouted wood at my age, you'd be lookin' to show it off, too."

"But I wouldn't be scaring young girls with it."

"That skinny young principal fired me on account of I was old and set in my ways. She told me so. Ha! I'll show her who's old." He withdrew his trowel from the soil. "I swear I didn't mean no harm. I mean, I never touched none of them girls. I wouldn't never hurt nobody."

For now, I spared him the lecture about physical hurt versus emotional hurt. Right now I needed the old guy to do a favour for me.

"Wilf you must promise me you'll never to do anything like that again."

"You gonna arrest me?"

"I'm going to think about it. And while I do, I'm going to ask you to do something for me. A little favor."

"Sure." He was suddenly very anxious to please. "What do you need? Yard work? Someone to mow your lawn? Do some painting?" Then he got an idea. "Hey, you want some of them boner pills?"

"The two women you work for – Lindsay and Sharon…"

He thought he was ahead of me. "You want to know if they like men, right?"

"No…" I lied.

"Everybody asks me that. How am I supposed to know? I trim their hedges not their bikini lines."

I assured Wilf that I was not interested in his bosses' sexuality. I was, however, interested in their recent habits and dealings. I asked him if he had noticed anything odd going on around the inn lately.

"Ain't seen nothin' weird," he said. "Unless you call fixin' up and decorating a…" He suddenly caught himself. "No, I ain't seen nothing weird."

The way he had braked himself to that sudden halt almost gave us both whiplash, so I pressed him on it. "Redecorating?" I asked. "What are they redecorating? Some guest rooms?"

He looked away, dug his trowel into the dirt, and muttered, "Just a room they want fixed up s'all."

"Fixed up how?"

"I… I ain't supposed to tell."

"Don't worry, I won't let on who told me. So, how do they want it fixed up?"

He hesitated then shrugged like this whole secret was a big deal over nothing. "Like for a nursery," he said.

"You mean, for a baby?"

"I don't mean for petunias." He shook his head in disapproval. "And it's gonna be one spoiled brat, let me tell you. They got me refinishing the hardwood floor so he won't have to breathe no carpet mites. Scraping off all the old trim so as he won't eat no lead paint. Installing a camera so as they can keep an eye on his little bare ass while they're in the kitchen suckin' back their apricot brandy. I even put a microphone over the crib so we can all give a cheer whenever the li'l fucker farts. They had me install a little bathtub thingy with solid brass fittings, up waist-high so they can wash the kid without bending over. You know what my old lady washed my ass in?"

I skipped his question in favor of one of my own. "Did the ladies tell you who this nursery was for?"

He answered his own question first. "A roasting pan. Very same one my old lady used for the Thanksgiving turkey. My old man used to say 'til I was two year old my little ass smelled like sage and onions."

"Wilf, has either of the women mentioned being pregnant?"

"I… I don't like to pry." Then he added, "But I made a crack to Sharon once. Said 'bout how I hoped nobody thought I was the father. I could, you know. 'Specially with them pills."

"Are the women in a hurry to get this nursery finished? Have they given you any timeline?"

"You know, that's the funny thing… If either one of them is pregnant you can see for yourself, she ain't *very* pregnant. And yet they want that damn nursery finished by the end of the month. How fast they think babies come nowadays?"

"Did you ever ask if they had plans to adopt?"

"I thought about askin'. But, well…"

"You don't like to pry."

"Seems kinda improper."

Right. This from a man who gets his jollies by cranking his Evinrude in front of young girls. On this subject, I made a deal with Wilf. I told him that, if he promised to keep his newly revived pride and joy inside his Dockers away from public display, I would try to convince the nice folks who run Cairnwood School not to press charges against him. Wilf was happy with my terms.

I started to leave the gardening shed, but then I realized I had one more question for my new snitch. A wild idea had been seeded in my mind when Wilf mentioned Lindsay and Sharon's baby nursery, and now that idea was taking root and sprouting.

"Wilf, do you know if either of the ladies owns any other real estate up here?"

"Real estate?"

"Like a ski chalet in the mountains, maybe? Or a condo in town?"

"One of them did talk once or twice 'bout a camp."

"A camp? What do you mean? Like a children's camp?"

"No. Just a camp."

Right. I'd forgotten Adirondackers use the word *camp* to signify anything from a one-room log cabin to a multi-million-dollar estate.

"Who? Which one mentioned it?"

"Think it was Lindsay. Said she don't use it no more. Belonged to her old man or something. I think he's passed." Then Wilf added, "You know, you're the second fella to ask me about that camp this week."

"Really? Who was the first?"

"Guy stayin' here. Guy what lost his wife."

"Paul Briar?"

"Said he'd give me a hundred bucks if I'd tell him where the place was."

"Did you tell him?"

Wilf smirked. "A hundred bucks buys a lot of them little blue pills."

"And now you're going to tell me?"

His smirk blossomed into a big toothless grin. "You got a hundred bucks?"

"No, but I have an arrest warrant waiting for the man who frightened those little girls."

His smile wilted like a daisy hit by early frost. "Off the Hahne Trail. Clear Lake."

I thanked Wilf for his help and left him to his gardening shed. I then continued on up to the main house. After all, it would be rude to leave without dropping by the inn and saying hello to the ladies.

As I strolled across the neat, freshly raked lawn I wondered if there was any tidy way to bring up this new baby nursery Wilf had mentioned. I couldn't just charge ahead and ask the women if either of them is knocked up. What if neither of them is? They'd think I was telling them they looked fat. Nor was there any way to ask if either of the ladies was preparing to adopt – I would only succeed in getting my new snitch into trouble for spilling beans he'd been specifically ordered to keep in the can.

As I climbed the patio steps, I could smell food cooking. And I thought about Windermere's sole guest, Paul Briar. I wondered if he had been sniffing around the new baby quarters Wilf was fixing up? If he had, is that why he'd asked Wilf about any other real estate properties the women might own? In other words, could Briar possibly be chewing on the same theory I was currently taste-testing?

As I approached the kitchen door, Lindsay greeted me, her warm smile instantly melting the cold edge off the crisp autumn air. She held the screen door open for me as she asked, "To what do we owe the pleasure?"

"An old guy who can't seem to keep his pants zipped up."

Her smile melted. "The flasher is back at Cairnwood?"

"Yup." I stepped inside. "I think we got him this time."

"Good for you. Those poor girls must have been terrified." She closed the door against the cold. "Stay for tea? Sharon just made some cookies."

From somewhere deep inside the house Sharon called out, "Biscotti. They're not cookies. They're fucking biscotti."

Lindsay corrected herself. "Can you stay for some fucking biscotti?"

I did. And the Italian biscuits were delicious. And so was Lindsay. And so was the coffee she gave me when I told her I didn't drink tea.

I kept my visit short. The women were in the middle of their workday, and so was I. Happily, Lindsay invited me to come back later for dinner. She said the menu would comprise gourmet leftovers – roast veal tenderloin, grilled eggplant parmesan, Vermont cheddar potatoes, and the whole artery-clogging mess would be finished off with a Grand Marnier egg-white soufflé. All by candlelight. Just the two of us. Apparently, Sharon was going out of town for the evening, and the inn's only guest, Paul Briar, had checked out this morning. This meant Lindsay and I would have the place all to ourselves. In several different ways, my pants strained at the very thought of it: Good food and the hottest-looking woman I'd seen since I'd left Buffalo.

And I said no thanks.

It broke my heart, but I had a previous commitment. Tonight, a new keyboard player was coming to the bar to audition for Simon's chair, and I'd promised the guys I'd be there. So I told Lindsay that, if there was any way I could wriggle out of the job, I would, but I can't. I'm the bass player. The band can't play without me. Lindsay understood. She said it must be nice to be so needed. I hoped she wasn't being sarcastic.

I suggested a rain check for the following night – if the leftovers were too left over, I'd even spring for a dinner in town – but she said that she couldn't do it. Apparently, a group of strict vegans was checking into the inn in the morning and staying for the weekend, and she was hoping tonight somebody with a hearty male appetite would help her clean out the fridge of all the meat and dairy products.

Yes, it is indeed nice to be needed.

As Lindsay walked me out to my car, I wanted to ask her about that camp Wilf had mentioned to me. Of course, I couldn't land on the subject directly, so I glided a circular approach.

I gazed out at the beautiful lake and said, "I've always dreamed of having a place on water. But I'm afraid shoreline property's a little steep for a cop's salary."

"It's expensive, all right. Taxes are rough. It's not easy."

"This is your only property, I take it. No ski chalets in the mountains? No cabins tucked away in the woods?" Okay, my technique was a bit on-the-nose, I admit. But I was pissed with myself about having to refuse her dinner invite just to keep my word to my friends. I mean, would any of them pass up a hot date to make a band rehearsal?

"No. This is it." Lindsay looked back at Windermere. "I'm afraid every cent I have is tied up in here. And if I could afford another place it wouldn't be a cabin in the woods. It would be a condo on a beach. Somewhere in the Caribbean."

"Yeah, I hear you." Then I buzzed low over another subject. "So, Paul Briar checked out, huh? I hope that means he's come to terms with his wife's death."

"That would be nice. But I doubt it."

"You don't buy this *closure* thing either, huh?"

"Not for a New York minute. He's been asking too many questions."

"Like…?"

"Like, 'How long did I think a woman could survive out in the woods?' and 'How well did I know the mountains? Do I know of any abandoned cabins out there?' Stuff like that."

"What did you say?"

"I said I'm sure there are lots of vacant places out there, but I don't know of any in particular."

"You don't think he's gone off to look, do you?"

"He didn't tell us where he was off to. But I have to say, you're not the only one who's been wondering about that."

I nodded. "You mean, you've been wondering too."

"No, but Len Holand has."

"Len Holand?"

"Called this morning. Wanted to speak to Paul. I told him he was too late. He wanted to know where Paul had gone. But like I say, I have no idea."

I thanked her again for the invite, bid her a quick goodbye, and got into my car.

As I watched Windermere Inn recede in my rear-view, I thought about the cabin that old Wilf had told me about – the one that Lindsay had just now pretty much denied owning. I'd given her an opening. Why would she not have been more forthcoming about the place?

Because she's keeping a pregnant woman hostage in it, that's why. So she can steal the baby.

Sure, the idea still sounded far-fetched. But my opinion wasn't the one I was concerned about. To a guy like Briar, in his desperate state, a kidnapping theory offers hope. And in that context, it may not sound all that nuts.

We both know that Lindsay and her housemate Sharon strongly disapprove of the abortion Paul's wife, Nancy, was about to have. Plus, as the two women had confessed to Briar last spring, they would love to have a child of their own. Now, for some unexplained reason, Lindsay and Sharon are building a nursery here at the inn. Individually, these three facts wouldn't add up to much. But to Briar, a man who is desperately looking for any ray of hope that his pregnant wife might still be alive, those individual twinkles combine to shine like the star of Bethlehem guiding him to a manger. Two pro-life women, who might have trouble obtaining a nice fresh baby of their own, have kidnapped his wife, first, to save the child's life and, second, to raise the baby as their own. Sounds extreme, but don't forget, just a few nights ago Briar spent the evening getting cozy with Rebecca Reesor, a beautiful and persuasive young woman who vehemently believes these two ladies are crazed anti-abortion terrorists who are responsible for the deaths of both her parents.

Of course, even to Briar's highly-biased reasoning, there are two problems Lindsay and Sharon, as babynappers, would have to deal with: First, what to do with Nancy Briar after she's given birth. That one's easy. They kill her. After all, she's already presumed dead. But after that, how do they explain the sudden new arrival? This one's a little tougher to deal with, but not impossible. The women could just tell their friends that they've adopted the child from some Eastern European country. After all, who checks records from war-torn Lower Slobovistan? Back in the city I used to see bad paper like that every day. Birth certificates, drivers' licenses, green cards. Heck, if thousands of illegal aliens are able to obtain forged documentation, I'm sure it wouldn't be difficult for two sophisticated women to phony up adoption papers and plug their blessed event into the system.

Shit, now Briar's crazy theory was starting to make sense even to me. Of course, I may have Paul Briar all wrong. The guy's runaway train of thought might not be speeding along these particular twisted rails at all. And he might not be out there somewhere right this minute combing through the woods for his wife and new baby. He might instead, at this very moment, be rolling merrily down I-87, heading back to New York City and waving goodbye to his ghosts in the rear-view mirror.

Curious, though, that he never said goodbye to me.

And then there was Len Holand's phone call this morning to Windermere Inn. Why is he so interested in Paul Briar?

Paul Briar, the man from the bar fight.

Paul Briar, the tourist who obviously has a grudge against Len's son.

Len's murdered son.

I stopped my car, grabbed my phone, and called Briar's cell number. No answer. I left a voice message. Then I texted him. Told him to call me. As soon as possible.

CHAPTER FIFTEEN

The new keyboard player turned out to be more than capable. He had fine chops and big ears. Not big the way the mayor's were – a navigation hazard to migrating waterfowl – I mean big in that they heard and could predict the changes to tunes the man had never played before. Yup, he was a real musician's musician. An asset to any band.

And I hated him for it.

Well, not so much hated him as I hated myself for enjoying playing with him so much. I felt as if I were betraying my old pal, Simon. That's why, after the first set, I invited the new guy to the bar and bought him a drink. I wanted to let him know that, if I'd seemed subdued on stage, it wasn't him – it was the situation.

The new keyboard player's name was Milo, and he was a tad older than the rest of us. I'd say late fifties. His head was shaved cue-ball smooth, but he sported a large bushy mustache that more than made up for the clear-cut forestry up top. He told me he was from Baudette, a little town on the northern edge of Minnesota, bordering Canada, and that he had moved to the Adirondacks last spring. This brought up the usual question. And for a change, I was doing the asking instead of the answering.

"So, what brought you to the mountains?"

"A Cessna 185." He smiled but this was nothing new. This guy was always smiling. He then explained, "I'm a pilot."

I took a pull on my Moretti. "Bush pilot huh?"

"The bushiest." He twirled his giant moustache. "Been working for Joe Cardillo up in Blue Mountain."

Joe Cardillo ran a float plane charter service out of Blue Mountain Lake where he took up sightseers, fishermen, and hunters. By way of small talk I said to Milo, "I guess, in your line of work, once tourist and hunting seasons are finished, things slow up considerably."

"I'm cool." He grinned, or continued to grin, as he added, "I got sidelines."

From the sly twinkle in Milo's eyes, it was clear that his *sidelines* did not include delivering pizzas or selling Mary Kaye cosmetics, so I decided this would be a good time to tell him about my day gig.

"Look, I think you should know something…"

But it turned out he wasn't finished incriminating himself quite yet. "If you guys need, like, any *supplies* or anything…"

"Thanks, but—"

"I fly to Vermont pretty regular. Canada, too…"

I laughed. "Listen, I think I'd better put you straight to something…"

But he was on a roll. "Tell you something about Canada: French strippers and hockey players ain't the only shit they grow good up there."

I tried again, "You see, music isn't my full-time gig. During the day, I—"

This time I was interrupted by a female voice. "Chief Tanager… I just want to thank you."

I turned my head just in time to receive a kiss on the cheek.

"You're very welcome," I said, recognizing the lady but having no idea what she was so appreciative about.

"Chief?" commented Milo, realizing what he'd just heard.

The woman, whose first name I knew was Jody, finished her thank you, "Took your advice. I put the duck decoys at the front of the store and the moose calls at the back. Haven't lost an item in three weeks. You were right. Who's dumb enough to try and slip a duck down his pants?"

"You'd be surprised," Milo offered her. Then he turned his attention back to me. "Chief, huh? You, like, an Indian or something?"

"Another kind of chief," I said. Then I made the introductions, "Jody, this is Milo. Milo, Jody."

But Milo still had my nickname on his mind. "You mean, like, a *Fire* Chief?"

"Mmmm, 'fraid not." I turned back to Jody. "Can I buy you a drink?"

Jody, who ran a local outfitting outfit, was quite attractive, in a wholesome, sturdy, freckled sort of way. She declined my offer of a drink. "Thanks, but I have to get up early. These days the shop is open Sundays."

"Right," I said. "Why should deer have a day to relax."

She smiled in agreement but gave me a good-natured poke about it. "We don't cater just to hunters. Lots of hikers like to explore the mountains in autumn."

"With ducks in their pants?" asked Milo.

Jody continued defending her business: "Today I sold a shit-load of very high-end camping gear to a guy who, I'm sure, wouldn't know which end of a rifle to point at the road sign."

Having straightened me out, she turned to leave. But I wouldn't let her go yet. "You say this guy had lots of money?"

"Enough to ignore the price tags. Pretty cute, too."

"Don't suppose you got his name."

"I was tempted, but these days I practise catch and release." She added, "Used a card, if you're interested."

"What did he look like? About your age? Slim? Five-eleven, six feet? Nice tan? Teeth so bright they attract moths?"

She winked. "Especially if they're female moths."

"And you say he purchased hiking gear?"

"A sleeping bag, hiking boots, knapsack, a GPS unit, a beautiful three-quarter-length down-filled khaki parka with a faux fur collar that went perfect with his grey-blue eyes. All top-of-the-line shit. *Kesler. Troy. Herschmitt and Kholer.* Stuff I thought I'd never unload. At least, not to hunters, fishermen, and vacationing teachers."

"Did this man say what he wanted the gear for? Where he was going?"

"No..." She had to think this over. "Did ask about one of the mountains, though..." Then she corrected herself, "No, not a mountain – a trail. It was the, uh... the, uh... Oh, shoot..."

I was tempted to prompt her, but I didn't want to prejudice the witness, so I waited, hoping she'd come up with the jackpot answer by herself. She didn't let me down.

"...Hahne. That's it. The Hahne trail. I remember because he asked if I thought he needed to purchase a tent. I told him he definitely should. Far as I know there's only one lean-to on the Hahne." Her curiosity was now piqued. "So, who is he?" Her eyes widened. "Have I helped an escaped convict or something?"

When I told her she hadn't she looked disappointed – I think she was considering a conjugal visit.

After Jody left, I turned back to my beer. I'd forgotten about Milo beside me. He, however, had not forgotten about me.

He said, "Chief of Police, huh?"

I clicked my bottle to his bottle to let him know he could relax, things were cool, but if he wanted to tell me any more about his business ventures, he might want to have a lawyer present.

My mind was on Paul Briar and the weather. It was supposed to get real cold tonight. Below zero. Maybe snow. I hoped the Hahne trail was easy to follow – some of the trails aren't, especially at this time of year when the greenery is gone and the ground is covered with leaves. But nature's fury wasn't the only devil out there. Len Holand seems to have a major hate-on for Briar. And then, of course, there's Len's son Clive, a practising psychopath who is still out there somewhere on the loose. And if those two aren't enough, there's always the hunters. This time of year the woods are loaded with guys in ear-flaps eager to shoot at anything that moves.

My morbidly deteriorating thoughts were suddenly interrupted by the dull thud of a bass drum. Earl was on stage letting us know it was time to make some noise. This was good news. We musicians are lucky this way. Transcendental Meditationists have to recite a mantra to empty out their brain pans. Buddhists have to buy Birkenstocks, drive their sport utes up a mountain, and shit bean sprouts to connect with their nothingness. But we blues players have it easy. All we have to do is slide into the groove and let that rhythm carry us downstream to that mindless pond we call the *pocket.* And that's where I floated for the next fifty minutes. Not an ugly thought in my empty noggin.

But soon the set was over, and I drifted back to reality again. And through no fault of my own I started thinking.

I hate it when that happens.

I thought about the mistakes I'd made so far. Like, not staying with Simon the night his wife had died. And after that, not contacting his daughter Rebecca personally to give her the news that her stepmom had been murdered and that her dad had taken his own life. And then there was my recent fuck-up with Arden when I didn't follow her into her residence to make sure her crazy boyfriend wasn't waiting for her inside.

By the end of our third and final set I had made up my guilt-marinated mind. I had decided it was finally time to do something smart.

I hate it when that happens, too.

*****

When I got home, I didn't walk the dog. Nor did I go to the kitchen and toast up my usual grilled cheese and onion artery-clogging thrill ride. Instead, I hopped onto my computer and raced it to a web site commonly used by cops, private investigators, and divorce lawyers to search land title deeds. It's a pay site, but luckily, the Buffalo P.D. hadn't yet cancelled my subscription.

I entered my password. Then I cross-checked Lindsay Porter's name for the counties of Hamilton, Essex, and Franklin. I had already checked that Porter was Lindsay's maiden name. She had never changed it when she was married.

The only item I dug up was a listing which named her as co-owner of the Windermere property. No gold there. I kept digging. But my shovel came up empty. So I extended my search area to the other counties, the ones that bordered on or overlapped the Adirondacks. Still no luck.

I was ready to give up when, in a last desperate dig, I burrowed into the site's archives, the ones that listed land transfers within the last twenty-five years. And this time I struck pay dirt.

Eight years ago, about the time Lindsay Porter bought Windermere Inn, a person named Mathew Lucas Porter had transferred title from a property on Clear Lake. I Googled up a map. As one might expect, there were several places in New York State called Clear Lake, but only a couple of them were in the Adirondacks and only one of those was near the Hahne Trail. This Clear Lake was about fifteen miles off Route Thirty, well past any old logging roads, and accessible only by that trail. Could Mathew Lucas Porter have been Lindsay Porter's father? Grandfather?

Now that I knew I was on the right track I returned to the land deeds site. And this is where things really got interesting.

The name of the institution to which Mr. Porter had transferred the land's title was *The Church of the Wondrous Cross* – the very same church run by my boss, His Worship the Reverend/Mayor Timothy Stinson. And what's more, Tim's good buddy Len Holand was also listed as a director of this church.

I sat back, my dim forehead brightened by the glow of the computer screen and my imagination sparked by the veins of flickering minerals.

About this time, my pooch, Stanley, came over to me and started grumbling that he had ideas of his own. I got the message. I grabbed his leash and threw my police chief's cap on.

Outside in the cold night air I watched my vaporized breath rise to the black sky and dissolve into frigid nothingness, and I thought about the digital vapor my computer had just coughed up. The findings were interesting, sure, but were they enough to take to the feds? Or to the state police? Or even to the Campfire Girls? I doubted it. All I'd really uncovered was some loose links between a few relatively upstanding folk, none of whom had criminal records. No, I was alone on this one. Or almost alone, that is.

I turned to my second-in-command who was busy investigating one of my neighbor's decorative solar-powered light fixtures. "What d'ya say, pal? You wanna to go for a walk in the woods with me tomorrow?"

Stanley looked up at me with his big sad eyes. Then he squatted on his haunches and deposited a steaming pile onto the neighbor's pesticide-free lawn. Damn it, I'd forgotten to bring a plastic bag. Then I remembered I had my official police chief's hat on.

What the hell, it's not like I was ever going to wear the thing again.

CHAPTER SIXTEEN

"A seaplane? You want the town to charter you a damn seaplane?"

"Just a short zip in and out. Should only take a couple of hours. Four, tops. Certainly no longer than six. Look, if I'm gone for more than eight, you can call the park rangers."

"Listen, Tanager—"

But I wasn't in the mood to listen. "I can probably get us a rate. There's this guy I met last night. Keyboard player. But he's also a pilot. Milo something-or-other. Nice guy. Flies out of Blue Mountain." I leaned forward and placed both my hands on my boss's desk for dramatic effect and to show my sincerity. "Mayor, I'm really worried about Paul Briar."

Tim looked a little taken aback. It was the first time I'd ever addressed him as *Mayor*. Apart from that, I had no more to say. I'd finished my pitch. Of course, I hadn't given Mayor Stinson the particulars of exactly what property Paul Briar was headed for and why I was so worried about him going there. After all, the mayor's church owned this camp property in question, and I still didn't know what his particular connection to all this might be.

Mayor Tim stood up. Preachers work best on their feet. "You say this man's gone for a hike. Left yesterday. You checked with local merchants. Sounds like he took enough provisions for a week. Your contact at the outfitters says he's well geared up – maps, GPS, survival gear, probably a cell phone. And the park rangers aren't concerned."

"Well, no. Not yet they aren't."

Stinson took a bottle of gin out of his liquor cabinet. Time for breakfast. He poured a shot into his organic orange juice. Then he unwrapped a high-fiber chocolate chip muffin. "I'm sorry, Tanager, I think you're way off base on this. I mean, a seaplane, for Heaven's sake. Even for you, this is extreme. I can't authorize an expense like that. And frankly, even if I could I wouldn't. Your record with official vehicles is not good."

He had me there. "Then I'm outta here."

"Pardon me?"

"Gone."

"What do you—"

"I noticed Darcy Grenfeld was here yesterday. I take it he's still in town?"

"Yes," the mayor said. A light behind his red, watery eyes was starting to glow. A light, we both knew, could lead us all to inner peace and eternal happiness. I led him toward that light.

I laid my cap on his desk and said to His Worship, "Normally I would never leave a job without giving at least two-weeks' notice. But I don't think you're going to miss me if I take off right away." I unclipped my badge and dropped it on the desk. The badge was closely followed by my cell phone and my Town of Glen Echo employee gas card. All-in-all this was the exact same striptease I had done seven months ago in Buffalo, so I had the moves down pat. "Sorry," I said. "But a man's life may be at stake."

Mayor Stinson picked up my cap. He examined the tooth marks on the brim where Stanley had chewed it. "You do realize that this will be deducted from your final paycheck."

"I wouldn't have it any other way, Tim." I ripped the official Glen Echo Police Department patch off the shoulder of my own personal suede jacket. It took two good pulls. On my next job I'll use Velcro.

*****

"I wish I'd been there." Marlene was searching through the cupboards trying to find an empty cardboard box for me. "You really called him a gin-soaked, self-righteous bag of raccoon shit?"

"Well... maybe not those exact words, but I'm sure he could read it in my eyes."

Marlene found a suitable-sized box and brought it to my desk. I started filling it with contents from my drawers while she sat down and patted Stanley. After a moment's thought she announced, "If you're leaving, I'm leaving."

"What? Why?"

"I can't work with Darcy."

"I appreciate the support, but don't be hasty," I warned her. "There aren't a lot of job opportunities up here."

She continued patting the pooch. "Been thinking of opening a pet store."

"Don't we already have a pet store?"

"It's not organic."

This from a woman who feeds my dog donuts. I grabbed my phone and looked up the number for Blue Mountain Air Charters. I called them and asked for Milo.

Happily for me, Milo was between flights. I pitched my case. I waited for his answer. It took him a moment to process my words. I may have been talking too fast.

Eventually, he came up with, "I'd like to give you a hand, man, but I just, like, you know… can't. You know?" Milo sounded slightly wasted. "Gotta pick up a party of hunters. Bear hunters. Man, I sure hope those fuckers didn't shoot straight."

"You an animal lover?"

"No, I just don't have room for any three-hundred-pound, flea-bitten passengers on the return trip." Then he asked, "So what's all this interest in Clear Lake all of a sudden? They spotted moose down there?"

"*All* this interest? What do you mean?"

"I mean you're like the third guy in two days to ask me to take him to that lake."

"Who were the other ones?"

"Oh, man, let me think. I'm not always on a first-name basis with first names. There was this guy. I met him couple days ago at that bar your band plays at. You probably know the dude. Let's see… About your height. Trimmer, though. And younger."

I helped him out. "Well-tanned? Expensive haircut? Posture like a game show host?"

"Throw in eyebrows plucked neater'n a porn star's twat and you got him pegged."

This made sense. I couldn't imagine Briar choosing to hike all that way into that lake if he could fly in. I said to Milo, "But you didn't take him?"

"Couldn't, man. It's hunting season. I been busier than a centipede with restless leg syndrome."

"Any chance he found someone else to fly him in?"

"During hunting season? Not much. We're all pretty booked up."

"And who was the other guy?"

"What other guy?"

"You said I was the third party who wanted you to fly to Clear Lake."

"Oh, you mean the chick."

"A woman? What was her name?"

"Sorry, man... But names and me..."

"Okay, what did she look like?"

"Geez, I'm not much at telling what they look like over the phone. I'm not on Skype."

"Did this woman say why she wanted to go in?"

"I work on a *Don't Ask, Don't Tell* policy. I told her same thing I'm telling you – call back tomorrow. 'Cause sometimes there's a cancellation. These hunters, they don't always show. Their wives decide not to let 'em off their chains. A lot of these boys are pussy-whipped. Frankly, I think that's why the dudes like killin' things."

I signed off with Milo and considered trying some other flight services but decided not to waste my time. After all, I doubted Milo was a first-call pilot, so if he was fully booked the rest must be busy as well.

I asked Marlene if she knew any local guides who might help me hike in to Clear Lake. But before Marlene could answer me, a female voice from behind me volunteered, "I might be able to help you out."

I turned to find Lindsay Porter standing in our office doorway. She looked great – high boots, tight jeans, and a short, car-length fur jacket. Faux fur, I'm sure. She didn't beat around the bush about why she had suddenly dropped by. "You still available for dinner tonight?"

I stood up and tucked in my shirt tails which had come untucked during my impromptu striptease for the mayor. "I thought you had a group of vegetarians you had to mow dinner for."

"Canceled." Lindsay stepped farther inside the room. "They decided hunting season might not be the best time to roam around the woods picking berries and wild mushrooms."

I introduced Lindsay to Marlene. After the usual pleasantries Lindsay turned back to me. She indicated my phone. "Sounds like you're planning a hike."

I didn't want to tip my hand and let her know that I was on to her father or grandfather once owning property that she's conveniently failed to mention. I had to do some pretty fast dancing. "Yeah, well, you see, I, uh… The thing is… well, I, uh…"

"Clear Lake."

"Yeah, right, well, you see–"

"I used to have a place on Clear Lake. Or at least, my family did."

"You don't say."

And that's how I got a guide for my hike. Hey, what else could I do? Lindsay said she was an experienced woodsperson and that she knew the trail like the back of her lovely hand. Apparently, she'd been hiking it ever since she was a little lesbian. She proudly told me that she was almost a Forty-Sixer. Seeing that I wasn't suitably impressed by this fact, Marlene explained that a *Forty-Sixer* is the title bestowed upon any person who has climbed all forty-six major peaks in the Adirondack Park. Apparently, Lindsay has only five more to go before she becomes a member of the club and learns the secret handshake.

When Lindsay got around to pressing me on why I wanted to go for this hike through the woods, I told her that I had reason to believe that Paul Briar may be hiking the trail to Clear Lake and that I was worried about him getting into trouble along the way. Lindsay agreed that the mountains were no place for a tenderfoot. When she asked why Briar would be hiking the Hahne – a trail that was nowhere near the area where his wife had disappeared – I outlined my crazy theory. I said that Paul Briar may have convinced himself that his wife is being held hostage in order that her captors could prevent her having an abortion and, subsequently, steal her impending baby when it arrived. *Pretty crazy idea, huh?*

Turned out she didn't think my theory was crazy at all, especially considering the state of mind poor Paul Briar was in. *But why*, she asked, *was Clear Lake his target? What was it about that area that attracted his suspicions?* To this I just shrugged and played stupid. I was a natural for the part.

Throughout our discussion, I had watched Lindsay's face for her reactions. But I never saw any sign of suspicion or trepidation. No worry that Briar – or I, for that matter – might be on to her scheme. On the contrary, she seemed quite eager to help find the poor, distraught widower.

Lindsay tightened her scarf around her neck, pulled her gloves back on, and asked, "So, what time you want to shove off?"

"Soon as possible."

She checked her watch. "It's almost ten. How's 'bout we meet at Windermere in a couple hours, say, noonish. I have most of the gear on hand – backpacks, cook ware, sleeping bags. You can leave your car at the inn – we'll take mine. That okay by you?"

"Huh?" She'd caught me thinking of something else. "Uh, sure, that's fine."

Now, I hate to sound like a horny teenager, but I had stopped paying attention to her after she'd said the words *sleeping bags.* Heck, we hadn't even had our first date yet, and here I was about to spend the night with her. Alone. In the woods. Just the two of us. Which reminded me…

"Okay if I bring Stanley along?"

"The more the merrier," she said.

Lindsay left to prepare for the trip, and I finished emptying out my desk. As I packed, I pondered further about Lindsay and her eagerness to accompany me to this cabin at Clear Lake. It seemed at odds with any theory I might have that she and Sharon were the kidnappers. On the other hand, maybe it confirmed that theory. After all, it's a common tactic, when you're doing something covert, to stay close to your opponent and know what he knows, hopefully before he knows it.

Anyway, by ten-fifteen I was carting my cardboard box, my laptop, and my dark suspicions out the door. The junk from my desk included handcuffs, a box of nine-mil cartridges that were long-past their expiration date, a couple of half-empty bottles of pepper spray that I use primarily to spice up meatball sandwiches, breath spray, a few bass strings that, although they'd gone dead, I can never bring myself to toss out, a tattered old Miranda card that I'd had since my days at police college, and a fresh new box of Ata-Boy Doggie Treats. I told Marlene I'd come back later for my band's gear that we'd stowed in the basement holding cells.

Stanley stuck close by my side as we bounced down the city hall steps, both of us free of our tethers. Sure, in Stanley's case it was a blatant infraction of village leash laws, but hey, now that I was off the job this town was wide open.

As we stepped onto the sidewalk we were greeted by a beautiful bright sunny November morning, the air crystal clear and celery crisp. I was still wearing my suede bomber jacket and a pair of soft black leather gloves. From what the natives had told me, in a few days I'd be switching to wool.

I took extra care walking down the hill. The sun had not yet burned the layer of hoar frost off the shady parts of the concrete. I had been worried about that frost earlier when I'd driven to work. The damn stuff can easily turn to black ice which is almost impossible to see and can make for treacherous driving. Happily, there had been no accident calls yet this morning. And now… well, it would soon all be Darcy Grenfeld's problem. Besides, the state boys handle most of our roads.

As usual at this hour, our town's main street was busy. In Glen Echo that means maybe a half dozen people in sight. I stopped to discuss the approaching winter with Hank Pengilly while he stacked a display of snow shovels in front of his hardware store. He said he noticed the squirrels had particularly bushy tails this fall so we were in for a cold winter. Plus, the woolly bear caterpillars had large brown stripes. As we spoke I looked into the window of the Riverview Diner across the street where old Alfie Lawson was flirting with his favorite waitress, Nola Bruckner, over his usual piece of pecan pie. Meanwhile, Chet Samuelson's old Dodge truck coughed by. Chet called out something obscene, but nevertheless friendly, to either me or to Hank Pengilly. We both laughed and flipped him the bird.

Geez, I thought, if a guy can't find happiness in a cozy little town like this, where can he find it? Sure, no situation is ideal, but this place, snuggled away in the mountains like this, was as close to perfection as I was ever going to find. Nice people. Easy pace. Pretty good blues band to waste my weekends with.

I looked up at the window of the mayor's office and thought, Would it really be so tough to go crawling back with an apology, a freshly filled ice bucket, and a pledge to be a good lap dog?

And then my box rang. I realized I had packed my own personal cell in with my desk leavings. I set the box down on the sidewalk and fished around for the phone. It rang another three times before I finally found it buried at the bottom between my fake plaster dog shit and my singing Billy Bass wall plaque. Both were birthday presents. "Hello?"

Marlene's voice answered, "State police just called."

"Uh, huh." I started repacking my box. The singing trout and the dog shit had sentimental value.

"They found your patrol car."

"*My* patrol car?"

"Okay, the town's patrol car."

"That's nice," I carefully cushioned the plaster turds inside my *Home Of The Whopper* underpants. Another birthday present.

"The patrol car was used to jack a Lexus. Just outside Schenectady. Some middle-aged couple thought they were being stopped by a cop."

"Aw, geez. Anybody hurt?"

"Husband was roughed up a bit."

"Any idea which direction Clive headed with the Lexus?"

"No."

I could see Marlene standing in the window of the police station as she talked. She saw me, too. So I waved to her and said, "Call me if there's any news. By that I mean news about Paul Briar."

"You taking your vest?"

"Won't Kevlar get kind of uncomfortable on a hike?"

"There's some dangerous folk with guns out there."

"You mean Clive and Len Holand."

"I mean deer hunters."

I went back and got the vest.

CHAPTER SEVENTEEN

When I pulled into the driveway of Windermere Inn I was surprised to find Lindsay strapping a canoe to the roof of her SUV.

"I thought we were hiking," I said.

She threw a rope across to my side of her car for me to grab and do something useful with. She said, "First rule of the woods: Never walk when you can paddle."

"And never paddle when you can drift."

She was impressed. "Are you sure you weren't born in the 'Dacks?"

I started tying my end of the rope to the roof rack and explained, "Story goes, my life got started in a sleazy motel in Niagara Falls, Canadian side. Nine months later I was born at Buffalo General, but they say my poop smelled like maple syrup.

She pounced on my comment. "See? You referred to your life getting started the day you were conceived – not the day you were delivered." She came around and poked me in the chest. "That, my friend, makes abortion murder." She untied my knot and tied it again into, I guess, a better knot.

I stepped back to give her busy arms and flailing dogma more room. "I'm not going to have to listen to this sort of stuff all the way, am I?" I smiled as I said this to soften the blow, but she knew I was dead serious.

She laughed. "Sorry. I couldn't resist."

"Next time, try harder." I checked her knot. It was tighter than mine.

She opened her car door and pulled out a map which she spread open across the hood of her vehicle. "We launch here, Loon Lake. Take Wilket Creek to Taylor's Pond. There's a couple of carries along the way but nothing that will bust our buns. From the pond it's a short walk to join up with the Hahne and we'll be two-thirds of the way to Clear Lake. We'll overnight at the pond." She folded the map.

"Overnight at the pond? You mean, we can't get to the lake today? It doesn't look that far to me."

"November. Gets dark early. Can't hike after dark. Too easy to twist an ankle, bust a leg, fall off a mountain."

This prolonged hike and change in schedule was not good news. Paul Briar had left yesterday, and I didn't like the idea of his getting to that cabin so long before we did. I had no idea what was waiting for him in there, but I did know that the Holand clan knows about this place. After all, the camp is presently owned by the church that Len Holand attends. The camp would be a handy place for his son Clive to hide out. Of course, if I see any evidence of Clive as we approach the actual camp itself I will order Lindsay to hang back so I can continue in alone.

We finished loading the car and the three of us – Lindsay, me, and Stanley – drove off. We arrived at the launch site for our trip at one-thirty. As we placed the sixteen-footer into Loon Lake I commented to Lindsay on how light the canoe was. She told me it was made of carbon fiber, like my bullet-proof vest. This only served to remind me that I'd forgotten to pack my Kevlar vest. It was too late now. Frankly, I doubt I'd have had the good sense to wear it anyway.

On the subject of good sense, Lindsay asked me if I'd brought my handgun along. I told her yes, and asked her if she was worried about anything in particular. She shrugged and said she was just curious, but I got the impression she was as concerned as I was about who might be waiting for us at that cabin.

Once our gear was stowed in the boat, we hid the car in the bushes and the three of us jumped into the canoe. Well, Lindsay and Stanley jumped in. I stepped gingerly into the tippy craft with Lindsay holding it steady. I haven't done a lot of canoeing. I must say, though, that it takes a real man, secure in his manhood and full of great manliness, to let a mere wisp of a woman hold a boat steady for him.

Lindsay made me strap on a neon orange P.F.D. which was fine with me. Besides keeping me afloat, the bright orange color will discourage hunters from mistaking us for a couple of moose paddling a canoe. With their dog.

Anyway, I took up my first-mate's position in the front end of the boat, or bow, while Captain Lindsay took her position in the back end, or stern. Stanley, our cabin boy, lay on the floor amidships. Or middle.

The trip started out smoothly enough. The wind was light, our craft was sleek, our paddles were strong, and in no time, I was turning around and whining to

Lindsay, "Are you sure we aren't dragging the anchor or something?" I pointed across the large lake which seemed to be getting larger. "I don't want to complain, but after half-an-hour's paddling shouldn't the far end of the lake be getting closer?"

Lindsay said that lake travel by canoe always seemed slow – with no nearby reference points you never feel you're making any headway. Soon, though, we'd be on a river where our minute-by-minute progress would be more noticeable.

When we reached the middle of the lake, which on this particular body of water meant a good half-mile from any shore, a stiff cross-breeze came up which presented two more problems. First, it constantly blew us off course. And second, it stirred up a chop that soon had our extra-light little craft bucking like a mechanical bull. The waves swelled and started swamping over our gunwales, forming a pretty good-sized puddle around my shoes. Stanley, who was lying in that cold puddle, looked up at me as if to say, *I told you I should stay back and guard the car.*

A half-hour later the breeze shifted from crosswind to headwind, and instead of washing over us broadside the waves now slammed into us head-on making further headway seem almost impossible. As the wind speed rose, the air temperature fell, but at least, sitting in the front end as I was, I was staying fairly dry. Stanley, not so much. And poor Lindsay, not at all. According to her, every time I yanked my paddle out of the water, I was slicing off the top of a wave which the icy wind would then grab and toss into her face. I apologized and assured her I wasn't doing this on purpose – I was just more at home swinging a bass guitar than I was swinging a damn paddle.

Somehow, forty-five minutes later, we reached the river mouth where Lindsay had promised things would get better. She was wrong.

The wind had died down, true, and the waves showed less anger, as she'd predicted, but the water level had sunk uncommonly low, which was common for November, and this meant we had to constantly zig-zag to avoid scraping our ass, against submerged rocks. Turns out, carbon-fiber cloth impregnated with acrylic resin stands up great against bullets, but it ain't worth shit against pre-Cambrian gneiss. And because I was sitting up front, Lindsay blamed me for every damn boulder we pranged the prow into. In my defense, I pointed out to her that we obviously weren't the first canoe to hit these rocks – their granite faces were streaked with smears of red, yellow, and green lipstick from similar intimate contact with previous vessels. She acknowledged my keen eye for detail, and said

I was certainly a better detective than I was a canoeist. I thanked her but I'm not sure why.

After bouncing off our tenth or twelfth rock, but who's counting besides Lindsay, I started to take off my life vest. I found the bulky garment restricting. Besides, the water through which we were now paddling was so shallow a super model couldn't drown in it if she fell face down. But Captain Lindsay was insistent I keep the thing on, so I did. At first, I thought she was just being a tight-assed bossy boots about the thing, but then I heard a distant roar coming from up ahead. Next thing I knew, we turned a corner and found ourselves at the bottom of a set of rapids called Manakawana's Crush. The name referred to a dead, mangled-up native American who was either an idiot or a show-off. It no longer mattered which. For once I was actually glad we were fighting our way upstream, because if we were coming the other way, I swear Lindsay would have been game to ride and buck our way over the tumult. The look in her eyes as she stared up at that white water crashing down over the corrugated concourse of cobbled granite was the same hungry look men get when they sit ringside at a strip club.

We wound and twisted our way through the maze of eddies below the falls and then beached our craft up onto the pebbled shoreline. Here, we hefted the canoe onto our shoulders and hiked, following a pathway that circled around the lethal rockslide that had originally formed these rapids. When I was a kid at summer camp we called this particular exercise a *portage*. In the Adirondacks they call it a *carry*. No matter what you name it, in my opinion, stumbling through dense underbrush while holding a canoe blindly over your head so you can't see the rock you're about to smash your toe into, is not an example of the human brain firing on its highest octane number.

After a quarter mile of scrapes, strains, and sweat, we removed our silly canoe-hat and placed it back into the calmer, friendlier water above the falls. Or at least it looked friendlier. Up here the river flowed glassy-smooth, dark, deep, and narrow. The increased depth made for easier navigation, fewer hidden rocks to dodge. Only trouble was, because of the more constricted watercourse we were now battling against a stronger current. The best thing about this quieter part of the journey was that it gave Lindsay and me a chance to talk. And pretty soon that talk got around to the story of her association with the property toward which we were headed.

The camp had been in her family for three generations. Her grandfather, and then her father, used the hundred-acre parcel primarily for hunting and fishing.

When her father died, he left the land, along with his house in the town of Long Lake, to Lindsay, his sole heir. At the time, Lindsay was recently divorced from her second husband. By the way, I must say I found this news about her having two male husbands rather encouraging. Maybe this whole lesbian-thing was just something she was trying out, much the same way I tried growing a beard. Maybe she'll find the whole experience makes her itchy, too.

When her father died Lindsay was newly divorced and living in Tennessee. Using the money from the sale of her father's house in Long Lake, she was able to move back to the Adirondacks and open the bed and breakfast she'd always dreamed of running, Windermere Inn. As far as her dad's hunting camp at Clear Lake went, she tried to sell the property, but because it was so isolated, it was hard to find a buyer. Her father had tried several times to clear a road into the place, but the property was within the Blue Line, so the Adirondack Park Agency vetoed the road's construction. The Blue Line, by the way, is what Adirondackers call the park's official border within which the Park Agency has an iron grip on all development. Unable to do anything with the property other than leave it as a hunt camp, Lindsay donated it to a local church. That way, she could not only unload a tax and insurance liability but also gain a nice write-off. She said the leader of that local church, my pal Mayor/Reverend Tim Stinson, had hopes of succeeding where Lindsay's father had failed. Stinson thought he had the political muscle to get the road okayed and subsequently open up the camp as a religious retreat – sort of a walk-on-the-water park. But alas, not even mighty Mayor Tim could beat the all-powerful Adirondack Park Agency. As a result, the Clear Lake property has lain fallow, completely abandoned and unused, even by hunters.

Make that, *especially* by hunters.

Because of her love of animals, Lindsay had added a restrict-of-use clause to the agreement of purchase and sale when she handed it over to the church. The contract stated that, in return for getting the land at below-market value, the new owner would agree never to allow the property to be used for hunting or trapping. Lindsay had added this codicil because, when she was a little girl, her father, having no son to teach his shooting skills to, had tried to make a hunter out of her. It didn't take. Seems little Lindsay went out with Daddy once, shot a furry little bunny rabbit and flipped out. That night, while saying her tearful prayers and asking the Lord's forgiveness for her murderous deed, little Lindsay vowed never to kill another one of God's creatures.

When I heard about this I was impressed. I'm sure Lindsay could have sold the land for a better price had she allowed its original utility – as a hunt camp – but she chose instead to put her profits where her heart was. On the other hand, I recalled a slight inconsistency in her views: She eats meat. In fact, hadn't she recently served veal at her Inn? I didn't call her out on this, though. What would be the point?

Anyway, we talked some more, and we paddled some more, and we carried some more. Our last carry took us to Taylor's Pond which, to my stiff legs, sore arms, and tired eyes, looked more like an ocean. Man, it's amazing how out of shape a guy can get simply by sitting in a patrol car all day and eating meatball sandwiches.

Once we'd traversed the pond – a pristine, uninhabited acre of water – we pulled our canoe up and onto a large flat table of rock from which the thin forest receded like hair from a middle-aged forehead. At this point I was thrilled to hear Lindsay proclaim that, for today, our journey had ended. It was rest time. The sun would soon be setting.

The first thing both Stanley and I did after beaching the canoe was to head for the nearest tree. Lindsay did the same but behind cover of an elderberry bush. The second thing we all did was walk to the far end of the clearing to check out our night's lodgings. No room key was needed to open the door. In fact, the man-made structure had no door. It was a three-sided wood-board affair with a steeply-slanted roof. Hence the name *lean-to.* Lindsay told me that the fronts of these things are left open so that the night's tenants can absorb the full warmth of their evening campfire. Plus, when the wind blows the interior space is self-cleaning.

This lean-to was set on a wooden platform, about a foot off the ground, making it appear like a small open-air stage. Or like Barbie's Dream House if Barbie's dreams had been considerably more modest. These Adirondack lean-to's are maintained by New York State's Department of Environmental Conservation The structures come in various sizes and sleep anywhere from four to a dozen campers. Because Taylor's pond was not part of a popular canoe route or hiking trail, our lean-to was one of the smaller ones.

Being November, darkness was checking in early, so Lindsay suggested we get our asses in gear and start gathering firewood before the day's light faded completely. I grabbed a small axe from one of the packs and started for the nearest tree, but Lindsay immediately grabbed the weapon away from me. Turns out cutting live trees for firewood is a big ecological no-no. Apparently, we had to restrict ourselves to picking up only confirmed-deceased wood that was lying on the forest floor. All fuel in the park must be DOA.

While I was collecting the wood, however, my keen detective's eye told me that other campers had been here recently and that these campers hadn't shown the same respect for park rules that we were demonstrating. I pointed out to Lindsay that these thoughtless jerks had cut perfectly healthy branches off young, living trees, stripping their bark for tinder as well. And since the carnage was limited to the lower four feet of the trees, I deduced that it was obviously the work of a well-organized gang of marshmallow-roasting short people, possibly jockeys with low blood sugar. For some reason, Lindsay disagreed with me. She said the damage was caused by foraging deer. Apparently, in autumn the animals change their feeding habits from grasses to tender tasty white cedar.

Lindsay knew a lot about the forest and its creatures. She also knew a lot about cooking over a campfire. No beans and beef jerky for this gourmet mountain gal. For our fireside dinner she prepared a meal that could have been served in any four-star restaurant. Since refrigeration was no problem at this time of year, Lindsay had been able to tote along a hunk of beef tenderloin which she roasted directly in the hot coals as a chateaubriand. She admitted that, although she opposed killing animals for sport, she has no problem with offing them for the table. And to make sure our particular meal was good and dead she finished it off by flaming the beef in brandy. I thought she was going a bit far with formalities, though, when she suggested we change clothes for dinner. I told her I hadn't packed my dinner jacket. But it turned out she just didn't want me eating in the same pants I was going to sleep in. Bears, she said, have an incredible sense of smell, and I probably didn't want them sniffing their way into camp and snacking on my grease-stained corduroys while I was still in them. Woodsman tips like this, Hawkeye never got from Chingachgook.

For our dining comfort Lindsay had packed a couple of light-weight folding chairs. And for our sleeping comfort she had packed a couple of slabs of foam to place under our sleeping bags. I asked her if air mattresses wouldn't have been easier to pack, but she said that the inflatables would be too cold for this time of year. Then she added, with a slight smirk, "Tonight we'll need to conserve all the body heat we can."

"I see," I said, seemingly oblivious to the wonderful opening she'd offered me for sexual innuendo. In my defense, I had something else on my mind.

I was thinking of something Lindsay had said while we were washing up our dishes. She had mentioned that yesterday Sharon had gone on an overnight shopping trip to Schenectady to pick up some chinaware from an outlet store mall. Sharon had promised that she'd be back early today. But this morning she had phoned Lindsay to say she'd had car trouble and wouldn't be back until late tonight. From Lindsay's account, Sharon had sounded a little vague about what exactly that car trouble was.

Now, the mention of Schenectady, alone, shouldn't have set off any special alarms for me – although the town is not exactly a shopping mecca, it could be just a simple coincidence that Sharon had been down there at the same time that Clive Holand had hijacked that Lexus in Schenectady. Still, I had to ask Lindsay, as casually as possible, "By any chance, does Sharon know Clive?"

"Clive Holand?"

"Yeah." I tried to be off-hand. "Like, did they ever, I don't know… meet… or anything?"

Lindsay smiled slyly as if she'd been caught doing something naughty. "You really *are* a good detective."

I sipped the delicious rum-spiked hot chocolate she'd brewed and waited for her to elaborate. My silence was soon rewarded.

"The Inn used to get its fresh produce from the Holand farm. Vegetables. Eggs. Clive used to deliver it. And yes, he and Sharon struck up a friendship of sorts. They had similar backgrounds. Similar interests. Cars, mostly. Clive used to help Sharon tune up her carburetor. And I don't mean that as a euphemism."

Most of what Lindsay was confirming I'd already noted. When I had first visited Windermere I'd seen the logo of Holand Farms on an egg carton. Later, when Arden Dawes, Clive's girlfriend, mentioned that Clive used to make deliveries for his old man I figured that Sharon or Lindsay might have, at least, a passing acquaintance with Clive.

Lindsay continued, "Sharon and Clive didn't go out for long. Just long enough for Sharon to learn that he was not her type." Lindsay blew on her hot chocolate, the froth curling into a question mark. "So tell me," she said. "Do you think Clive did it?"

"Did what?"

"Bomb that car. And then kill Robbie."

"Kill his brother, yes. Blow up Simon's car, no. It doesn't feel right. He doesn't strike me as the type to have an agenda."

"Agenda?"

"Terrorism... pro-life terrorism or any other brand of terrorism." I pulled the collar of my jacket close around my neck and poked the fire with a stick to coax more heat out of it. "But sounds like you know the guy better than I do. What do you think?"

My prodding made the campfire blaze hotter, but turned Lindsay suddenly cooler. "I really don't know. You'd have to ask Sharon." Lindsay stood up. She tossed a fresh log on the fire. A shower of sparks flew skyward. She added, "But please don't call it *pro-life* terrorism. There's nothing pro-life about killing people. *Any* people."

"No? Not even *guilty* people?" The minute I said it, I knew I'd gone too far. I was leading the witness to where she didn't want to be led.

Lindsay selected a second log to add to the fire. But this time, to avoid excessive sparks, she placed it on the coals carefully and precisely – the same way she placed her next words. "I'm as against capital punishment as I am against abortion and hunting for sport. To me, all life is sacred. I'd kinda hoped you'd know that about me by now." She stepped away from the fire and from me as if she'd had enough of both of us.

I'd clearly insulted her, and I felt like shit about it. I got to my feet. I gently grabbed her shoulders and turned her to face me. "Of course, I know how you feel about taking a life. It's obvious. In fact, I don't think I've ever met anyone so utterly consistent in their convictions. I'm sorry. Please... I... I didn't mean anything."

Lindsay didn't say any more. Neither did I. The log she'd placed on the coals did enough talking for both of us. It snapped and crackled and slowly caught fire, bathing our bodies in its glow. It felt warm. In fact, it was the first time I'd felt really warm since we'd set out on this trek.

With my hands still on her shoulders I gently pulled her toward me. If she'd resisted for only a moment I'd have let go. After all, this poor woman was alone in the middle of the dark woods with a horny idiot. That sort of thing can scare some women. But it didn't scare her. She didn't resist. In fact, she seemed to encourage the idea.

Her lips felt as warm and as intoxicating as the spiked hot chocolate and as tasty as the chateaubriand. And the touch of her hand on the back of my neck made me forget that the cold grass at our feet was crisp and white with frost.

We lay down on that sparse grass. And for the first time since I'd taken my last leak, I removed my leather gloves.

Things happen fast in the north woods in November. They have to, otherwise, they get frozen in place. So there was no slow striptease. No long, lingering kisses to tease ourselves stupid until one of us finally removed her earrings and announced it was time to change into something comfortable. In fact, the only comfortable thing either of us got into that chilly evening was our sleeping bag. And yes, I meant that as a singular noun.

Somebody once said sex was the most fun you can have without laughing, clearly implying that the participants shouldn't giggle while doing it. Well, That *somebody* has clearly never had sex in a sleeping bag. And that *somebody* must have been a man because I've found that many women enjoy sex more when they're laughing. And Lindsay was one of those ladies. And I must say, without drawing any graphic pictures, *feeling* Lindsay laugh was even more fun than *hearing* her laugh.

Yes, sex can be a lot of laughs, all right. Especially when you're trying to do it wrapped up tight in a puffy zippered cocoon with your pants off but your socks, your sweater, and your wool cap still on. Luckily, Lindsay didn't seem to mind. She told me that, to a native 'Dacker, knitted wool was an aphrodisiac. She also said that she found the tight bondage of the sleeping bag to be as big a turn-on as silk ropes and velvet handcuffs. I must say I saw her point. But thanks to the cold, that's about all I saw of her that night. It was far too chilly to prance naked around in the autumn moonlight.

Yes, we filled the woods with plenty of laughter that night. A lot of high-pitched screams, too. Many of them from Lindsay. I don't want to say she was wild, but it was lucky that the rickety old lean-to platform was set on solid concrete blocks. At one point, our sleeping-bag gymnastics got so enthusiastic poor Stanley had to get up off the plank floor and move to quieter, more solid ground.

After the action was finished, and before our wool-socked feet had torn the bottom out of our quilted polyester burrito, Lindsay asked if I wanted her to move back to her own sleeping bag. I told her I'd rather she remain right where she was, thank you. This cozy arrangement worked great for about twenty minutes, by which time we'd both decided we'd sleep better with a little more elbow room. So I kissed her goodnight and gave her cab fare home. Stanley, who was finally satisfied that the humans were through their nonsense for the night, crawled back up and lay between us.

The silence that falls over the forest on an autumn eve is other-worldly. No crickets chirping, no mosquitoes buzzing. It's like sleeping on the moon. I presume. Kind of frightening, if you have a chance to think about it. Happily, I didn't. I went out as soon as my head hit the goose down pillow which Lindsay had so thoughtfully packed. And for the next three hours I slept the sleep only an exhausted, out-of-work cop who'd just had sex with a gorgeous woman can sleep.

But the peaceful slumber didn't last long. And as with so many nighttime intrusions, this one started as a dream.

A cute little spotted fawn was standing on the main street of Glen Echo, across from town hall. Suddenly the town's new Chief of Police – rock musician Ted Nugent – came down the steps and shot the young animal with a crossbow. To Ted's surprise, the deer, having been previously loaded with high explosives, blew up, leaving a huge crater in the middle of the road. Mayor Tim heard the noise and came running out of his office carrying his empty ice bucket. He saw me standing nearby and immediately started berating me for not directing traffic more efficiently around the brand new bomb crater. Then he asked me to get him some ice. But instead of words emanating from the Reverend/Mayor Tim's mouth, the man was barking like a dog.

And then things got weird.

Tim's breath smelled of left-over chateaubriand. And it was at this point I realized I must be dreaming – I mean, when did Mayor Tim not smell of gin?

I opened my eyes. Where the hell was I? I turned my head. Oh, yeah, right. I was in the middle of the forest with a lovely part-time, non-committed lesbian who, for some strange reason was now shining a flashlight into the forest. I wonder why she's doing that? And why is she barking? No, that isn't her. That's Stanley.

"What's happening?" I mumbled.

"A bear."

I hoped I was still dreaming. "A what?"

"Maybe not a bear…"

"'Maybe'?"

"Could be raccoons. But they don't usually come out when it's this cold."

Stanley was facing the woods and barking his head off at something. I propped myself up on my elbows. "Don't bears usually hibernate?"

"Not 'til the snow comes."

We listened. And we waited. And we listened some more. Meanwhile, Stanley continued to bark. For variety, he also growled a bit. He didn't move from our feet, though. He was staying to guard his pack.

"Smell a bear out there, boy?" I whispered. I don't know why I whispered.

"Something's definitely out there," Lindsay said. "Down by the lake. I can hear it."

"Probably just the wind." I said, always happy to head straight for the warm comfort of denial. "Or maybe a moose."

"Kind of late in the day for moose to be out. No, I'm pretty sure it's a bear. Now you see why I didn't want you to wear your pants to bed?"

I silently thanked her. No, *blessed* her would be more accurate.

We listened. Heard nothing. After a minute or two Lindsay said the magic words, "I think he's gone."

"I'll go see." I reached into my knapsack and took out my service pistol.

But Lindsay put her hand on my arm. "Put that thing away. He won't bother us. The food's out there, not in here."

She was referring to our knapsacks full of provisions, which we'd left hanging high from a tree limb that stretched out over the lake.

After a few more minutes of silence, Lindsay turned off her flashlight and lay back. Stanley had settled down as well. He put his big head on his paws and closed his eyes. Lindsay too, shut her eyes. This left only me staring wide-eyed up into the blackness of our lean-to's roof. Eventually, even I drifted off. That's how utterly exhausted I was. Besides, when it came to the forest and its critters, I trusted Lindsay's instincts. And Stanley's nose.

Still kept the pistol under my pillow, though.

CHAPTER EIGHTEEN

"Morning."

"Morning," I answered.

"It wasn't a bear."

I rubbed the sleep from my eyes. "What wasn't a bear?"

"Last night. Wasn't a bear."

"Oh. Good." At the time, I honestly considered this to be welcome news. Silly me.

Still lying flat on my back, I stretched my arms up toward the lean-to's ceiling to try to work out the kinks. It seems Lindsay had let me sleep in while she had gotten the fire started. Have I mentioned I like this woman?

Clouds blanketed the sky, so I couldn't tell what time it was. I'd have checked my wristwatch, but sometime during our sexual gymnastics last night the thing had slipped off and was now probably lying in the bottom of my sleeping bag. I could have checked the time on my phone, of course, but that was still in the pocket of my pants, wherever they were. I watched Lindsay hang a pot of water over the campfire. She wore wool slacks and a thick parka, and for a change she sported mittens instead of gloves. Stanley was still lying at my feet, fast asleep. He's not a morning person.

I squirmed out of my bag and quickly looked around for my corduroy pants. I didn't immediately see them, so I got back into my bag again.

"Here," Lindsay lifted my pants from a branch near the fire and tossed them to me. "I put your phone in your pack."

I slipped into the pants. Mmmm, toasty. I stood up to zip and asked, "So if it wasn't a bear, what was it? A raccoon?"

"Something with two legs, not four. You like your porridge thick or thin?"

"I generally prefer it thin so it won't clog the pipes when I toss it down the drain. No offense, but I'll just have eggs, if you don't mind."

"Eggs?" She chuckled. "You haven't gone tripping much, have you."

My sleepy head was still lagging a paragraph behind her. "Two legs? You mean we have company?"

"Looks like. Glad they didn't show up earlier, huh? Could've been embarrassing. Geez, you don't think they heard us, do you?"

"You kidding? I think they heard us in Lake Placid." I sat on the edge of the lean-to and pulled on my boots. "So have you seen them? Do they have a tent?"

"Nope. No sign of anyone at all. Just their canoe."

In the far back corner of my mind a small alarm bell started to ring very softly. I asked her, "And this canoe wasn't there when we arrived?"

"Not that I noticed. I wish I knew where they were. I'd invite them to join us for coffee."

"What color?"

"Huh?"

"This canoe… what color is it?"

She took a couple of packets of instant oatmeal out of a backpack. "Yellow, I think. Why? You expecting company?"

My inner alarm bell rang louder. "Where?" I asked.

"You like your coffee black, right?"

"The canoe," I said. "Where is it?"

"Down shore. Far end of the bay. Just past where we beached ours. Tucked behind some bushes. I'd never have noticed it if it weren't for Stanley. Do you know that furry little pervert of yours likes to watch women pee?"

I did know that. But I didn't bother to answer her. I had more important things on my mind. I zipped up my jacket and hurried down toward the lake.

"Don't go far," she yelled at me.

I followed the shoreline to the area Lindsay had indicated. And that's where I found it. The craft was hidden behind some low scrub. The owner hadn't bothered to flip it upside down to keep it dry. He must have been in a hurry. But it was Clive's, all right. There was no mistaking the yellow fiberglass canoe with the black-trimmed wooden gunwales that I'd seen so often sitting in the back of his old pickup behind Blues and Cues.

The first thing I did was grab my cell phone from my pack where Lindsay had stowed it. The second thing I did was turn the phone on and check the signal. The third thing I did was curse the surrounding hills. The phone was useless down here.

I hurried to the fire and explained the situation to Lindsay: Clive Holand must have leap-frogged past us during the night. He must be on his way to Clear Lake, which he knows is abandoned, to hide out after hijacking that Lexus in Schenectady yesterday. When he beached his canoe, late last night, and stumbled upon our campfire, he must have been thrown off balance for a moment, but he then continued on with his hike. I imagine Paul Briar, too, will be a surprise to him – a surprise Clive won't be able to ignore quite as easily as he'd ignored us.

My instructions to Lindsay were simple: She must take the canoe and Stanley back the way we came and call for help as soon as she gets a cell phone signal. Meanwhile, I'll continue the rest of the way alone. Lindsay had said that we were now close to the trail, so I should be able to follow it to the camp.

But Lindsay didn't like this idea. She thought we should all turn back and head for home. Clive was likely outfitted with a deer rifle and she didn't want me confronting him alone with only my service revolver. I told her this was not an option. Paul Briar needed help, and he needed it *now*. And that meant Lindsay was going back alone.

But Lindsay wasn't buying it. She said I'd never find my way to the trail without her. My GPS was useless here, and the Hahne was a minor trail, not a marked road. I'd soon lose it. So, if I insisted on going on, she had to come with me.

Frankly, I knew she was probably right. I had no good choice. And more important, no time to argue the point. So, the only thing I could do was make her promise that, once we reached Clear Lake, she would hang back, stay clear of any action. She agreed. She even called me *Chief*, although I detected a hint of sarcasm when she said it.

Now that our new chain of command had been established, I ordered that we leave the lean-to immediately. Lindsay suggested we eat first, claiming that our bodies would need the fuel for the cold, arduous hike. She had a point. After a quick breakfast we set off.

At first, there was a trail. Of sorts. But it didn't last long. At this time of the year, when the ground is shag-carpeted with dry pine needles and dead leaves, it's hard to see much evidence of any pathways. And even at those rare times when the trail did tease us and make itself known for a few yards, the thing would suddenly come to an abrupt halt, usually at a stark rock face or at a patch of wetland, leaving me gazing off into the naked trees and scratching my wool-capped noggin about which way to turn. Lindsay had been right – if she weren't with me I'd have lost my way within minutes.

At the start of today's trek, back at the lean-to, Lindsay had estimated that within an hour we'd meet up with the larger, main trail, at which point the going would get easier. Well, I didn't check my watch, having never found it this morning, but it seemed like an hour had passed and we were still blazing our way through the same thick virgin underbrush. Our one blessing was that our backpacks were not heavy – we'd left our cooking utensils and sleeping bags back at the lean-to. One thing I did bring along, though, was my cell phone. Whenever we got to higher ground, I turned it on and prayed for a signal. But my prayers were ignored. Lindsay said I shouldn't blame God but the Adirondack Park Agency for this. While they do allow some unobtrusive cell towers, like the new ones that are spruced up to look like pine trees, they like to keep them short.

By the time we reached the main trail – the Hahne trail –snow had begun falling. Being the first snow of the season, the big, wet fluffy flakes drifted down so slowly they seemed suspended in mid-air, refusing to honor any ugly, earth-bound notions of gravity, and they soon turned the forest into a magical, mystical fairyland. Quite nice if you liked that sort of thing. Personally, I did not. Under these circumstances, with the air temperature being low and the relative humidity being high, the flakes stayed huge and moist making the rocks as slippery as non-stick cookware.

Stanley was the first to go on his ass. Lindsay and I were both wearing boots with rubber soles, but poor Stanley's paw pads were like the leather tips of pool cues – a little moisture and they lost their grip and next thing the pooch knew he was whacking his balls off the rails and into the corner pocket. The poor guy struggled up the first couple of granite slopes, but after falling on his chin a couple of times I decided enough was enough. As I picked up the mid-sized lab in my arms he looked at me as if to say, *You sure they don't need cops in Arizona or California?* Dry, Stanley weighs about fifty pounds, but by the time we'd reached the third hill, the wet snow had added another five or six pounds to him. And by the time we started up the fifth ridge I was thinking seriously about how much I'd always liked Shih-Tzu's.

After a mile or so of this nonsense the Hahne trail mercifully leveled out and so did my aching back – the pooch was back on all fours again. At this point Lindsay suggested a time out, mostly, I think, for my benefit. But I was too worried about what was going on at that camp. So we pressed on. In hindsight, this probably wasn't a great idea. When a hiker's muscles get tired, he gets sloppy, and when he gets sloppy, he can easily end up picking pine needles out of his butt, which is exactly what happened.

The trail had become easy, fast, and straight, so we were almost at a trot when my toes caught the sucker root of a pin cherry bush hidden beneath the snow. I went down hard, bruising my elbow on a rock and twisting my ankle. When I tried to stand up the pain shot up my spine and struck a cymbal crash in my brain. I had no choice. I had to sit and rest for a minute.

Lindsay gently pulled off my boot. Stanley, of course, promptly grabbed the boot and ran off into the forest. While the dog waited patiently for me to join his game, Lindsay examined my ankle. She decided the bone probably wasn't broken but the injury certainly meant the end of our hike. I disagreed. I told her that all I needed was a short rest, and if she really wanted to help me she could chase the pooch and get my boot back before my foot froze.

Moments later, as Lindsay and Stanley returned with my footwear, we heard a rifle shot. And then a second one. Both shots came from behind the hills somewhere. Not far off.

My first question was, How close were we to Clear Lake? Could the shots be from Clive at the camp? But Lindsay said we weren't that close – the sharp cracks had to be hunters' guns. She went on to explain that a first prediction of snowfall always brings the hunters out. The precipitation gets the young deer all skittish and disoriented and easy to sneak up on, and the fresh white carpet makes tracking them a breeze.

I pulled my boot on, and we resumed our hike. As I limped along, I took a hint from the hunters and watched for footprints in the new snow, human footprints, that is. I didn't see any. Clive had hiked in before the snow had started.

The topography stayed reasonably flat for the next hour-and-a-half. But as we neared Clear Lake the going got rough again. Lindsay had warned me this would happen, what with the lake being encircled by high rocky hills. Actually, she called them mountains, but Adirondackers are like that. They'll stick a ski lift on a parking lot speed bump and call it a mountain.

When we'd reached the summit of the final hill, or mountain, we stopped to survey the vista that lay stretched out below us.

Except for the dark green splotches of pine, the panorama below us was presented mostly in glorious black and white, the hardwood trunks being black, everything else, freshly white. At the center of this high-def picture lay a large flat screen of slate grey, its dull surface seemingly waiting for someone to turn the power on. Clear Lake seemed, from up here, just about large enough to take a quick, three-minute turn on water-skis before ending up back where you started. This particular lake, however, was guaranteed never to feel the cruel cut of a water-ski. Like many such lakes within the blue line, the A.P.A. has ordered it to remain power-boat free.

From our lofty elevated position I could see a small river and gulley to my right that either fed into or emptied out of the lake. On the far side, I could make out a clearing with a lone large building planted in the center. Lindsay said there were a couple more small cottages tucked into the dark evergreens behind this main structure, but from up here I had to take her word for it. I looked for signs of smoke coming from the buildings, but I didn't see any. The most prominent feature of the camp was its small wooden water tower. Lindsay said this tank had been constructed forty years ago when her father had installed indoor plumbing and a gasoline-fueled electric generator. Being as inaccessible as it was, most of the buildings were constructed of native logs with any necessary board timber and sheet metal dragged in during high winter over frozen lakes and bogs.

We resumed our walk down the slope and soon found ourselves on the flats, just a hundred yards or so from the lake shore. From here, Lindsay said, it should be an easy fifteen-minute walk around the lake to the camp. But of course, nothing in this country is easy. And frankly, our next obstacle was close to impossible to overcome.

Lindsay was the first to see it. "Aww, for fuck's sake. Jesus Herbert Christ. I mean, Holy fuckin' shit."

Didn't sound like good news. My eyes followed her gaze. "Oh," I concurred.

Seems the fucking suspension bridge was out. And I do mean the *fucking* suspension bridge. Lindsay had told me about how she used to play on this thing when she was a little girl and how she had eventually lost her cherry on it. Her words, not mine. Apparently, the swinging motion of the suspension ropes added to both the challenge and the thrill.

Well, nobody was screwing on the bridge now. Nor would they anytime soon.

Constructed with thick hemp, short planks, and a lot of blind faith in the builder's knot-tying abilities, the structure normally spanned a fifty-foot-wide gorge. But not anymore. Today, the limp ropes dangled impotently, their ends still attached to the opposite side of the embankment and their flaccid remains snaking down into the gully where their frayed toes danced like skeleton feet in the quick-step current of the small river.

Lindsay threw up her arms and repeated a phrase I imagine she'd first said many years ago on this very same spot. "That does it. We're fucked."

Her assessment of the situation was terse but accurate. I stood at the edge of the little gorge. Twenty feet below me the narrow river raced fast, deep, and cold.

I said, "Looks like Clive wanted to make sure he wasn't followed." My eyes followed the stream, down toward the lake. "So where's the next good place to cross?"

Lindsay showed little patience with my question. "If there was a better spot, would Granddaddy have built the bridge here?" Then she smiled the whole matter off and patted my back. "Well, Chief, you tried. You did your best." And she continued to cheer up even further. "You know, I bet Paul Briar never made it into the camp. After all, we don't know that Clive cut this bridge down today. I bet Paul found the bridge broken and decided to turn back. Hell, I bet, right now, he's back home in the city sitting in a hot tub while we're freezing our sorry asses off in the snow."

Her attitude, or I should say her *change* in attitude, worried me. It was too fast. One minute, anger and frustration over the bridge being out, the next minute, total acceptance. It was as if she'd known this was coming. As if, when she'd first seen the busted bridge, she'd been only acting surprised and angry.

I turned my attention back to the broken structure, grabbed one of the short vestiges of rope, and examined the frayed end. It had obviously been cut, all right, but it wasn't a fresh cut. There was black mold growing up inside the loosened jute, mold that wouldn't grow inside a tightly wound rope. Lindsay was right. If Clive did do this, he hadn't done it today. Or even this week. But that didn't mean she was right about Paul Briar not being at that camp. It just meant he didn't go in by way of this bridge.

There was one more curious thing about this bridge – it was clear that it had been sabotaged not from the far side, as one would expect from someone who was trying to prevent anyone from following him in, but from this near side, which would prevent someone from getting out from the camp not into it. Somebody wanted to turn the camp into a prison. This left an obvious question.

"There another way into the camp?" I asked. "Round the other end of the lake?"

She shook her head. "The other end of the lake is ringed with some vicious cliff faces. Some bad rock falls. You'd have to be part mountain goat. We wouldn't have a hope. Not with Stanley. And certainly not with your bad ankle. Of course, if we had a canoe we could just paddle across, but–"

"So why didn't we bring the canoe?" I asked.

"You kidding? All that way? You said you were in a hurry. Besides, how was I to know the bridge would be out?" Lindsay looked up at the sky. "Looks like more snow. We better get back." And she turned around toward the direction we'd come.

But I stayed right where I was, my attention focused on the river. "How deep?" I asked.

"This time of year? Four, maybe five feet. Some deeper holes. Forget it." Lindsay continued walking away. She clearly had no intention of hanging around to discuss the matter. We'd reached the end of the road. No sane person would do anything at this juncture but call it quits and turn back. We'd done our best, but hey, sometimes you gotta kick hope in the nuts and face reality. As I say, no sane person would consider wading across the river.

I started inching toward the water. Down the embankment.

Lindsay was incredulous. "You… you aren't thinking of swimming that thing."

"Four or five feet deep? It'll be more like wading."

"Are you crazy? You'll freeze solid when you come out."

"You packed my spare jeans and undies this morning, right? I'll hold my pack over my head."

She gestured to the stream. "Look how fast that thing is? Have you ever tried just standing in water like that?"

"I have very slim legs. And large feet. I'm built like a heron. You'd know that about me if you hadn't been in such a rush last night." I grabbed a juniper bush for a handhold to lower myself over the edge as I said, "The water's what, forty, fifty degrees? It's not that far to the other side. I'll be in it for just a minute or two. The way I see it, as long as I can get out and change into dry clothes fast enough, I should be okay. The trick will be keeping my pack high and dry."

"What if you trip and get your pack wet? We'll never get you home. You'll die of hypothermia before we're halfway there. And... and..." For the first time since I'd known her, Lindsay had run out of words.

The pooch was trying to follow me. I pushed him back. "You stay here, boy. You're the man of the house now. Be a good fella and take care of the womenfolk, okay?" His tail wagged. I think he liked the idea of finally having Lindsay all to himself.

I lowered myself further over the edge. A few loose stones gave out under my weight and avalanched down the slope. I would probably be better off sliding down on my ass than trying to climb down, but I didn't want to commit yet to such silliness. I didn't want to turn this bluff over a bluff into a reality. If Lindsay didn't say what I wanted her to say soon I might have to actually go through with this dumb stunt. I called up to her, "Darn it. I forgot. My pistol's in my pants pocket. But that's okay, bullets still work when they get wet. I think."

Lindsay had heard enough and seen enough. Resigned, she announced quietly and reluctantly, "There's another way."

I paused in my suicide mission. "Pardon me?"

"It's a long walk. No trail. Tough scrambling. And it will add at least another hour to the hike, but..."

I scrambled back up to the lip of the gorge. "And you were going to keep this to yourself because...?"

"Because I'm pro-life. Especially pro the life of people I care about. You said yourself, you don't know what's waiting for us at the camp. Clive Holand is crazy. His old man is crazy. Maybe his old man is in there with him. Maybe the rest of his crazy extended family. And you're just one brave man with a handgun. That whole Holand clan is a cult of self-reliant nut-jobs with rifles and high explosives. You could be going up against a damn militia."

I dusted the snow and granite grit off my hands. "You seem to know quite a lot about these people."

"Yeah, well... about Sharon... it wasn't just *Clive* Holand who was interested in her.

"You're kidding. His brother?"

She shook her head, no.

"You don't mean... Big Daddy?"

I'd hit the target. She said, "He hung around a lot. I think he had eyes on Sharon becoming Mrs. Holand Number Five."

We started walking again. "Number five? I met two wives at the house, and I know one died in childbirth. There was a fourth?"

"Still is. Name's Julia. Nice woman. A little more sophisticated than the others. I used to run into her in town. Haven't seen her all summer, though. Rumor has it she left him."

"And you say Len Holand had eyes for Sharon?"

"She thought it was a joke. You know Sharon… when he came on to her she laughed in his face. Sharon's a dear, but she can be a little direct sometimes."

Since she had brought the subject up, I seized the opportunity. "You know, uh… a lot of people think you two are, uh…"

"Lovers?"

I chuckled. "Crazy, huh?"

"I've heard crazier." And with that said, she left me hanging.

I'd gone this far, so I figured I might as well go all the way. "Wanna hear what's really crazy? Paul Briar… he thinks you two might have—"

"Kidnapped his wife."

I was beginning to feel unnecessary to this conversation. I said, "Paul may even think you're keeping her out here at the camp."

Lindsay didn't seem surprised by any of this. She turned and asked me, "That what you think?"

I looked into her eyes, and I hate to say it, but I didn't like what I saw. The warm bright sparklers that had warmed my soul for the past two days had suddenly extinguished and then frozen into two cubes of cold, dead ice that chilled me through to my wool socks. I paused and buttoned up my coat. But it didn't help. I answered her question with a silence that simply paid tribute to my own cowardice. Then I changed the subject, "So, where's this trail?"

We walked on in silence, Lindsay leading the way. I felt lousy, but I couldn't help but be suspicious. Sure, maybe she did have my welfare at heart when she lied to me about there being no other way into the camp with the bridge out. But she should definitely have told me earlier about Sharon's connection to Clive Holand and his old man. And she should have told me earlier that she knew about Paul Briar's suspicions. All along, she'd known exactly why we were making this trek, and yet she let me carry on with my charade. She also could have confessed a little sooner about once owning this Clear Lake camp. But no, she made me discover everything for myself. Naturally, this made me wonder what else she was holding back. All in all, I simply no longer trusted her. Despite her guidance through the woods yesterday and today, I wasn't convinced she had come along with the intention of making my job any easier.

The walk around the lake proved to be difficult both emotionally and physically, our bonds of trust having been severed and frayed like the ropes of that bridge. Neither of us felt much like talking. Added to that, we were both exhausted.

Physically, the toughest part of the march came when, hiking close along the east shore, we came to a rockslide. A *talus* or *scree*, the 'Dackers call it. Hundreds, maybe thousands, of years ago a cliff at the top of the mountain had crumbled spilling a stream of boulders down the hillside and leaving a river of rubble that now trailed from the top of the mountain to the water's edge. We didn't have time to go around the slide – the climb was too long and steep – we had to go over it. For Lindsay and me this would prove a slow and difficult task. But for Stanley it would be impossible. So, once again, the pooch became luggage. And not the kind on wheels.

I hefted him once again up onto my shoulders, and the three of us struggled up, over, around, and through the rock field like ants clambering across a gravel driveway. Our one good fortune was that the noontime temperature had risen above zero, so the rocks weren't slicked with black ice as they had been in the morning.

By the time we'd crossed the rock slide my ankle was throbbing. Lindsay suggested we sit down for a rest, and this time she got no argument from me. We shared a bottle of water. Since relations between us were already rocky, I took the opportunity to address a couple more touchy questions.

"So what's the new nursery for?"

Lindsay was not shocked by the sudden reference. Nor did she display any curiosity as to how I'd learned about the freshly decorated room. "My niece," she answered with no particular emotion. "She's having a baby."

Her niece? How was that possible? Lindsay had told me that she was an only child. How does a person have a niece without first having a brother or a sister to manufacture said progeny? I guess Lindsay realized her little mistake, because she quickly amended her story.

"Tracy's not an actual niece. Her mother was a roommate of mine in college." Lindsay picked up a blade of switch grass as she talked and started fiddling with it, tying it into a knot, giving herself time to twist her words just so. "Her mom's pissed off at her, getting knocked up and all. Wants her to have an abortion. I'm not sure what young Tracy's plans are, but I thought maybe if I offered the girl a place to stay, everybody would have time to cool down, think things out. Tracy might make the right decision. And heck, if it turns out Tracy has the baby but doesn't want to assume the responsibilities of motherhood just yet, maybe I could take care of the baby for her. Who knows? Maybe even adopt the child if things don't work out."

Well, there it was: Lindsay's neonatal cover plan. All laid out nice and neat for me like that map she had unfolded on the hood of her car at the start of our journey. Lindsay was going to explain the newly-arrived pink bundle as a cast-off from an old college pal's careless daughter.

Lindsay waited for me to make a comment of some sort. But I didn't. So she tried baiting one out of me. "You probably think Tracy should go ahead and have an abortion."

I didn't take the bait. "Not really any of my business."

"Come on. It's all right. Don't be afraid. I won't bite your head off."

"Well, since you're pressing me… I believe what a woman does with her body is a private matter. A matter between herself and her body shop. In most cases a good oil spray once a year should do the trick. But up here in the north we use a lot of salt on our roads, and too much salt can lead to high blood pressure which in turn leads to over-inflated tires. Now, let's have no more of this sort of talk." I pointed at Stanley. "I'd rather the boy not see us fighting."

"Shit." Lindsay stood up, shook her head in utter awe. "Is there any situation you won't try to joke your way out of? Any subject you take seriously?"

I stood up in defiance. "Yes, of course there are subjects I take seriously. My children, for instance. I never joke about my children."

"You told me you don't have any children."

"That's because I had a vasectomy, which, by the way, was nobody's decision but my own."

"A vasectomy? You can't compare a vasectomy with an abortion."

"Sure I can. For one thing, you don't want to ride home from either of them on a bicycle."

She laughed, "You know your problem?"

"If I say *yes* is there any chance you'll drop this line of questioning?"

But she was on a roll. "You know why I think you really left the Buffalo police department?"

Oh no, here it comes. An eighteen-wheeler full of Psych 101 headed down a darkened, icy hill, and I'm the deer caught in the headlights.

Lindsay didn't touch the air brakes. She just kept on rolling at full speed. "It wasn't because you'd shot that little girl's dog. It was because that job in Buffalo was a *real* job. A job you had to give a damn about. Every day, you were dealing with serious stuff. Murders. Assaults. Robberies. Rapes. Unpleasant stuff. Stuff you couldn't joke your way out of. Stuff you had to take seriously or not take at all. So you chose to not take it at all. You ran away, straight to sweet little Glen Echo where the nastiest thing you ever have to do is tell the Johnson twins not to play Frisbee golf on the town's bowling green."

"Well, it does fuck up the grass."

"I don't buy it."

"That's because you don't bowl."

"I don't think it's the mayor who's keeping you from getting involved in the important cases. I think it's you. I think you're happier handling the kitties stuck up in trees so you can pass off the sad and ugly chores to someone else."

"That's not true. Well, not completely true. But I—"

"And if I were already in a relationship with anyone – man or woman – do you think I'd be having this affair with you?"

"*Affair*? We're having an affair?"

"Whatever you want to call it, do you think I'd cheat on him or her?" Lindsay slowed down her speaking tempo to more of a ballad. "I'm a loyal, one-lover-at-a-time kind of chick, and so far, all those lovers have been male." Then she added, "I know what they've been saying about Sharon and me. But what can I do? You know what small towns are like."

"I'm learning."

"A woman turns down a few offers, bruises a few male egos – she must be lesbian. How else would a hound like Darcy Grenfeld explain his constant strike-outs?"

"Darcy Grenfeld? The guy who wanted my gig? Darcy Grenfeld was hitting on you?"

"Constantly. It quickly went from flattering to tiresome to annoying. I complained to Grant Hindle. He told me not to worry, Darcy would be gone soon."

"Well, funny you should mention that…" I started to give her the bad news that Darcy might soon be back on the job, when I was interrupted by…

Bang!

And we both froze. Statues. No talking. No breathing. We just listened to the echo of the loud gunshot bounce off the mountains and rock faces.

"Close," uttered Lindsay.

"Let's hope it's hunters." And this time I was dead serious.

CHAPTER NINETEEN

I snuck my first close look at the camp from the edge of the clearing, careful to keep myself hidden by the thick cover of cedars.

According to Lindsay the main lodge comprised six rooms including one in the attic where a small eyebrow window squinted out at the lake from under the mossy forehead of a green shingled roof. There was no basement, just a two-foot tall foundation of cinder blocks cemented directly onto the granite. From there to the roofline the rest of the structure was built entirely of logs, big bold logs, the kind of logs mother nature isn't given time to grow anymore.

Behind this main building squatted two smaller, newer, guest cottages. Both of these structures were framed and faced with boards rather than logs. No lights shone from any windows, but then, it was mid-afternoon and still daylight out here. No smoke rose from any chimneys either, but I could tell someone was here besides us. Fresh footprints in the newly-fallen inch of snow testified to that.

Down at the water's edge, a small rickety dock tongued out into the lake. The only other notable feature in the front yard, standing halfway between the lakefront and the main lodge, was a large stone and mortar barbecue. One other more modern piece equipment caught my eye.

Being careful to keep us both within the shadows of the evergreens, I turned to Lindsay, "Your dad watch sports or the Playboy Channel?"

She didn't understand. I pointed to the small, pizza-sized satellite dish perched high atop the water tower where it was screwed to the sheet metal tank. Lindsay said, "I haven't been out here for eight years. The dish wasn't here then."

I took Stanley's leash from my pocket, clipped one end onto his collar, and handed the executive end to Lindsay. "If I don't come back in fifteen minutes get the hell out of here. Okay?"

She nodded her okay. As I turned to step out of the bushes, she grabbed my arm. "The gun?"

"You take it." I started to pull the pistol out of my pocket. But she shook her head. "You keep it."

I didn't argue. I patted her shoulder and left, threading my way through the line of trees around the perimeter of the clearing. A couple of months ago, these oaks, birches, and maples might have offered some decent cover, but at this time of year their naked skeletons were almost useless. On the plus side, I was grateful to mother nature for laying the carpet of fresh snow over the dried leaves to muffle my footfalls.

As I neared the main lodge, I kept my eye on the windows for any signs of life inside. I couldn't see anything obvious, so I made a quick dash to the structure's back wall. From here I hugged my way around towards the front of the building. I couldn't sneak a peek directly into any windows as I passed because they were set too high off the ground – the cement block foundation kept the whole building well off the ground. So, I had no choice but to climb the porch and see if I could get a look into the big front window.

I gingerly put my full weight on the first of the wooden steps, ready to freeze should any old joints creak, mine or the cabin's. They didn't. So, I continued up the three additional steps to the top.

Now, at this point, if I were absolutely sure nobody but Paul Briar was inside, I would have called out so as to not frighten him and hopefully not get myself shot as an intruder if Briar had a gun. But with the possibility of Clive Holand being inside I couldn't take that chance. So I continued skulking.

Like a backwoods B&E artist, I sidled up to the front window and peered into it. But it was too dark in there and too light out here, so all I got from the reflective glass was a big, dirty, unshaven face staring back at me – a face I couldn't believe Lindsay had slept with last night. I gave up with the window idea and turned back to the front door.

The old black pine-board door whispered original equipment, but the gleaming brass knob and Yale lock screamed brand new upgrade. I placed my gloved hand on the knob. The shiny brass handle turned freely.

I edged the door open. Just a crack at first. Then a wee bit wider. Finally, I stuck my whole dumb head in. Not good. I immediately pulled it back out.

I gulped a deep breath of fresh air. And then I threw up. Just a wee bit. I couldn't help myself. The stench of rotting flesh always does that to me. It's a stink no cop ever forgets. Something in there was dead. Or if it wasn't, it soon would be.

With one hand clutching the doorknob for support I readied myself for a second charge. I hyperventilated like a pearl diver readying himself for a long submersion. But just as I was about to make my plunge, I heard a voice call in a loud stage whisper from the forest to my right.

"No, no. Come back, you idiot."

Naturally, I assumed she was talking to me. But I turned to see Stanley come loping out of the woods. The pooch must have gotten away from her. A few feet behind him Lindsay followed, awkwardly trying her best to step on his trailing leash. But her feet weren't as big as her bravery.

When Stanley got as far as the stone barbecue he stopped. He barked, took a couple of sniffs, then lifted his leg and pissed on the grill. I laughed aloud. Why not? If there was anyone around, our cover had already been blown. So I opened the door.

And a gunshot rang out.

The shooter was close. But not in the room I was now staring straight into. The shot had come from above me, above the porch roof under which I was standing – probably from that attic window over the front entrance.

A second shot rang out. And this time, I witnessed the results of the bullet's travel. With a puff of dust, the lethal projectile smashed a chunk of mortar off the stone barbecue that Lindsay was now crouching behind.

Stanley didn't have the brains to hide there with her. Instead, he ran straight into the line of fire. Maybe he was coming to my aid. Maybe he was just anxious to join the party. I don't know. But happily, the shooter didn't waste any bullets on the running target.

"You okay?" I yelled out as I grabbed my dumb pooch.

Lindsay thought I was talking to her. "Yes," she answered from behind the brick barbecue.

I hastily tied Stanley to the porch railing. Then, with my handgun drawn, and both hands clutching it, I advanced inside through the door and deeper into the building. "Police," I called into the darkness. "Glen Echo Police. Put your weapon down."

Dead quiet. No obvious sign of life nor much light to see it with. The cabin's side windows were small and no electric light fixtures were turned on. But now that I thought of it, I had heard no electric generator running.

I knew that at least one shooter was upstairs in that attic. If there was another waiting down here for me, he had a hell of an advantage – I was still a little blind from looking at that white snow outside. I called out again, "Clive, I know you're here."

I waited for my eyes to adjust to the gloom. Slowly, an image started developing. To my right, a living room. Fully furnished, complete with a modern flat-screen television bolted to the wall. To my immediate left, a coat closet. Ahead of me, a staircase, one of those circular space-saving ones that corkscrewed itself tight around a support pole until it disappeared up into a large opening in the ceiling. I imagine the sniper had chosen to secure himself up there in the attic because the height offered him a wide view of the grounds. Now, though, it just made him my prisoner.

I kept my pistol trained on the top of the staircase. I didn't attempt to climb the stairs, of course. If I did, as soon as I stick my head over the top Clive will pick me off like a kid popping a gopher at a carnival game. So I called up to him, "Throw down your gun."

He wasn't dumb enough to do any such thing.

The way I saw it, there was only one way out of this situation – find a can of barbecue starter, light a match, and grab anything that comes running out of the blazing building that looks like Clive Holand. But first, I'd have to check and make sure nobody else was here inside the structure, particularly Paul or Nancy Briar.

Keeping one eye on that staircase, I searched around the main floor.

Two bedroom doors rested partially open. A quick glance inside the first told me it was used as a storeroom, mostly for junk and discarded furniture. The second room, however, testified to more recent occupation. A crumpled bed lay sheeted and blanketed but unmade. Various clothes and toiletries littered the floor and dresser. Most of them seemed to be a woman's things.

Still keeping my eye on that twisted staircase, I continued to the third room, at the far end of the hall. This door was shut, and as I neared it I started to understand why. The stink grew stronger with my every step.

I tried to edge the door open, but the bottom of it seemed to be stuck on something on the other side. I put my knee against the door and inched it a little farther until I'd finally cracked it open wide enough to stick my head through.

And there I saw her. Lying in an iron cot. Filthy. Bedclothes in tatters. Her thin mattress stained like an old parchment map.

She didn't look anything like her pictures. The photos her husband had emailed me months ago had been taken in better days, back when Nancy Briar was healthy and vibrant. Paul's camera had caught a sly, devilish smirk and sultry, hooded eyes that looked sideways at the lens daring the photographer to snap a bad picture of her, which I'm sure she knew would be impossible. Today, however, was a different matter. Today those eyes were bursting wide with terror. And she had no mouth at all, her lips hidden tight under silver duct tape. Her arms and legs were taped to the iron crossbeams of her cot with the same plumbers' tape that sealed her mouth.

But at least she was still alive. And still pregnant. Ready to pop at any minute, by my quick, uneducated assessment.

"Hello, Nancy," I said through the half-open doorway. I still hadn't pushed my way fully into the room. "I'm a policeman. Name's Tanager." I smiled at her. "Don't get up."

She motioned toward the ceiling with the only part of her that was still free to move – her eyes.

"Yes, I know he's up there. Don't worry. We'll take care of him."

Since I wasn't fully in the room yet, I checked behind me, up the hallway to that corkscrew staircase, to make sure we were still alone. We were. I turned my attention back to Nancy. "Let's get you out of here."

With the pistol still clutched tight in my right hand, I squeezed myself through the partially open door, feeling like a baby being born. When I was fully delivered into the bedroom, I glanced behind the door to confirm what I'd expected to find lying on the other side, acting as a doorstop.

From the smell, I'd figured it to be a corpse, and I was right. And from the circumstances, I'd figured that corpse to be the body of Paul Briar. But on this count, I was wrong. It was the body of a woman. And although I'd never seen her before, I had a pretty good idea who that woman was.

At first glance she seemed to be in her fifties, but on closer examination I realized she was younger than that. What had added the years was her long gray hair and lack of makeup. I guess that's the way Len Holand likes them. His other two wives, Carol and Charlotte, wore their hair in exactly that same manner and also had to decline any help from Max Factor. The main difference between those two wives and this one, however, was the bullet hole in this one's chest.

For no particular reason, I racked my brain for her name. I knew Lindsay had just told me, but I couldn't remember it. Finally, it came to me. I turned to Nancy for confirmation. "Julia?" I said. "Julia Holand?"

She nodded yes.

I quickly, but respectfully, urged the corpse of Mrs. Holand Number Three out of the way so I could open the bedroom door to its full extent. I kept my eyes and my ears on that hallway while I put the gun down and worked on freeing Nancy.

I knelt down, laid my pistol on the bed, just inches away from my hand, and started peeling the tape away from Nancy's mouth. I was strongly tempted to rush the job, but I didn't, fearing that if I ripped the tape off too quickly, most of Nancy's dry, chapped lips might come with it.

As soon as those lips were free to speak, Nancy said in a weak, hoarse voice, "Upstairs... he's upstairs."

"I know." I tore my fingernails into the tapes that secured her arms and legs.

"He has a gun," she added.

I knew that, too. So, I asked her something I didn't know, "Where's Paul?"

She looked at me blankly, as if she didn't understand. She must have been in worse shape than I'd thought. So I repeated my question. "Your husband. Paul. He's here, isn't he?"

"Yes." It was a simple declaration of a simple fact to a simple man, as if *I* were the confused one.

I asked once more, "Nancy, where is Paul?"

She didn't get a chance to answer. Someone beat her to it.

"I'm right here." The voice came from behind me.

I didn't bother to grab the gun. I recognized Paul's voice. He wasn't close, though. Not yet.

My first reaction, when I saw him standing there at the bottom of the circular stairs, was a happy one. Great! He's alive. Clive hadn't killed him after all.

But then I realized that the rest of the picture didn't add up. *Were those guns that Paul was holding? A rifle in one hand? A pistol in the other? And was the pistol pointed intentionally at me?* I turned back to Nancy. Maybe she knew what the hell was going on.

"I'm sorry," she said, speaking not to her husband but to me.

And that's when everything fell into place. The needle finally dropped, and the record started spinning.

I turned to Briar, speaking my thoughts aloud as the needle found the groove. "She didn't want the baby. But you did."

"Tell me, Chief Tanager," he said. "Why is it always up to the mother to decide? Why shouldn't the father have a say?"

I traded his question for one of my own. "Where's Clive?"

Paul walked along the hall toward our door. "Don't worry. He won't be starting any more bar fights ever again."

As he got closer, I recognized the rifle as a .243 Winchester. "Clive's rifle?" I asked.

"Yes." Briar then indicated his pistol. "He, of course, was shot with my Glock."

I indicated Julia Holand's dead body on the floor. "But she was killed with Clive's rifle."

"Of course."

I added, "Just as Nancy and I will be."

"I wish there were another way. I truly do." He looked at his wife. "I pleaded with you to have the baby."

Nancy said nothing in response. I summed up the rest of his upcoming plan. "So, Clive Holand shot the whole lot of us before you, the big hero, finally got him."

Paul said, with genuine regret, "No witnesses, I'm afraid."

Nancy indicated her ripe belly. "Except one."

Briar smiled. "Yes."

"So what went wrong?" I asked. "You hired the Holands to kidnap Nancy, take care of her until the baby came. Then what? They get greedy? They hold you up for more money?" I now realized something. "Is that what the fight was about? That fight at Blues and Cues?"

"Clive Holand reneged on our prior arrangement. He decided not to disclose where he was keeping Nancy unless I paid three times his agreed-upon fee. Otherwise, I would never see my child."

"Of course," I added. "He didn't have to worry about you going to the law – you would be an accessory to kidnap and confinement. Man, he really had you over a barrel."

Briar said, "Human resources was never my strong suit. I actually thought the Holands believed in what they were doing."

I asked, "So it was Len Holand who blew up Evelyn Reesor's car?"

"Len Holand had nothing to do with any of this, including the bombing of your friend's car."

I believed him. Len Holand truly didn't seem the type. But then, neither does Paul Briar. So I asked him, "Why'd you help me? Why lend me a hand with Evelyn's body that night?" I turned to Nancy. "Your husband was quite the hero."

Briar answered, "Let's just say I wanted to stay on your good side. At that point I thought I truly needed pro-active assistance in locating my child."

I said, "But then the handyman, old Wilf, told you about this place." Paul Briar was now standing well inside the bedroom doorway. If I was quick, I might be able to grab one of his guns, but not both of them. "How about Robbie's murder?" I asked. "What was that – a pro-active enticement to get Clive to tell you where Nancy and your child were being held?"

"I never laid a hand on Robbie," Briar offered.

Nancy explained to me, "Clive said he had to do something about his brother. Robbie was chickening out, talking about letting me live after the baby was born. Clive was afraid Robbie might even tell the old man about me. He'd already told his girlfriend."

This was news to me. "Arden Dawes knew you were out here?"

Nancy said, "Clive makes sure she keeps her mouth shut."

He certainly does, I thought.

While the three of us were gabbing I kept my gaze frozen on Paul. Or more correctly, frozen on what was happening behind Paul. And what I was seeing brought my heart to a stop.

At the far end of the hallway, framed by the cabin's open entranceway like John Wayne in *The Searchers*, stood Lindsay. And in her hands, she clutched a hatchet – the same hatchet she'd stopped me from using last night on a live tree. I hoped she felt differently about using it on live people. Carefully, she tip-toed towards us, towards Paul Briar's back.

I locked eyes with Briar. I had to keep his attention fixed on me. "So, Paul," I said. "Whatever made a stable, upstanding fellow like yourself go into the hostage game?"

"Tell me, Tanager, if a father is responsible for his child's financial welfare why is he not also responsible for said child's very right to live?"

Lindsay was now halfway up the hall. And my heart was halfway up my throat. All Lindsay needed was for one of those old dry floorboards to creak and…

"You've got a good point," I replied a little too loudly. "Why don't you put those guns down, and we'll talk about it. I'll fix us some martinis. Let bygones be bygones. Your wife Nancy, here, looks like the forgiving sort."

Briar chuckled. "I always liked that about you Tanager. Always ready with a quip. Never taking yourself too seriously."

"Thanks, but I'm told that it can wear thin." Ironically, the person who had told me this was presently just a few feet behind Briar, her axe drawn back over her head, blunt end aimed at his head. *You'd better commit yourself to this*, I screamed silently to her. *Put everything you got into that first swing, babe, 'cause you ain't going to get a second one.*

And that's when I realized I'd made a big, fat, dumb, mistake. I hadn't tied the dog up well enough.

Stanley's claws clattered on the clapboard floor like canine castanets as he clambered down the corridor. Leash dragging, tail wagging, tongue flapping, the crazy pooch was anxious to join the party.

Briar turned at the noise. Lindsay was in mid-swing. A large mutt was bounding down the hall. For that split second, Briar couldn't decide which assailant to shoot first.

I reached to grab my pistol from off the bed. But I was too late. Nancy Briar had beaten me to it.

Her gun and Briar's pistol exploded at the exact same instant. Briar's bullet travelled slightly off target, hitting Lindsay in the leg. Nancy's aim was far more lethal.

Nancy Briar watched in horror as a sizeable chunk of her husband's precisely coiffed skull – carefully styled to look tousled but not ignored – exploded. A large piece of it flitted off toward the ceiling like a shiny, well-moussed moth. The gray hunk of brain landed in a freshly woven cobweb that stretched across the top corner of crown moulding where a large black spider was patiently awaiting dinner.

The spider pounced.

Paul Briar collapsed, dead when he hit the floor.

And Stanley finished his leap, landing on Nancy's bed. He gave her face a big wet lick that spoke for all of us. *Nice shootin', lady.*

I stepped over Briar's body and hurried to Lindsay. She appeared to be in good shape – not too much blood. I asked Nancy if there was a first-aid kit anywhere around.

"The bathroom," Nancy said, somehow ignoring the cold wet nose that was now sniffing her nether regions. "And when you're done with her I might need a hand."

"You hit?" I asked, thinking maybe a ricochet or stray splinter had hit her.

"Nooo…" she groaned, as she cramped up. "About four hours ago I went into labor."

CHAPTER TWENTY

My cell phone was as dead as Paul Briar. On our hike into the camp I had drained the battery trying to get a signal. When I asked Nancy if there was a cell phone in the cabin she told me that Julia Holand, the lady whose body was still lying on the floor, normally kept one, but Paul Briar had taken it from the woman when he'd arrived. I checked Paul's pockets for it. No luck.

Lindsay wasn't in bad shape. Paul's bullet had gone straight through her leg, missing any bones and large arteries, so once I had her cleaned up and bandaged, she was able to stand. She wasn't well enough to walk, though.

Regarding Nancy, our impending mother, there was nothing I could do now but wait. Wait and try to remember what the hell I was supposed to do once the action started. It had been a long time since my first-aid classes at police college. And ever since then, while I was busy raiding crack houses and busting gang bangers, the subject of birthing babies had rarely come up.

Nancy's water broke at ten o'clock that evening, and the baby popped his head out about twenty minutes after that. Happily, everything seemed to proceed as we all thought it should. Sure, the cord did get wrapped around the baby's neck a bit, but it wasn't wrapped tightly, so I didn't think it was ever a real problem. And one of the baby's shoulders got stuck at the gate for a moment, and this wouldn't have been a problem either if the mother, who tended to always want to take control of the operating room, didn't keep reaching down to pull her baby out with her own two hands. Lindsay had to restrain her while I continued to support the baby's head and let the contractions do the work.

By about ten-thirty the baby was all the way out and resting comfortably face-down on its mommy's tummy. Regarding the child's sex, let's just say Stanley and I were still the only boys at this garden party.

All in all, the infant appeared healthy and ready to sing unplugged, but I wasn't anxious to cut the cord yet. Two things worried me. First, the baby's heart rate seemed rather slow, about sixty or seventy beats per minute – the tempo of a slow ballad. If memory served me right, it should have been more of a medium-tempo swing. Second, the little girl had a green tinge to her skin. Not jaundiced, but green, especially her wee fingernails. The amniotic fluid had also been green. And thick. The two ladies, who were both surprisingly clueless on this entire subject, didn't know what any of this meant, but I thought I did. I didn't tell Nancy about my suspicions, though. I didn't want to worry her.

Eventually, that evening, I did decide to tie off and cut the cord. And for a while everything seemed fine. But then around sunrise the baby seemed to be in distress. Her heart rate, which had finally come up to normal speed, now seemed irregular. Plus, in my opinion she looked a little pale. Her breathing wasn't great, either. The mother was in good shape, though. And Lindsay, although in some pain from her bullet wound, was able to hobble around fairly well.

While the sun finally rose over the eastern hills, I loaded more wood into the kitchen stove so Lindsay could cook us some breakfast.

"We'll just wait here," Lindsay suggested as she cracked some eggs into a cast iron skillet. "In a day or two I'm sure Nancy will have enough strength to walk out with us."

"I'm sure you're right," I said, not wishing to cause any undue alarm. Truth was, I was planning on walking out myself. Today. Alone. I would stick to the Hahne trail all the way if I could and then return in an EMS chopper. I was afraid the baby might be suffering from a condition called MAS. I couldn't remember at the time what those letters stood for, but if my amateur diagnosis was correct, the infant might need antibiotics and oxygen. Fast.

After breakfast I outlined my plan for a solo hike. I spoke as casually as I could so as not to alarm Nancy. Nancy had no problem with my leaving, but Lindsay didn't like the idea at all. She was sure I was going to spend a couple of days wandering around in circles until I finally died of hunger, exposure, and stupidity. Nice to see I'd impressed her with my outdoorsy skills. I assured her that I'd be fine. I started loading my backpack.

But then something happened to change my plans. And at first, I thought it was a good thing. In fact, we all did.

Lindsay was cleaning up the breakfast dishes, and Nancy was sitting in her bed trying to encourage her fresh new daughter to drink from the tap when we heard it. Lindsay was the first to express her joy.

"A plane," she shouted.

I ran to the door, with Lindsay hobbling close on my heels. Together, we stood on the porch under the overhang and watched the floatplane circle the lake. Then it skimmed down over the water. But after making that one low pass, the plane rose and banked away, toward the north.

"No, no," Lindsay cried. "Come back." She started to hobble down the steps so she could wave at the departing plane from the snow-covered lawn, but I stopped her before she got her stocking feet wet.

"He just checked for rocks and dead-heads," I said, "Now he's circling on final." We stayed under the cover of the porch roof and watched as the plane retraced its circuit before committing to a proper water landing. At this point Lindsay suggested I go down to the dock and greet our visitors. But I didn't like that idea. "Let's see who it is first."

Lindsay looked at me as if I were nuts. "Why? Paul Briar's dead. So is Clive. Who are you afraid of?"

"Big Daddy." I knew Len was still looking for Clive.

Lindsay didn't give me any argument as I ushered her back into the cabin. Neither did Stanley when I pulled him by his collar into an empty bedroom. I closed the door to keep the pooch quiet. Then I grabbed the rifle that Paul Briar had taken from Clive. I took up my post just inside the open front doorway, tucked well back into the shadows. Meanwhile, in the adjoining front room Lindsay knelt on the sofa in front of the window so she could keep an eye on the dock and beachfront.

The Cessna turned onto its final approach. The roar of the engine softened as the pilot throttled back.

The pilot had a tough job ahead. This little lake was ringed with steep hills. The pilot had to drop down fast while somehow keeping his airspeed low. I'm no aviator, but I've flown enough in small planes to know how difficult a maneuver like this can be.

As he descended, the pilot kept his speed down by crabbing and slipping sideways to increase his forward drag. Then at the very last second, he straightened himself out so his floats hit the water in line with his forward momentum. If he misjudged, he would flip the plane onto it's back. But he didn't. He greased the thing onto the water without a single bounce. Whoever was at that wheel knew his stuff.

The pilot pulled his aircraft up to the leeward side of the dock. This could not have been an easy maneuver either considering the stiff breeze he was fighting and the fact that the dock wasn't much longer than one of his plane's aluminum floats. Finally in position, he shut the engine down and opened his door – the one closest to the dock. He jumped out onto the float, anxious to tie his plane to something solid before the wind blew the craft back out into the lake. When he turned my way I saw his face. I laughed. I wasn't surprised to see that he operated his plane with as much skill and finesse as he had handled his keyboard two nights ago.

My first reaction was to call out, *Hey, Milo! Good to see you, buddy. Nice landing.* But I held back. I wanted to see who his passenger was before I made my presence known.

With the wind trying to weathervane his plane's tail away from the dock, Milo wasted no time. He grabbed a line from one of the floats and hurriedly secured his craft to a ring on the dock. Meanwhile, his passenger was already starting to climb out. Milo noticed this and, like any good limo driver, rushed to help his paying client step out onto the float. But the passenger ignored the kind chauffeur's outstretch hand. Typical of Len Holand, I thought as I watched the passenger's legs stretch out of the open door. Len Holand would have to be drowning in a sea of sharks before he'd ever accept a helping hand.

But I was mistaken. The passenger was not Len Holand – not unless Len had lost a couple of inches from his height, slid into a pair of tight jeans, and slapped on a mop of blonde curls.

From her post in the living room Lindsay called out to me, "That's not Len Holand."

"Sshh…" I suggested.

But Lindsay was on a roll. "That's Rebecca Reesor."

Nancy heard her and joined the news broadcast. "Rebecca…" she announced from the bedroom. "That's Clive's girlfriend."

I assumed that Nancy was mixed up, of course. I knew for a fact that Arden Dawes was Clive's girl, not Rebecca Reesor. But then, to confuse things further, I heard Rebecca call out to us from the dock, "Hey, Clive. Come on out. I know you're here."

Rebecca started walking this way, up the slope toward the cabin. I turned to Lindsay who was now standing by my side and said, "Rebecca knows Clive?"

"They met last spring when she was working at Windermere."

"They date?"

Lindsay rolled her eyes. "Who *didn't* she date. I told you, Rebecca was... popular. That's why I had to fire her. She's a serial flirt. At least, that's the nice way of putting it."

At this point I heard Rebecca shout out, "I told you to stay by the plane." This time she was speaking to Milo. He had been following her up the hill toward us.

Milo protested, "But I have to take a leak."

"Who's stopping you?" She swept her arm out towards the lake like a model showing off a car.

Milo grumbled as he proceeded to walk back to the dock and unzip his fly. And that's when I saw the light, the penny dropped, and all the pieces fell into place for me. I turned to Lindsay and whispered my revelation, "She doesn't want Milo to see Nancy."

Lindsay said nothing. It was a lot to take in.

Meanwhile, Rebecca continued up the hill toward our door. As she walked, she called out to the cabin, presumably to Clive, "Gotta get outta here. Fast."

"Of course!" Lindsay whispered to me, quickly doing some deducing of her own. "She must have been the one who introduced Paul to Clive."

I didn't understand. "But... I introduced her to Paul. At the bar."

"That's what you thought."

Shit. It all made sense now. Rebecca must have been working at Windermere that weekend when Paul and Nancy had stayed at the inn. She met Paul. Maybe things clicked between them. If Paul then confided to her that he needed help with an unsavory task involving his wife, Rebecca could have introduced him to just the men for the job – Clive and his old man. Of course, there was one last loose end to this rope bridge of deductions that still needed tying up. And I wondered if Rebecca could help me knot it.

It was time to reveal myself. But not in the way Milo was currently doing, down on the dock.

I stepped out of the cabin, onto the porch.

CHAPTER TWENTY-ONE

Rebecca Reesor froze the moment she saw me. Her soft moon face crystalized to solid ice. Her eyes alone moved, panning the scene before her. After a moment's assessment her lips thawed enough to part without cracking. "Chief Tanager, what… what are you doing here?"

Milo, in mid-piss, saw me as well. He waved his free hand. "Hey, man."

By now Rebecca had warmed herself up to a slight smile. "This is a nice surprise."

"Is it?" I asked.

Without waiting to be asked, the young woman offered a defence for her presence. "Paul Briar told me he was coming out here. I was getting kinda worried about him."

"You were, huh?"

"Hey, I'll bet that's why you're here too," she spoke as if the idea had just occurred to her.

Milo, who was just stuffing himself away, called up, "This was the chick I told you about – called me yesterday. Remember? Turns out I had a cancellation. Like I said, those hunters are all pussy-whipped." Milo zipped up as he walked. "You should have waited, man. I could have saved you the hike."

"So, how's Paul?" Rebecca asked, her eyes darting to the windows. "He find his way here all right?"

Before I could say anything, Lindsay stepped out from behind me and answered, "Paul's dead."

I really wished Lindsay hadn't said that. Not yet, anyway.

Rebecca's mouth fell open. "What? No!"

"Tell me, Rebecca," I said. "When you arrived here why did you call out Clive's name and not Paul's?"

"Dead? Paul's dead?" Even from this distance I could see Rebecca's eyes welling up with tears.

"Why Clive's name?"

She wiped her eyes with the back of her wrist and pulled herself together. "I… I used to know Clive. We kinda dated. Not long, though. Daddy didn't like him." Rebecca then looked pointedly to Lindsay. "Nobody did."

For a welcome change, Lindsay said nothing.

Rebecca wiped a tear from her eye and continued, "This… this camp used to be, like, Clive and Robbie's retreat. A place to get away from their crazy old man. So I figured when Clive got into trouble – you know, stole your police car and all – he might come out here. And then when I heard Paul was heading out this way, well, I didn't want them butting heads. Clive can be a little… well, you know."

"So you came all the way out here to help Paul Briar," I said.

"Paul…. he's really dead?" Rebecca was truly shocked. And saddened.

Lindsay stepped in closer. "I should have known it." Lindsay tossed her hard, sharp words straight at Rebecca's face, "You were screwing Paul. Is that why he let his wife go out canoeing alone that morning? He was otherwise occupied, fucking the maid?"

Rebecca snapped back, "Paul didn't love her. Not anymore. Not for a long time."

I brought the subject back from the past to what was happening right here and now, "Rebecca, why didn't you want Milo to enter the cabin?"

"Milo?" With a tug of her hair, Rebecca switched on her sweet, innocent look. "I never told Milo he couldn't go into the cabin."

But Milo had heard my query. "Told me she had a crazy grandma livin' here who went all batshit when she saw strangers. So I should stay by the plane. Course, I knew it was a load of crap. Figured she was probably growing weed." He looked up at the water tower. "Lots of water for the 'ponics, I see."

I turned back to Rebecca. "Why would you tell Milo a story like that?"

Rebecca's face hardened. "It was none of his business. Or yours."

I turned to Milo. I had a more urgent matter for him to take care of. "We have a mother and her newborn here. Gotta get them to Adirondack Medical Center. Fast." I noticed Rebecca's eyes open wide at this bulletin. But she kept her mouth closed, bit her bottom lip. I continued to Milo, "How many people can you take out in one trip?"

"Including me?" Milo asked.

"Yes, including you," I answered tolerantly. Frankly, if I hadn't just seen this guy land that plane so expertly, I'd now be seriously reconsidering that walk out.

"Might squeeze in four. But she has a full tank, and we'd need a good long run, which we don't really have on this puddle." Milo surveyed the small lake. "Might scrape the tops of those hills a bit. Three'd be better."

"Take Nancy, the baby, and Lindsay. You can come back for Rebecca and me." And then I added, seemingly as an afterthought, "And Clive, of course."

This odd addendum baited sudden interest from both Rebecca and Lindsay. I prayed Rebecca would be the first fish to bite. My prayer was answered.

"Clive's here?" she asked.

My eyes flitted to Lindsay. She got the message and kept her mouth shut. "He's tied up," I lied. "Locked in the bedroom."

Rebecca did not welcome this news. She suddenly looked like a kid on a high school basketball team who was watching the other squad march onto the court and learning that every player was over six feet tall. Suddenly, the whole game was changing right before her eyes.

I set the hook. "And Rebecca, he's told me everything."

"Everything? What do you mean?"

"You know… about your mother." I hated to play dirty like this, but I needed her to believe her accomplice was alive and willing to testify against her.

"My… my mother?"

I corrected myself. "Your stepmother. About Evelyn."

Rebecca still didn't understand. Or at least, she pretended not to. So I pushed a little harder. "He told me why you wanted her killed."

"Killed…? Evelyn? That… that's crazy. Why would I want that?"

"Ironically to save your father's life. Didn't work out that way, though, did it. Quite the opposite, actually."

I was flying blind here, but I had to take this chance. If I was full of shit with my quickly forming theory, this was a dangerous maneuver that could crash and burn. If I wasn't… well, I had to seize this opportunity while I could. So, I took another pass at the runway. "Evelyn was the one who talked your dad into performing terminations."

"Did Clive tell you that?"

"No, your dad told me. Before he married Evelyn, he'd always refused to perform abortions." Okay, so far, I was telling what I knew to be true. What I said next, however, was pure conjecture. But I took a shot anyway because it explained a lot. "Your father said his first wife – your mother – she didn't approve of the procedure."

"That's not true."

"Yes, it is," Lindsay butted in. "I knew your mother. She was pro-life all the way. There's no way in hell she would ever let your father perform abortions."

Rebecca knew she'd been caught on a technicality. "What does that prove? I'm not against abortions. Why in the world would I want to harm Evelyn?"

I said, "It must have been tough. I mean, even in the best of circumstances, no daughter likes to see a new woman barge in and take over her father's life. Her father's heart. But when that woman imposed her own social agenda on your dad, an agenda that put your father's life in danger, that was too much. Hell, she even had the poor guy flying halfway across the country, risking his life to do work the southern doctors were afraid to tackle. It was risky stuff. Especially for a guy from a little place like Glen Echo. I mean, it's one thing for big city doctors to offer controversial procedures – those guys have some anonymity going for them. But your dad – up here, where everyone knows everyone else's business – his ass was hanging out every day. And not just *his*. I'll bet you got hit with some of the flack, yourself. It couldn't have been easy for you either."

I'd struck a nerve, a nerve so raw and sensitive it drew more tears as Rebecca spoke. "Daddy had to send me away to school. Kids at Glen Echo High were giving me a hard time. But that doesn't mean…"

"I'm sure you begged your father to get out of the whole messy business, but by then he couldn't. Or wouldn't. He didn't want to let Evelyn down."

"He'd do anything for her, and she knew it." Rebecca wiped her eyes and straightened herself up. And with that renewed posture came a renewed confidence. And it wasn't an attractive confidence. "Even if what you say is true, which it isn't, all you've got is Clive's word against mine. And who is a jury going to believe – a young college girl whose father is a respected surgeon or a backwoods hick whose old man is a polygamous, gospel-quoting nut job?"

"Frankly, I'm betting they'll believe the evidence."

Rebecca's confidence faded. "Evidence? What… what are you talking about?"

"I'm talking about Evelyn's cell records. The call she received twenty-one minutes before she got into that car. I'm not sure exactly what excuse you used –

my guess is you told her you had some personal problem that could only be solved by a cozy stepmother-stepdaughter chat. After all, you'd always seemed to be close to her."

"I *was* close to her."

"Records show you made that call from across state, your school residence. But I distinctly remember your dad saying you were coming home that weekend. You must have pretended to be making the call on your way, probably telling Evelyn you were just outside Glen Echo. You had to guarantee Evelyn would start that car first and not your father. That was easy – you knew your dad would be otherwise occupied on stage all night with the band."

"Did Clive tell you that?"

I ignored her question and said, "You're a smart girl, Rebecca. You knew everyone would assume the bombing was terrorist-related. I certainly did. You even had Lindsay, here, as a handy scapegoat. Everyone knew about her pro-life activities. I never seriously considered Clive for the bombing – it didn't fit his profile. Pro-life... pro-choice... It all means pro-fuck-all to a guy like Clive." I added, "Or to most guys, I hate to admit."

Milo, tried to help me out, "I know I never gave a fuck about it."

I said to Milo, "Fire up your engine. We gotta move." Then I turned to Lindsay, "Your leg well enough to give me a hand with Nancy and the baby?"

Lindsay indicated that she was fine and began walking up the hill to the cabin. Rebecca started to follow her, but I gently nudged her back with my rifle barrel. "Not yet."

"But I'm cold."

"After they leave. We'll have a warm chat by the fire."

Rebecca pouted, and on behalf of horny assholes everywhere, I could see why a horny asshole like Clive was so willing to do the odd favor for her, like blowing up a meddlesome stepmother.

Rebecca tried another approach. "I have to go to the bathroom."

What could I do? Let her freeze to death out here, squatting in the snow? She may have been complicit to abduction, forcible confinement, and conspiracy to murder, but she was still my pal Simon's daughter. "Okay." I said.

The three of us walked up the hill, Rebecca between Lindsay and myself. As young Rebecca stepped through the doorway into the cabin ahead of me, she asked, "So, where is he?"

"He?"

"Clive?"

"Upstairs. But you're staying down here."

From the far end of the hall, an anxious Nancy called out, "Everything okay?"

Lindsay yelled back, "Everything is fine," and she hurried down the hall to Nancy's room.

Rebecca smiled. "Can I see the baby"?

"I thought you had to use the bathroom."

"Just a quick look."

"I don't think that would be a good idea." I was thinking of the loaded pistol that I'd left lying on Nancy's nightstand. So I watched Rebecca step into the bathroom. Watched her close the door. Heard her lift the lid and sit down. Satisfied she was settled in, I then continued on into Nancy's bedroom to get that handgun. Yes, Rebecca could now make a break, but where she would run to?

Once in Nancy's bedroom, I tucked the pistol safely into my waistband. This meant that I now had possession of all known firearms in the place – my service revolver, Briar's Glock, and Clive's Winchester rifle.

Meanwhile, Lindsay had started dressing and preparing Nancy Briar for the plane ride. It would be a short flight but a cold one, and to keep Nancy and the baby warm they would need plenty of blankets. Nancy informed me that there were some clean ones in the closet of the spare bedroom – the same room in which I had secured my dog – so I went to go get them.

As I passed the bathroom door I knocked. "Everything okay in there?"

No answer.

I wasn't terribly happy when I opened the door and discovered Rebecca gone. But I wasn't terribly worried either. As I said, there was no place for her to run to, I had all the guns, and it wouldn't be the end of the world if she went upstairs and found out I'd been bluffing about Clive.

I walked to the foot of the corkscrew staircase and yelled up, "Rebecca, you up there?"

No answer. But I did hear a bark come from Stanley's room down the hall. The pooch was obviously eager to come out and join the party. "Settle down, buddy," I said as I proceeded down the hallway to grant him parole and set him free.

I approached his room. I noticed the door was already ajar. This was curious. I mean, Stanley is a talented mutt and all, but he hasn't learned how to turn doorknobs yet. I was equally puzzled that, once the door had been partially opened like this, he hadn't nosed it the rest of the way and walked out. He is bright enough to do that.

I slowly edged the door wider.

Stanley looked up at me with his big brown eyes, his tail wagging happily. But he didn't budge. He seemed perfectly happy standing right where he was, thank you, on the far side of the room with the pretty young blonde lady holding his collar. All of this would have been fine and dandy for me, too, had it not been for the open, eight-inch scissor blade Rebecca was holding against Stanley's furry throat. They were the scissors I had used to cut bandages for Lindsay's leg. I particularly recalled noticing how razor sharp they were. Then I'd returned them to their drawer. For safe keeping. In the bathroom.

Rebecca crouched down so she could keep the blade clutched firmly to my furry buddy's throat as she spoke, "I never wanted Evelyn dead. I only told Clive to scare her, that's all. I figured maybe if she had a first-hand taste of the danger, she was putting Daddy through she might ease up on him. Cut him some slack. So I told Clive to mess with her car. He said he'd bleed out the brakes, loosen some lug nuts, fuck with the steering, something like that. I just wanted her to shit herself, maybe crumple a fender or something. That's all. I didn't know the crazy idiot would take it as an invitation to get out his chemistry set and play terrorist."

"And Nancy Briar?" I asked.

"Paul told me he had some sort of plan to keep his wife from having an abortion, but he needed help. So I hooked him up with Clive. I can't help it that Clive saw an opportunity to make a big score. By that time I was long out of the picture."

"I believe you." I couldn't take my eyes off that scissor blade touching Stanley's moronically happy throat. "Makes sense to me."

"You're lying. I want you to bring Clive down here. Tell him to confess the truth or I'll kill his dog. And I'm not kidding." To punctuate her point Rebecca yanked Stanley's collar tighter. Stanley responded, of course, by turning his big trusting face up to hers and licking her nose.

I gave her the first news bulletin: "That's not Clive's dog."

"It isn't?"

"No, he's mine. Or at least, he lives with me."

"Clive told me he has two dogs. He said he planned to keep one of them here as a watch dog."

"He does have two dogs. Irish wolfhounds. Beautiful. Well-trained. But they're not here. They're back at the farm." I now added the second news bulletin: "And Clive isn't here either."

"But you said… Where is he?"

"I don't honestly know." And this time I was telling the truth. Paul Briar hadn't told me where he'd dumped the body.

Rebecca didn't know what to do next. I could see the gears turning as she assessed her situation. She still had a sharp instrument clutched to my dog's throat. There must be some way she could use this to her advantage. She got her answer when, from outside, she heard Milo's airplane engine cough and then fire up.

"I'm going down to that plane," she announced.

"What do you plan to do – have Milo fly you to Canada?"

"I'll figure that out once I'm in the air. All I know is I'm not going to jail for Evelyn's murder." She edged the scissor blade slowly down Stanley's breastbone, closer to his heart, as she ordered me, "Now get out of my way."

I was too far away to try and grab her. If I lunged, she'd still have time to plunge those scissors into Stanley. I could, of course, use the rifle that was currently clutched in my left hand and simply shoot the young woman dead before she had a chance to do anything to anybody. Trade a human life for a dog's life. But I wasn't going to do that, and she knew it. So I did as she ordered and stepped backwards into the hallway.

"All the way," she demanded. "Into the back bedroom."

As I followed her instructions and backed into the busy bedroom, Lindsay, unaware of my and Stanley's predicament, said to me, "We're ready. You got the blankets?"

"I'm afraid there'll be a slight delay."

Noting the look on my face, Lindsay craned her neck around the doorway to see what the hell I was looking at down the hallway.

She saw Rebecca backing away, out the front door, still holding Stanley's collar firmly by one hand. The lethal scissors were no longer actually touching his fur, but they were close enough to keep my attention. The pooch, of course, didn't put up a fight. He's always happy to go for a walk with a pretty girl.

Lindsay summed up the situation rather well, "What the fuck does she think she's doing?"

"She has no idea," I said. "That's what worries me."

From a safe distance I followed Rebecca and Stanley out the cabin door.

By the time I stepped onto the porch Rebecca was ten yards down the hill, holding Stanley's collar, but still looking back to make sure I wasn't following too closely.

Frankly, I didn't know what I was going to do next. But I sure as hell wasn't going to let her get on that plane and use Stanley's life to force Milo's into doing something stupid.

So I walked down the steps. And when I reached the bottom something caught my eye. It was a few yards to my right. In the snow. A drop of blood. Not fresh blood. In fact, it wasn't even red anymore. More of a rust brown. But it was blood, all right.

Then I noticed another drop. And another. And more. The gruesome trail led up from the woods to this main building. The drops intensified in frequency until they disappeared right here, beside me, under the...

As I bent down to look under the porch, he jumped me. He came from somewhere behind, smashing me face-first onto the granite. The half-inch of snow did little to cushion my fall. The blow sent the rifle flying out of my hands.

I hadn't seen my attacker's face yet, but I didn't need to. Turns out I hadn't been lying to Rebecca after all. Clive was indeed still alive. True, Paul Briar may have shot him, but he hadn't killed him. The guy must have been hiding in the woods and then under this porch.

As soon as I started to raise my face off the rock, he booted the back of my head back down again. My forehead hit the granite. My world spun. My vision blurred. I lifted my chest off the ground and immediately lost the contents of my stomach. But I managed to roll over in time to see Clive picking up that rifle.

In one motion I whisked Paul Briar's pistol out from under my waistband and thumbed off the safety just as Clive cocked a cartridge into the rifle's chamber. Happily, I pulled my trigger first. Unhappily, there was no bang. Not even a metallic click. Paul Briar's fancy auto magazine had jammed. I should have gone for my own handgun in the other pocket. But it was too late now.

Clive smiled down at me. I noticed the large red stain on the front of his jeans, at the belt line, where Briar must have shot him. Gut shots like that work slow. That's why he hadn't died right away. But he would soon. Not soon enough for me, though.

To my left, I saw Lindsay step out of the cabin onto the porch. Once again, she had that big axe in her hand. This time she didn't waste any time sneaking up on her target – she just hauled off and threw the thing like a tomahawk.

Clive didn't have time to duck. But that didn't matter. The axe missed him by a mile and hit my foot. Up 'til now it was the one part of me that wasn't hurting. Meanwhile, to my right I saw Stanley come running up the hill to join the party. He must have broken free from Rebecca.

Clive decided who should go first. He turned and drew a bead on the charging, vicious dog.

Using every last drop of energy I had left, I leapt to my feet and put everything I had behind one good punch to the side of his neck. I heard his atlas vertebrae crack. Clive went down. By my guess, he was dead before he hit the ground which was damn lucky for him considering that Lindsay had jumped over the porch railing and was now kicking him in the nuts. The woman was wild. Despite her bad leg, I actually had trouble pulling her off the guy. You've got to watch those social activist types.

They take things very seriously.

EPILOGUE

I flipped the steaks on the grill with one hand and pulled the hood of my parka up over my head with the other. Didn't do much good, though – the cold wind was hurling the snow and ice pellets horizontally. I fumbled with the pepper mill and dropped my barbecue tongs in the snow. Tried to fish them out of the drift, but my ski mitts were too bulky, so I used my bare hands. By the time I managed to get hold of the tongs my fingers were too cold to operate them. I shook the snow out of my sleeve and looked back over my shoulder.

And I laughed. What else could I do?

Behind me, at the far end of the path that I'd shoveled through the three-foot drifts, yellow sparkles of candlelight flickered like fireflies behind the dining room window of Windermere Inn. Of course, if they were real fireflies, they'd be frozen solid just like the turkey that has been sitting for hours in the Inn's ice-cold electric range.

Christmas Eve in the North Country. Power out, big bird still frozen, and a table full of hungry guests. Luckily, Lindsay and Sharon kept a well-stocked meat locker for just such emergencies.

Holding my little LED flashlight between my chattering teeth, I stacked the lukewarm sirloin steaks on an ice-cold platter and closed the lid of the gas barbecue with my elbow. I just hoped everybody liked their beef rare – the propane tank had run empty two minutes ago. On the plus side, with the electric lights out nobody would be able to see how undercooked their meat actually was.

I opened the back door of the Inn and stepped up into the darkened kitchen where Stanley was eagerly waiting for me. Or at least, waiting for the steaks. Using the narrow beam of my flashlight, I carefully placed the platter of steaks on the table. From the next room I could hear the short, raspy riffs of Nancy's baby crying her tiny lungs out. I guess, for Christmas music, we could have done a lot worse.

Nancy's little girl was now almost six weeks old. After Milo had flown her and Nancy out of the mountains, an ambulance whisked mother and child straight to the Adirondack Medical Center where the doctors proclaimed Nancy and the baby to be in good health. The little girl did indeed have Meconium Aspiration Syndrome, a condition which, if untreated, could have been serious, but the doctors assured Nancy that somebody we all know and love had done something right when he delivered the baby. Since then, Nancy has stuck around to boost up her own vitamin deficiencies and to assist Detective Manwaring and the district attorney's office with their investigations.

The district attorney charged Rebecca Reesor with criminally negligent homicide in connection with her stepmother's car bombing and with accessory to first-degree kidnapping for Nancy Briar's abduction and confinement. We'll have to wait to see what a judge and jury have to say about the matter. Either way, the young woman gets little sympathy from me. Len Holand, on the other hand, has already received my condolences. He claims he had no knowledge of what his late sons were up to, and Nancy has backed up his story. As far as she could tell, Robbie, Clive, and Julia Holand seemed to be acting without Len's knowledge.

Nancy has regained her strength, so tomorrow, if the roads are open, she plans to drive home to the city. Hence our little Christmas celebration here tonight.

I picked up the platter from the kitchen table and kicked open the door to the dining room. As I carefully walked into the candle-lighted room I warned Nancy, "I wouldn't feed any of this to the baby – might be a little rare for her."

Lindsay really liked that joke. In fact, she laughed so hard she shit herself. That's right, Nancy Briar has named her daughter Lindsay after the woman who helped save her life. This despite their ongoing arguments about a woman's right to choose. It's nice to see two people who can agree to disagree. And that's exactly what they were doing as I placed the platter of steaks on the table.

"Bullshit," said Nancy.

"You're just rationalizing," Lindsay countered.

I asked, "What's it about this time, ladies? Gun control? Immigration? Plastic straws? The metric system?"

Nancy Briar tossed back a big swallow from her wine glass before pointing a freshly-manicured finger at Lindsay. "She says I'm poisoning my baby by having one lousy glass of wine."

Lindsay looked at me and pled her case, "The alcohol goes directly into her breast milk."

"Bullshit," Nancy suggested. "Doctors say one or two glasses won't hurt."

I said to Nancy, as gently as possible, "But you can't drink just one or two, can you." It wasn't a question, it was a simple statement of fact.

Nancy Briar has been open with us about her problem. She's a functioning alcoholic. Has been for years. It was the reason she was afraid to have a baby. She didn't trust herself to stay sober for a whole eight months. Of course, this problem was solved when she was locked away in that mountain cabin where her jailors had been ordered not to give her any booze. As a result, her baby was born healthy. And this was all thanks to the baby's daddy, whose motives, of course, were anything but altruistic.

Irony can be as cold and hard as an Adirondack blizzard.

Lindsay, our hostess for tonight's party, dealt out the steaks, and after a quick toast to friends, family, and good health we all sliced into our Christmas beef. Awash in the candles' warm glow, sat Nancy, Lindsay, Sharon, Milo, Marlene, and myself. Just beyond the twilight, little Lindsay lay in her crib, behind Nancy.

"Good job on the steak," Milo said as he chomped into his first bite.

"Any bunnies?" asked Sharon.

"Nope," answered Marlene.

"Hamsters?"

"No live animals of any kind," I said.

"How about fish?" Sharon asked.

Marlene explained, "Just supplies. Food, shampoo, dog collars, squeaky toys."

"We figure Lake Placid is best," I said. "Very pet-friendly. Do you know almost every hotel in that town allows dogs?"

Milo said, "I'll remember that next time I get lucky with a schnauzer."

I laughed. But Lindsay just looked at me. Then she looked at Marlene. "I just can't buy it," she said. "I wish you both all the luck in the world, but I just can't buy you guys running a pet store. I don't think people like you can be happy selling flea and tick spray."

"Why not?" Marlene said. "We both like animals."

"And neither of us likes fleas and ticks," I added.

Lindsay addressed her argument more to me than to Marlene, "I just don't think you'll be happy. You need action. Stimulation. Sitting behind a counter all day… it's not you."

I took a sip of wine. "Manwaring has offered me a job with his people."

"Well, there you go. Perfect. A New York State detective." Lindsay thought this sounded peachy keen. "You'll love it."

"I don't know," I said. "A lot of hours. On call day and night. Weekends. No time left for music."

From across the table Nancy Briar asked with true concern, "Do you really need to play that much?" Nancy didn't know me well.

Milo answered for me. "Without music he'd go bat shit." Milo did know me well. "Music keeps him sane."

And with Milo's smart insight as the perfect cue, the electricity suddenly flashed on. The room was bathed in warm, bright light.

Yea. Yippee. We all cheered and applauded as if a solar eclipse had just ended. But then…

"Yech." It was Sharon. She was looking at her steak with bitter disgust. "I can't eat this!! It's hardly cooked. It's still blood red. Just look." She held up a forkful for all to see.

Lindsay placed her hand on Sharon's uplifted arm. "But you were enjoying it, weren't you?"

Sharon thought this one over for a moment. "Yeah… I guess so…" Then she shrugged and popped the piece into her mouth.

Everybody laughed. And the party went on.

But I knew better. I got up and flicked the light switch off, plunging us once again into that cozy, candlelight universe where nobody gets a close look at what exactly is sitting on his or her plate.

I often think life works out better that way.

THE END

ABOUT THE AUTHOR

Richard Adamson has worked as a scriptwriter and story editor on several American and Canadian TV series, as a script doctor for film and on-Broadway stage productions, and as a contracted writer for such diverse talents as David Letterman and Yakov Smirnoff. Previous to becoming a professional writer, Adamson earned his living in Toronto as a jazz pianist.

NOTE FROM THE AUTHOR

Word-of-mouth is crucial for any author to succeed. If you enjoyed the book, please leave a review online—anywhere you are able. Even if it's just a sentence or two. It would make all the difference and would be very much appreciated.

Thanks!
Richard

Thank you so much for reading one of our **Crime Fiction** novels.
If you enjoyed the experience, please check out our recommended title for your next great read!

Caught in a Web by Joseph Lewis

"This important, nail-biting crime thriller about MS-13 sets the bar very high. One of the year's best thrillers."
-*BEST THRILLERS*

Made in United States
North Haven, CT
03 March 2023

33503370R00136